Anna gripped Lily's forearm and pulled herself high enough to hook her elbows over the ledge, giving her the needed leverage. When Lily dropped to the other side, Anna continued upward and through, falling in a heap amidst the pile of lace and satin lining the trench that bisected the store. Racks of wedding gowns had rolled into the gaping hole and toppled, layering the earth floor with a strange blanket of plush cloth.

"God, I could sleep for a week!" Lily exclaimed.

"Maybe we should stop and rest a while," Anna suggested casually, falling beside her savior. She was already exhausted from her ordeal with the bookcase, not to mention hungry and thirsty. And her knee was screaming in pain.

"As tempting as that sounds, I'm still worried about the aftershocks. The ceiling dropped a little more back there during the last one, and the next one might finish the job. If that happens, I'd realize my worst fear."

"What's that? Being buried alive?"

"No, being caught dead in a bridal shop."

Visit

Bella Books

at

BellaBooks.com

or call our toll-free number

1-800-729-4992

WITHOUT WARNING

KG MacGregor

Bella
BOOKS

2008

Bella Books, Inc.
P.O. Box 10543
Tallahassee, FL 32302

First Edition

Editor: Cindy Cresap
Cover designer: Stephanie Solomon-Lopez.

ISBN-10: 1-59493-120-8
ISBN-13: 978-1-59493-120-8

To my partner Jenny, who makes it possible for me to write about love.

Acknowledgment

A few years ago, I published a book called *Shaken*, an epic story of two women who first met when they became trapped in a collapsed mall after an earthquake. Upon their escape, they embarked on a three-year journey of romance, adversity and utter joy. *Shaken* was the first story I ever wrote, and the first book I ever published. It is now forever out of print.

When I signed with Bella Books, publisher Linda Hill agreed to publish my backlist, which also included *The House on Sandstone*, *Mulligan* and *Malicious Pursuit*. We were all set to bring back *Shaken* when a casual conversation launched us onto a different track: Bring back the story, but make it deeper, longer and more intense. And then see if these characters have more stories to tell. I'm grateful to Linda for the chance to have another crack at this story.

Without Warning is a classic romance, the first book of The Shaken Series. I hope you agree this isn't the work of a first-time novelist. It's written in a style I've developed over several years of working closely with editor Cindy Cresap, who deserves a ton of credit for helping me draw out the story's most important element—the characters of Anna Kaklis and Lily Stewart—and for shaping the tale into its natural arc. I'm excited about this new beginning, and I hope you enjoy it.

I want to thank my dear friend, Tami, who read and responded to every draft of the original story and encouraged me to stay with it. And I also want to express my deep appreciation to the fan fiction readers from the Xenaverse, whose hunger for uber-inspired lesbian fiction led to an explosion of our stories. Without their early support, I wouldn't be writing today.

About the Author

Growing up in the mountains of North Carolina, KG MacGregor dreaded the summer influx of snowbirds escaping the Florida heat. "If it's tourist season, why can't we shoot them?" she said. Now older, wiser and intolerant of extreme temperatures, she divides her time between Miami and Blowing Rock, NC. A former teacher, KG earned her PhD in journalism and mass communication, and her writing stripes preparing research reports for commercial clients in the publishing, television and travel industries. In 2002, she tried her hand at lesbian fiction and discovered her bliss. When she isn't writing, you'll find her either on a golf course or a hiking trail.

Chapter 1

Anna Rutherford nudged her luxury coupe one lane to the right, determined to get out of this jumbled mess. Freeway traffic was usually snarled in LA, but today's was even worse than usual. With a GPS subscriber service, she could have checked for construction or accidents, but that option wasn't available in 1999, the last model year for her classic BMW 850. Her next car would have the GPS . . . if she could ever bring herself to part with this one.

She felt sorry for the drivers around her, because they probably did this every day. Her usual commute, from her home in Bel Air to the dealership in Beverly Hills, took twelve minutes. Lucky for her, she made this downtown trip only once a month, for the breakfast meeting of the Greater Los Angeles Chamber of Commerce. As treasurer of the organization, her presence was mandatory.

At least this morning's program had been interesting, she thought, a slide show on various community organizations involved with the area's at-risk youth. Anna liked the idea of using Chamber resources for making the whole community a better place. The way she saw it, it was good for business because they were building a foundation for future employees, vendors and customers.

For more than forty years, Premier Motors of Beverly Hills, southern California's top BMW dealer, had lent its support to LA's thriving symphony, its opera, three of its theaters and at least a half-dozen art museums. The dealership was a major underwriter for an afternoon business update that aired on the local public radio station. Anna's father believed charitable donations were best spent on those who bought luxury cars.

Anna, who at thirty-one served as vice president of the family's dealership, agreed that supporting the arts was good business, probably the best advertising their money could buy. But she had been moved by today's program, especially by the teenage girl who told a personal tale of how one organization had helped her overcome an abusive home, poor school performance and a flirtation with drugs and alcohol to become a college-bound senior with hopes and dreams of one day being a leader in the LA business community. Why couldn't Premier help with things like that too?

Despite losing her mother at an early age, Anna knew she was blessed by the hand dealt her, lucky to have never known such hardships as those she saw displayed today. For all the good those organizations did for the community, it seemed such a small price to—

A blaring horn interrupted her ruminations, and she hurriedly accelerated to close the thirty-foot gap between herself and the car in front, lest someone squeeze in and delay them all by ten seconds. Spotting the off-ramp for Endicott Avenue, she continued to pick her way to the exit lane. Endicott eventually dumped into La Cienega Boulevard, where stoplights and surface streets were preferable to this creeping, growling mass of motorized inhumanity.

This morning's look at the struggles of troubled youth had been an ironic respite from her own problems, which had consumed her like a cloud for the past three months—even longer if she was honest with herself. Her control had been slipping away gradually for over a year, to the point where she no longer had any sense of direction. Strong and confident in the business world, Anna had always felt clumsy when it came to her personal life. If only she could have plotted contingencies like she did with her sales models, or studied engineering blueprints for clues like she did with her cars. Romance didn't come with a kit. At least hers didn't.

"Two hundred dollars, counselor," Judge Rusty Evans barked, slamming his gavel against the desk.

Lily Stewart cringed, not just at the fine, but at the anger on the judge's face. Of course he was furious. She couldn't blame him for that.

Eager to wrap up this case, she had led her client, Maria Esperanza, into the family courtroom at the Los Angeles County Courthouse, where they were to have squared off against Maria's ex-husband Miguel for primary custody of the couple's two children. Lily knew the facts of the case cold, and Maria was perfectly prepped on what to tell the judge about her ex-husband's volatile behavior.

As Lily looked back now on yesterday's conversation with Maria, she recalled the confusion. Her office calendar said Thursday—which was today—but Maria's cell phone reminder was programmed for Friday. That had to be a mistake, Lily had told her.

Unfortunately, the mistake was hers, not Maria's. The case

file that Pauline, the legal aid clinic's newly-hired secretary, should have pulled was that of Maria *Espinosa*, Lauren Miller's client, whose final divorce hearing was to have been today. It all came to light only moments ago when Maria looked across the aisle quizzically at Mr. Espinosa and whispered into Lily's ear. "Who is that man and why does he want custody of my children?"

She scribbled a personal check to the clerk to cover her fine—she would have to move money from savings right away to cover it—and turned to face a fuming Maria. "I'm really sorry. I don't know how that happened."

"I knew it was tomorrow."

"You were right." No matter how irritated Lily was with Pauline at this moment, it was nothing compared to how furious Lauren would be when she discovered Judge Evans was fining her too. "At least let me give you a ride home."

Though the screw-up hadn't been entirely her fault, she felt awful for trusting the eraser board in the office instead of checking the file herself. If she had, she wouldn't have dragged her client out on the wrong day.

Maria had another letdown when they reached Lily's car, a ten-year-old Toyota RAV4, with more dings than a wind chime. Lily saw the disappointment on her face when she realized they weren't getting into the Lexus in the next space. Yes, she needed a new car, but not a new car payment. All of her extra money went to her house fund on the off-chance she ever found something decent that didn't require a second job.

Lily gathered up the pile of folders and books on the front seat, making room for her passenger. "There you go. Sorry about that." Then she removed her suit jacket and laid it across the backseat. The day was unusually warm for February, and the RAV4's air conditioner had been out of commission for four years.

Most of Lily's clients at the Braxton Street Legal Aid Clinic lived in Watts or East LA, but Maria was staying with her sister until the custody of her children was resolved. "Culver City, right?"

"*Si.* I mean yes."

Lily bit her lip and started the vehicle. She deserved Maria's condescension after the fiasco today. It wasn't that her client had a dozen other places to be today. It was that a court appearance involved a new blouse she couldn't afford, her sister missing work to babysit and three buses to get her downtown to the courthouse.

As she coasted to the bottom of the ramp to the stoplight, Anna checked the digital clock on her instrument gauge: 11:40. Today's meeting had lasted until ten, after which the officers met in closed session to discuss the new membership drive. Her morning was shot, but that didn't worry her. Staying late at her office was routine, especially since her troubles at home began.

A wave of her hand over the infrared eye on the doorframe produced a dial tone. "Premier Motors," she stated succinctly. A few moments later, her call was answered with the same two words. "Carmen, it's Anna. Is Dad there?"

"Yes, and he's driving us all crazy. Please tell me you're on the way."

"I am, but I'm stuck in traffic."

"Did you bring that book for Hal? He called a little while ago and said he'd come by for it."

Anna banged her fist on the console, irritated when she suddenly realized what probably had happened. Last night, she had laid out the book about the car business to bring to her brother-in-law, but Scott must have picked it up this morning on his way out the door, assuming she meant for him to read it. "No, I don't have it with me, but I can stop at the mall and get another copy. I want Hal to have his own anyway."

"Okay, I'll tell him if he calls again. Hold on. I'll get George for you."

A few moments later, her father answered, obviously out of breath. "Where are you? They're driving me crazy."

"So I heard." Except she had heard it was the other way around. "I'm on Endicott. I have to go pick up a book, but I'll be there in less than an hour."

"Can you call Steve French? He needs the run-of-press order."

Steve was their account representative from the *LA Times*. "I sent it to Brad yesterday for the VIN numbers. Just get him to forward it."

"Fine. I have to get Morty Schneider's car off the rack in the next five minutes or I'll never hear the end of it."

"What's the problem?"

"Thomas didn't show up today. I've got two trucks due in this afternoon and no way to get them processed. I'm going to fire him the minute he walks in here."

"He had a doctor's appointment this morning. He'll be in this afternoon."

"Why didn't he tell anybody?"

"It's on the calendar behind Carmen's desk. You need to check that first. And please don't go firing anybody." Anna had inherited many things from her father, but fortunately, not his temper.

He sighed, clearly exasperated. "I'm getting too old for this."

"No, you're not. Just go worry about Morty. I'll be there as quick as I can." She hung up and shook her head. Since taking over most of the day-to-day operations at the dealership, she had managed to streamline processes for everyone but her father, who still thought he had to oversee everything, just as he had since the early 1970s.

❧

Five minutes into the ride to Culver City, Maria decided to phone the sister she would see in less than a half hour. Lily's working knowledge of Spanish was just enough to find the conversation distracting, so she tried to concentrate on other things.

At the top of her list today was why on earth she had decided on this line of work. Sure, it was full of intrinsic rewards, but the fancy firms downtown didn't suffer snafus like hers today. Of course, those secretaries probably made twice what Pauline made at the law clinic, and they would be fired for an error like that. Pauline would be forgiven, but all of the attorneys would double-check their own schedules from now on.

Lily had never truly second-guessed her decision to accept the job at the legal aid clinic. The downtown firms were notorious sweatshops for young lawyers, who worked endless hours to line the pockets of the partners. Their goal was billable hours. Hers was actually doing some good in the world, like family attorney Katharine Fortier. When Lily was only seven years old, Katharine rescued her from an unfit mother, Karen Parker, and saw to it she was placed for good in a loving home with Eleanor Stewart, the woman Lily always considered her real mother.

Lily fell in with the traffic flow and continued her musings. Given her background as a child, it wasn't surprising at all that she had followed a career path to helping people like Maria. She was working now with people just like herself.

Clutching the steering wheel of the RAV4 a little tighter, Lily fought back the emotions her early memories always brought to the surface. The difficult moments in her life had given her empathy for others . . . others like the woman beside her, a divorced mother who needed a champion to help her escape a life of domestic violence.

Lily reached Culver City, depositing Maria in front of a small stucco home. She bid farewell with characteristic optimism. "Only one more day, Maria. Then you'll know your children will be safe."

With one last wave, she neatly executed a tight U-turn, and headed back to her office.

Anna reached an important decision as she drove toward Culver City scouting for a bookstore. She wasn't going to languish in this marriage mess another day, just waiting to see what life would hand her next. It was time for her to wrest back some control, to make the tough decisions that had to be made and live with the consequences.

There was no easy answer. She and Scott would both have to work hard for their marriage to survive—if they even wanted it to survive. The alternative was admitting her failure and walking away. That would be humiliating and a huge disappointment to her family, especially her father. Either decision would take all the courage she could muster, which was precisely what had her stuck in this quagmire.

It had been easy in some ways to retreat emotionally and act on the outside as though nothing was wrong. For the past three months, she had gone to work early most days, and stayed late in the evening because she couldn't bear to be at home with Scott. But she couldn't keep this up, and it wasn't going to just fix itself. She had been avoiding her family, and people had begun to comment on her weight loss and tired features.

What Anna realized she missed most over these past three months, even more than personal happiness in her marriage, was being in charge of her life. She had quietly stepped back from the world, allowing things to proceed as she watched from the outside. She needed to come out of the safe corner she had backed herself into, no matter how hard it was, or things would only get worse. So while the resolution was unclear, she knew she couldn't put off dealing with it any longer.

Turning on her blinker, she pulled into the parking garage of the Endicott Mall. Finding a space on the ground level, she parked and pulled her long frame from her car. She straightened her shoulders as she walked, as if physically demonstrating the resolve she now felt to break this impasse. She tapped her key-chain to set the car alarm, and turned toward the breezeway leading into the stores. Out of nowhere, a battered RAV4 careened around the corner and continued its rapid climb to the second floor.

"Crazy driver," she muttered as she rolled her eyes with disgust. Unfortunately, the whole world seemed as self-absorbed as she.

At precisely 11:40, Lily's phone vibrated against her waist to announce a new text message calling her to a one o'clock arraignment for another client's abusive boyfriend. She just had time to pick up lunch at the In-N-Out Burger on Endicott Avenue and to stop by her office to gather the files she would need. She placed her order and circled around to the small window to wait, justifying the greasy cheeseburger with the argument that she couldn't very well eat a salad while driving.

Her mouth watered as she pulled away from the window. This was a rare treat, and she was going to savor every bite. With one hand on the wheel, she pulled into traffic. As she took the first decadent bite of her sandwich, she felt something hit her chest.

"Oh, fuck!" Her cream-colored top now sported a prominent blob of ketchup right below the neckline, too high for her suit jacket to cover. Not only was her nicest silk top ruined, she would have to replace it before going to court. She couldn't very well walk in looking as if she had been shot in the chest.

Disgusted with her carelessness, she dropped her burger on the seat beside her and quickly sidled across four lanes of traffic. Signaling left, she turned into the Endicott Mall. Peeling around the corner to the second floor of the parking garage, she barely missed a tall, beautiful woman with long dark hair exiting her fancy BMW. "Careful, gorgeous," she muttered, checking out the stately figure in her rearview mirror. "With the kind of day I'm having, you don't want to be stepping in front of my car."

The second floor parking deck was wide open and she grabbed the space next to the breezeway that led to the upper concourse. Hurriedly, she dialed her office.

"Pauline, it's Lily."

"Did you get my text message? You're supposed to be in court at one with the Washburns."

"Yes, I got that message. Did you get my earlier one about Maria Esperanza?" she asked testily.

"Yes, I'm so sorry, Lily."

"I'll forgive you this once. But I'm not going to be the one to tell Lauren she owes Rusty Evans two hundred dollars for missing her court date."

"I feel so bad."

"It happens, Pauline. But you have to be very careful not to get these names and dates mixed up. We depend on you for that." She took one more bite of her burger, making sure not to let it drip on her skirt. "I need you to call a courier and send the Washburn files to the courthouse for me. I spilled something on my top and have to get a new one."

"I can do that."

"And please, Pauline—"

"I know. I'll double-check to make sure it's the right one."

"Thank you." Lily hung up and dropped the phone inside her console. Leaning over to the passenger side, she grabbed her wallet before shoving her briefcase under the seat. If she got in and out really fast, she would have time to finish her lunch in the parking lot at the courthouse.

Entering the mall on the lower level, Anna looked about for a bookstore. Not seeing one right away, she scanned the directory near the entrance. "Come on, come on. Every mall has a bookstore," she pleaded with the silent sign. There it was—Binders Books, just to her right about halfway down the concourse.

It was now a few minutes past the noon hour, and the mall was buzzing with lunchtime shoppers. But the only other person in the bookstore was a friendly young clerk with orange hair, Skye, according to her nametag.

"Excuse me. I'm looking for a book called *Top Down*. It's about the car business. Do you have it?"

"Sure, I remember seeing that. It's got the picture of the Ferrari on the front." Skye hopped down from her perch at the register by the shop entrance and led Anna to the business shelf located along the left wall. "It's here somewhere."

Anna quickly located the book, not bothering to point out that the car in the picture was actually a Maserati. She was oddly satisfied her nerdy accountant brother-in-law had expressed interest in a book about the car business. She had often thought about asking him to leave his accounting firm and join them at the family dealership, but she didn't want to be presumptuous. Not everyone shared her fascination with the car industry.

"Thank you. I'd like to browse for just another moment, if you don't mind."

"Help yourself."

Anna tucked the book under her arm and checked the shelf labels as she walked toward the back of the store. She had always been skeptical of self-help books, but she had to at least consider the possibility a pop psychology strategy might work to help her solve the current crisis with Scott.

Coming straight from the second floor of the parking garage, Lily entered the mall on its upper level. She scanned the directory and located Sycamore, a women's apparel store, at the far end of the building on the lower floor—about as far away as it could be.

The layout of the mall was confusing at first. The main entrance appeared to be at the far end on the top level, opposite where she was standing. Then she remembered the mall was built into a hillside, so the ground floor entrance on this end was directly below her.

She started down the escalator to the lower level and got her bearings for a hasty retreat once she found what she needed. She charged past Lacy Lady, not failing to notice the mannequin in the window wearing a red satin teddy. Next was a gift store, a dress shoe store, Peggy's Bridal Shop, a bookstore, Foot Locker, and finally Sycamore.

An online and catalog shopper, Lily rarely set foot in a mall. Though she usually only hated shopping, she absolutely despised it when she needed something in particular and was short on time. When she reached Sycamore, she was relieved to find right away a rack near the door holding the perfect style blouse in a variety of colors, and on sale.

Of course none were her size. It was that kind of day.

Her size was available among a new shipment in a slightly different style, but at a much higher price. Out of options, she pulled off the tag. "Excuse me."

The sales clerk rushed to her side. "Would you like to try that on?"

"No, I'm sure it will fit. I just need your dressing room to change in, if that's all right." She fingered the blob on her other top. "Here's the tag and my debit card."

The clerk took the items and began to process the sale as Lily ducked into the fitting room at the very back of the store. When she yanked the stuck louvered door, it caught her knee with a sharp crack, and a splinter in the wood neatly pierced her hose.

"How could this day get any worse?"

❧

If the picture on the cover—a man and woman standing back to back with their arms folded stubbornly across their chests—was any indication, this was the book Anna needed to start the process of dealing with her personal tumult. In truth, she held all the cards in their relationship right now, but she was too paralyzed to play.

As she grasped the book, she lost her footing and stumbled against the bookshelf. It took her a moment to realize what was happening, that the steady vibrations beneath her feet signaled an earthquake. These rarely lasted more than three or four seconds, but each one was an adventure.

"Hold on!" the young clerk yelled.

Anna did, grabbing the bookcase for support as the fluorescent lights began flickering and raining sparks around the store. The rumble grew louder and books fell from the shelves around her—at first only a few at a time, then in bunches as the floor suddenly tilted.

Then it went dark.

Anna strained to get her bearings as the shaking grew louder and more violent. This was no minor quake. A glimmer of light filtered from the atrium to where she was hunkered in the back of the store, enough that she could make out the shadows of the bookshelves as they crashed to the floor, blocking her escape.

With every breath, she prayed for the quake to subside, but it only grew more intense. She clung to the shelf as her anchor, even as it shook free of its bolts and tipped precariously toward her. A creaking sound drew closer and passed near where she stood. The smell of fresh dirt told her the earth had opened up within inches of where she was standing.

The shaking lessened for several seconds, and Anna held her breath in hopes it was over.

Suddenly the whole room seemed to pitch upward. She felt her feet leave the floor as she lost her grip on the bookshelf. Then with as much force as the thrust upward, she was thrown back down. As she collapsed onto her back, the floor lurched once more and the bookshelf hit her full force as it fell. The room convulsed one last time, followed by a deafening crunch of something heavy and large falling in the space between where she lay trapped and the way out.

Chapter 2

The worst part was it was completely dark.

Or maybe the worst part was the throbbing of her head just above her eye. Rolling onto her side, Lily traced with her forefinger the rim of the wide gash responsible for the sticky mess on the left side of her face.

She had no idea how long she had been out of it. This was her fault for asking what else could go wrong.

"I was only frustrated. It wasn't intended to be a challenge."

What happened after that was a blur. When the floor beneath her began to shake, she had reached to brace herself in the doorway. From there, she was flung headlong into the angled mirrors on two walls of the fitting room. As she lay on the rolling floor, her last thought before blacking out was to wonder if the sales clerk had run her debit card already, since without moving money from her savings account, her check to Judge Evans was going to bounce.

Lily sat up and tried to orient herself to her dark surroundings. She hated dark surroundings. Groping around on the floor, she located the top she had intended to purchase and held it to her wound, pressing hard to stop the bleeding. Her eye was sore and swollen, and no doubt full of the dust she had seen flying from the crumbling drywall just before the lights went out.

She reached out to get her bearings. Glass was everywhere. The mirrors, she figured. The floor—if it was still the floor— was uneven, and the wall to her right was crooked. She knew it was the mirrored wall, as she felt a few of the jagged fragments still attached. Behind her, the place she remembered as the back of the store was now a bare concrete block wall, and it leaned toward her.

"Where the hell did that come from?" she asked aloud, not expecting but half hoping to hear a reply. It seemed to Lily she was still in the tiny fitting room, such as it was. To her left was another wall and she recognized in front of her the splintered texture of the wood from the louvered door. That meant the way back into the main part of the store was past the door and straight ahead.

But where was the light? Even if the power had been knocked out, there had been an atrium in the center of the mall that should have provided some light. Maybe she had been unconscious for awhile and it was evening already. Too bad she wasn't wearing her sports watch, the one with the back light. No, that one didn't exactly go with her court clothes.

"Is anybody in here?"

Silence.

Louder this time, "Hello! Anybody!" Lily strained to hear another sound.

Nothing.

She struggled to stand, bumping her head sharply on the ceiling, which had sunk to a height of less than four feet. The uneven floor and the low ceiling made it difficult to navigate the darkness, but she picked her way along the edge of the hallway and emerged on her hands and knees through a doorway into what she supposed was the main store. Again, she called out, "Anyone here?"

From her crouched position, she realized the floor directly in front of her now sloped downward, and when she slid feet first in the direction of what she thought was the entrance, she stopped at the bottom of a crevasse. Racks of clothes had gathered where the floor had given way, and she lost her balance as her feet tangled in the garments, hangers and metal racks. The odor of fresh dirt was strong, and Lily guessed the ground had literally broken through the bottom of the store. She knew from living her whole life in California—twenty-nine years—that this was a very significant earthquake, and she was probably near the epicenter.

She was lucky to be alive.

Reaching forward, her hand came to rest against a wall of earth. The mall had collapsed, she realized, as she wondered what had become of all the people who had been inside. Was she the only one still inside? Or were the others . . . ?

With alarm, Lily acknowledged the truth: The worst part was she was trapped.

"Unnnnhhh!" Anna grunted, struggling against the bookcase that pinned her firmly to the floor. She hurt all over. Why hadn't she run for the door when the shaking started?

Breathing heavily, she regrouped for another push. "Unnnnnhhhhhh!" she groaned again, moving the shelf only an inch or two from her chest. With every effort, more of the books that were bracing the heavy bookcase fell away, leaving her left knee to bear even greater weight under the lower shelf. Her twisting and pulling as she tried to get out had only exacerbated her predicament, and now her knee was throbbing and trapped firmly in a vise.

"Help! Somebody!"

Anna had heard nothing since the loud boom. She kept expecting to hear people shouting and screaming, rescuers searching the mall to see if anyone was trapped or hurt. She had to let someone know she was here, but if others were in worse shape, she was all right to wait. She was uncomfortable, but not in danger . . . unless they had an aftershock.

"Help!"

Something had shifted in the bookstore after that last crash, something large enough to block all of the light from the atrium. And without the sound of shouts and voices, she had to consider the likelihood she was completely cut off from everyone else.

This wasn't Lily's first experience at being trapped in a dark space. Time had a merciful way of stealing memories from her early childhood, but one she clearly remembered was being locked in a dark closet on several occasions when her mother went out. To this day, Lily slept with a nightlight.

Fighting the urge to kick at the dirt and scream, she gathered herself for what she knew might be the strongest test of her life. The situation called for calm and control, not childish panic that no one would ever come back for her.

First, she tried to get her bearings with respect to where the store was situated. She had entered the mall from the garage and taken an escalator to the lower level, where she had walked to the opposite end of the concourse. Remembering the image of the mall from the outside, she figured Sycamore was in the part that was carved into the hillside, so she was below ground level. That meant there would be no service doors to the outside. The atrium was the only way out.

From what she could gather, the V-shaped crevasse where she sat seemed to be about five feet deep. One side was carpeted, which meant it was the original floor. The other side was dirt, where the ground had thrust upward. Most of the crevasse was jammed with merchandise, but that was good since she could balance herself on the overturned clothes racks to feel around the ceiling for a way out.

After what seemed like an hour of groping along in the dark, Lily came to the conclusion that getting to the center of the mall from here was probably impossible with this wall of dirt in front of her. It was as if the back of the store where the fitting rooms had been had fallen into a hole.

She had two choices. She could wait in this protected pocket of dark, damp space until rescuers found her. Or she could follow the crevasse into one of the adjacent stores and hasten her exit. If she was right about being underground, her best bet was to go back toward the parking garage, where the stores emerged from the hillside to sit at ground level.

Anna was exhausted. She had no idea how much time had passed since the quake, but she had been working almost constantly to pull herself from her prison. The shelf now rested firmly on her left leg, its sharp edge digging into the soft tissue around her knee. Her toes had begun to tingle, and she feared she soon would lose feeling in her lower leg.

Her repeated cries for help had gone unanswered, and she knew she was alone. The orange-haired clerk was the last person she had seen. Had she gotten out safely, or was she crushed beneath whatever fell? Anna shuddered to think what might have happened to the girl, and what surely had happened to others in the mall.

It was too soon to panic, but she would feel a lot better if she knew for certain the people outside were trying to find her. She had read somewhere a person could survive for several days without food or water. All she had to do was stay calm and wait for the rescuers . . . assuming they even knew where to look.

"Help!" she yelled again, her voice rasping in the still air.

She calmed herself, deciding she ought to save her energy and voice until she heard someone who might be near enough to help. She had no idea how large her confinement area was, but she had to consider the possibility her air supply was limited. Or worse, that the air was teeming with poisonous gases from ruptured pipes.

This would certainly solve her problems with Scott, she realized grimly, pushing the thought away as macabre. She assumed he was in his second-floor office on the campus of USC when the earthquake struck, just as he probably assumed she was at the dealership. Even though they weren't talking much these days, she liked to think they would have touched base, provided the phones were working.

At least she had called Carmen and told her where she was. But if this was anything like the aftermath of Northridge, it would be a few hours before people around the city were able to get damage reports. They wouldn't know right away the Endicott Mall had suffered damage. And while the ground splitting nearby likely meant the epicenter was close, it was impossible to know for sure. The very worst scenario would have her on the fringe of something catastrophic, something that caused thousands of casualties and calamitous destruction to the region's infrastructure . . . something that rendered trapped shoppers at the mall a low priority.

For a moment she was almost sure she heard a voice, but when she strained to listen it was gone.

After hours of combing the walls in the dark with her fingertips, Lily found herself crawling on her stomach at the bottom of the crevasse where the earth had split. The wall that separated the clothing store from the one next door had remained intact, but she discovered a small gap between the wall and the dirt at the lowest point on what used to be the floor. With both hands, she scooped the soil toward her until she had made an opening wide enough to squeeze through.

Pulling herself to the other side, she inhaled deeply, instantly recognizing the smell of new athletic shoes. This was the Foot Locker, she recalled. She knew she was still a long way from getting out of this tomb, but even the small lateral progress was exhilarating.

"Could I get these in a six?" she joked aloud. "I'm not picky. Purple is fine . . . orange . . . lime green." She had lost her own pumps in the fitting room. "Just make sure they're the same. I wouldn't want to crawl out of here with all of America watching my miraculous escape, and me wearing two different colors. My mom would be mortified. 'No, that's not my daughter!'" She laughed at the image, feeling strangely relieved at the mock interaction. "Fashion police arrest earthquake survivor. Details at eleven."

Lily rested a moment when she reached a pile of what seemed like sweat suits and T-shirts. She was tired, but she knew she needed to keep moving. Two things worried her. One was the possibility of aftershocks, which might bury her deeper. The other—just as dangerous—was that her exertion in the damp, dusty air would trigger an asthma attack. Prone to breathing difficulties since childhood, she always carried an emergency inhaler, but it was in her briefcase.

She took another deep breath, and was relieved to feel no sign of the tell-tale wheezing that precipitated an attack. If it came on, she would just have to take it easy and hope it subsided.

Best she could tell, the Foot Locker was just like Sycamore, where the back of the store—about a third of its depth—had fallen into some kind of gaping hole, with the front two-thirds apparently flattened against a fallen ceiling. In the dark, Lily envisioned a triangular-shaped tunnel, bound by the dirt wall on her right, the fallen floor on her left and the ceiling. The ceiling seemed about a foot higher in this room, and she took that as a sign she was one room closer to finding a store that had held up in the collapse. Apparently, the back wall of the mall had simply given way on the end that was built into the hillside. She was lucky the floor had dropped into the crevasse, or she would have been pancaked. Had she not been stuck in the fitting room, she would have dashed out to the atrium and crouched beneath the stairs. She hoped the woman who had helped her in the store had done that.

Her eyes had grown accustomed to the dark, and there wasn't even a speck of light coming from anywhere. Of course, she had been knocked out, so it was possible it was dark outside by now. Her stomach seemed to think it had been ages since she ate.

She groped around the perimeter at the top of the dirt wall, finding nothing but earth and ceiling tiles. With no way to access the atrium from here, she had to keep moving. She hoped the narrow crevasse she had followed this far extended into the next store.

In Sycamore, she had wrestled with the twisted piles of clothing and metal racks that had fallen into the deepest part of the hole. Here, that same gap was filled with what seemed like hundreds of boxes of shoes. Lily had never worked in a retail store, but like everyone, she envisioned endless piles of stock in a place always referred to as "in the back." That's where she was now—in that mysterious place called the back of Foot Locker.

She stumbled several times as she picked her way along the piles of boxes. Still fighting the urge to panic, she cheered herself with a running monologue. "Only someone with my luck would have trouble finding her footing in a shoe store."

Her efforts to remain upbeat and hopeful suddenly faded when her hand brushed against what was unmistakably a human arm, and she nervously traced it to the cold, stiff face of a man pinned on a ledge by the fallen ceiling. A wave of nausea passed through her at this stark evidence of what had happened. People died here. Overwhelmed with both horror and guilt, she knew this man was someone's loved one, and he deserved a final dignified brush with humanity. With her hand on his shoulder, Lily fought back tears as she soulfully paid her respects.

"Peace, my friend."

On her belly again, Lily felt along the far wall for an opening to the next store, now wary of what carnage her hands might find. She didn't find the opening at the ground that had been in the last store. This wall extended all the way to the bottom of the crevasse. That meant she was in for some serious digging, unless . . . Maybe if the wall had sagged along with the floor, there would be an opening at the ceiling.

Hiking up her skirt, she tried first to crawl up the incline that had once been the floor, but she couldn't get traction on the tile. That left scaling the dirt wall on the other side, which proved slippery as well, since the earth was crumbly and moist. When she finally reached the ceiling—about seven and a half feet from the bottom of the crevasse, she guessed—she was able to hold on to a light fixture with one hand while she felt for an opening with the other. Just as she hoped, the opening was directly above the lowest point of the floor, but it was narrow. She would have to flatten herself to squeeze through.

On her first attempt to pull herself up to the hole, her hands slipped and she fell clumsily into the pile of shoes. Again she tried, this time scraping her wrists viciously when she lost her grip. Now more determined than ever, she tried a third time, finally getting her head and shoulders through the hole. "Yes!" She inched her shoulders, chest and stomach through, at which point she fell forward, tumbling in a heap into a pile of books at the bottom of the crevasse on the other side.

"Shit!" she cried as she clutched her shoulder, which bore the brunt of her fall.

"Please, help me."

Lily was stunned by the sound of a woman's weak voice and she twisted in the dark to try to determine where it was coming from. Before she could react to the sound, the earth began to quiver again. Fearing the worst, she curled into a ball at the lowest point of the angled floor and covered her head with two books. The shaking grew stronger, and she could hear things falling around her as the ceiling threatened to give way once and for all.

Then it stopped.

Chapter 3

"Hello!" Lily called out. The aftershock had brought the ceiling down some more, but she was safely crouched at the lowest point in the bookstore. A scant thirty seconds earlier, and she would have been crushed between the wall and the ceiling, which she heard collapse in the room behind her. The decision to move toward the ground level entrance had been the right one.

Desperate to find the source of the voice she had heard, she yelled into the darkness. "Where are you? Are you hurt?" Hearing nothing, she feared the worst for the woman who had cried out. If the woman was up higher, she may have been crushed when the ceiling fell farther. "Talk to me! Where are you?"

Still no response.

Lily understood the danger she was in. The next tremor

could bring the ceiling all the way down, sealing her underground with no hope of rescue. But she couldn't forge ahead knowing there was someone else trapped here, someone who likely had no chance at all without her help. Her mind made up, she started to scramble toward the direction of the sound.

The bookstore was larger than Sycamore and Foot Locker combined, and lined with several shelves that had clung tight to their brackets rather than fall to the low point of the crevasse. Lily's only option was to pick slowly through the debris, careful not to put her weight anywhere that might cause the structures to shift. From every vantage point where she could balance, she groped in the darkness for the feel of flesh or clothing that might belong to whoever had called out.

After combing the room for what seemed like an hour, she was left with only one possibility, and it wasn't good. At the top of where the floor had fallen, along the back wall of the store, there was a ledge about six feet wide, similar to the one she was on in the fitting room. The ceiling had fallen on that side too, but not all the way. As best she could tell, there were some places that had at least two feet of clearance, enough to shelter someone who was trapped. But if the woman had been in one of the lower places during the aftershock, there was no guarantee she had survived. Lily steeled her resolve and pulled herself up.

The side closest to Foot Locker was where the ceiling was lowest, and she stretched her arm into the space and swung it from side to side. "Can you hear me? Are you there?"

After several minutes of crawling prone on the ledge, her hand brushed upon a full head of thick hair, then a warm face. She was flooded with relief, and almost giddy to finally find her quarry. "There you are. Thought you could hide, did you?"

She wriggled into the space alongside the woman, who was lying on her back. As her fingers traced the surroundings, she determined the woman was pinned by a fallen bookcase that seemed to be attached to the wall by a single bolt at its base. The top shelf lay across her chest and another across her hips. Lily found a strong carotid pulse, and gently patted the woman's cheek until she felt her stir.

Another tremor began to shake their dungeon, prompting Lily to lean forward instinctively to shield her captive companion from falling debris. So great was the comfort of knowing she was no longer alone, she never gave a thought to how much precious time and energy it would take to free the poor woman.

Anna's eyes fluttered open, but in the darkness, she couldn't see who was touching her face. Nonetheless, she felt calmed by the presence of another person. "Thank god," she murmured, shaking her head slowly from side to side. "I'm . . . the bookcase is . . ."

"Yeah, I can feel it across your chest. Can you move?" It was a woman's voice, a young woman by the sound of it.

"It hurts. My leg . . . the whole weight of the shelf is on it. Every time I try to push it up off my chest, it presses harder into my knee," she said. Taking a deep breath, she went on. "That last tremor made it hurt more. I think something fell on it."

"That's because it's pivoting on a bolt where it's still attached." The woman knocked her knuckles on the ceiling. "It's pretty low up here."

Anna felt the woman's hands wander across her abdomen. Then fingers slithered along the edge of the shelf where it held her hips firmly in place.

"Under normal circumstances, I'd buy you dinner first," the stranger said, the lightness in her voice a welcome relief. "I'm Lily, by the way, in case you wanted to know who was feeling you up."

Anna did her best to laugh, not minding at all the hands that brushed against her. "I'm Anna, and I can't tell you how happy I am to meet you. I've been screaming for hours."

"Yeah, well . . . sorry. I was busy trying on a new top."

Anna was comforted by the woman's gentle humor. She caught Lily's hand and squeezed it. "Thank you for coming to help me."

"No problem," Lily returned the squeeze. Then she pulled her hand away and reached lower to gently touch Anna's knee where the lower shelf pinched the swollen flesh. "I can see why this hurts so much. This shelf is digging into your leg. Let's see if we can take some of the pressure off."

"I can't lift it." From what she could hear, Lily was crawling around the area, shuffling books into stacks. "Please tell me you're not straightening up."

"Oh, good. A smartass."

"Sorry. I just had a vision of being rescued by an obsessive-compulsive neat freak."

Lily grunted, apparently struggling to move in the small confines. "Okay, here's what we're going to do. I need you to get ready to push up on the shelf on your end. I'm going to lift this end up at the same time and try to slide a couple of books under it. Then I'll put some more books under your shelf. Little by little, we should be able to get it all the way off." She crawled deeper onto the ledge until she was next to Anna's knee. "Hang on . . . I just barely have enough head room to do this."

"Just say when," Anna said, gripping the shelf.

"Ready? Now."

Lily grunted, apparently straining to hold the bookshelf with one hand while she used the other to slide the books. As soon as she got the lower ones positioned, she moved a stack next to the top shelf Anna was holding.

"Okay, you can let go."

Anna did, immediately noting that while the shelf was still touching her knee, it was no longer digging in. She could have cried with relief. Her foot began to tingle as the blood once again surged through her lower leg.

"Is that better?"

"God, I can't tell you! Most of the pressure is off my leg now."

"Think you can do it again? One more time, and I think I'll be able to pull you out."

As the circulation returned to her leg, so did the pain, especially around the joint. "Ready when you are."

They repeated the procedure, Lily adding another book to each stack. "How's that? Can you move?"

"Yeah, it's free. It hurts like hell." Anna squirmed, trying to no avail to slide out of her prison. "I need to get out from under this thing."

"Let me help." Lily scooted behind her head and Anna clasped her hands together across her chest as Lily's hands slid underneath her arms. "I'm going to back up a little at a time, and you tell me when you're out."

Inches at a time, Anna felt herself slide backward.

"Are you out?"

"Not yet."

"Good god, woman! How tall are you?"

"About five-ten."

"You're an Amazon."

Anna invoked the line she had used since she was twelve. "I'm perfectly normal for people my height. What are you, a Pygmy?"

"Only one of us is normal, and it ain't you. I'm a respectable five-four."

With every silly jibe, Anna let go of the tension that had gripped her since the earthquake. Almost overcome with relief, she grabbed Lily's hand again and squeezed it hard. "I'm so glad you found me."

Lily squeezed back. "Me too. Maybe two of us can make faster headway getting out of here."

Anna sat up, stifling a yelp when she tried to bend the leg that had been pinched by the bookshelf. "Do you know what's happened?"

"If I were guessing, I'd say the top floor collapsed. The only reason we're still alive is because we were both so close to the back wall. There's a huge crack in the floor that made the wall tilt forward. That kept the ceiling from coming all the way down back here, but every time there's an aftershock it drops a little bit more."

"Where were you?" It was weird talking to a stranger in total darkness. From her voice, Anna guessed she was relatively young, but mature—late twenties or early thirties.

"I was about to change my top in the fitting room at Sycamore. That's two stores back. I came through a Foot Locker to get here." Lily tugged her elbow. "Let's move down to the lowest part in case there's another aftershock."

They slid slowly down the incline of the fallen floor to the lowest part of the room. Anna's knee was throbbing, and she quickly discovered it wouldn't support her full weight, but it was useless to complain. She followed Lily to the far wall, and sat while Lily shuffled about among the books. "How did you get here from the other store?"

"There's a method to my madness, but I'm not totally sure what it is."

"That gives me a lot of confidence. Please go on."

"Like I said, this is the third store I've been in, and the space seems to be getting bigger, like maybe the ceiling hasn't fallen as far. The dividing walls between the stores shifted too. In the first store, there was a gap at the floor right at the bottom of this trench and I dug out some of the dirt and crawled under it. This one didn't have a gap at the bottom, but it had a hole at the ceiling because the wall sank with the ground," Lily explained. "If we can keep moving in the same direction, I'm hoping we'll find an opening, maybe some light from the atrium or even outside. There's no way out back the way I came."

"I don't know about the light from the atrium. I think it's dark by now."

"You're probably right. Do you have any idea what time it is?"

"No, but I'm wearing a very expensive watch."

"Figures. I don't suppose you have a cell phone?"

"It's hooked up to my Blue Tooth in the car." Anna hadn't meant for every word out of her mouth to make her sound like a spoiled brat, but she was sure she was leaving that impression.

"And I bet your car has one of those little emergency systems, where you can punch a button and find the closest Starbucks."

As a matter of fact, her luxury coupe was equipped with the top-of-the-line service assistance package from BMW. She decided not to offer that information, but Lily saw through her silence.

"All those fancy doo-dads and not one in your pocket. Now don't you feel stupid?"

"Somewhat. So where's your cell phone? Don't tell me. Let me guess. You're one of those technophobes."

"No, but I dropped it into my console because I only intended to be in here for five minutes." Lily sighed. "I bet you're right though. It's probably dark by now. Otherwise, we'd be able to see some light if there was a way out."

"So what's the plan?"

"It would be a shame to waste all that marvelous height." Anna felt a pair of hands on her shoulders turning her in another direction. "The front of the store is this way. Why don't you try feeling around the ceiling for a breeze, or even just air that's a different temperature?"

"That would mean there's a hole somewhere between here and the center of the mall."

"Right. Oh, and I don't want to scare you or anything, but when I was feeling around with my hands in that other room, I found a man who'd been killed."

Anna gasped as the grim reality of their situation struck her. No matter how much they tried to make light of their predicament, today was no doubt a tragedy for many people. "That's awful. So he was . . ."

"Yeah, I'd like to think it happened very quickly, though . . . you know, that maybe he didn't suffer. All of those people . . ."

"I know what you mean." Anna nodded in the dark, not even thinking of the fact that Lily couldn't see her. "Maybe most of them got out."

"I know I would have if I'd been closer to the door . . . and if I hadn't been knocked unconscious when my head hit the wall."

"You were knocked out?"

"Yeah, but I don't know for how long."

"I guess I was out of it too for a while, so who knows how long we've been in here."

"Have you heard anything at all from the outside? Like people or machines trying to get in here?"

"Just some crazy woman talking to herself." Anna chuckled. "Oh, wait. That would have been you."

"Very funny."

Whoever this Lily was, Anna knew she was brave and decent. And her confidence was contagious, she realized as she began her task, assured they would find a way out.

But after more than an hour of feeling with her fingertips along every nook and cranny at the ceiling's edge, Anna had found no clue of a break in the collapsed walls at the front end of the store. And to top it off, her leg was aching badly, but that she kept to herself.

"I've got something!" Lily suddenly called, breaking a long silence.

"What?"

"It's another pass-through near the top of the wall." Her voice was coming from the far end of the store, directly opposite from where she had first entered the bookstore. "There was this little crack in the wall and I followed it all the way up. It gets bigger toward the top."

"Is it big enough to squeeze through?"

"Maybe. Come give me a boost."

"Keep talking in case I make a wrong turn and end up outside."

"You're a laugh a minute, Amazon."

"You don't want me to find the cookbooks. You think this is a disaster . . ." Anna scrambled along the dirt embankment, wincing as her weight came down on her injured leg. She braced herself against the wall, supporting herself almost entirely on her good leg, and offered Lily a two-handed boost to the top.

"Yeah, it's definitely big enough," Lily announced triumphantly. "Give me your arm and I'll pull you up."

Anna gripped Lily's forearm and pulled herself high enough to hook her elbows over the ledge, giving her the needed leverage. When Lily dropped to the other side, Anna continued upward and through, falling in a heap amidst the pile of lace and satin lining the trench that bisected the store. Racks of wedding gowns had rolled into the gaping hole and toppled, layering the earth floor with a strange blanket of plush cloth.

"God, I could sleep for a week!" Lily exclaimed.

"Maybe we should stop and rest a while," Anna suggested casually, falling beside her savior. She was already exhausted from her ordeal with the bookcase, not to mention hungry and thirsty. And her knee was screaming in pain.

"As tempting as that sounds, I'm still worried about the aftershocks. The ceiling dropped a little more back there during the last one, and the next one might finish the job. If that happens, I'd realize my worst fear."

"What's that? Being buried alive?"

"No, being caught dead in a bridal shop."

Lily closed her eyes for a minute, silently thanking whatever deity had sent her a helping hand. Anna probably wasn't the

33

strongest woman, or even the most confident, but she seemed to Lily like a survivor, someone who wasn't going to let herself be beaten by this situation or any other. And anyone who could keep her sense of humor under a pile of concrete like this one was all right in her book.

"I think the ceiling's even higher here than it was in the bookstore," Anna said.

"Yeah, that's a good sign. Maybe it means we're getting closer to a part that hasn't collapsed."

"Look, I know it's a risk to stay put," Anna said. "But my stomach tells me it's getting pretty late, and if we stop and take a break for the rest of the night, we'll have more energy for whatever's next. And we'll also have a better chance of seeing an opening in the daylight."

Lily considered Anna's point, but she couldn't quell her anxiety about the aftershocks. "I'm still worried about the ceiling coming down. I really think it's best if we keep moving for as long as we can."

"So do I," Anna admitted. "Except I don't think I can go on right now. My knee is killing me. I need to rest it, at least for a couple of hours."

Lily felt awful. She hadn't even asked Anna if she was hurt. "Do you want me to check it? Maybe we can wrap it up with some of this cloth." Lily reached in the darkness toward Anna's leg and ran her hand up the shin to the inflamed joint. She heard Anna's breath catch in her throat as she anticipated the tenderness. Lily was shocked to discover how swollen it was. "Why didn't you say something? God, it must hurt like hell. We need to get that swelling down." She groped around on the floor until she found what felt like a small display pedestal. Pulling it over to Anna, she piled several cloths—probably ten thousand-dollar wedding dresses, she guessed—on top to soften it, and gently lifted Anna's leg to place it on the cushion.

"That feels good. Maybe you should go ahead by yourself. I

can try to catch up when the swelling goes down. Or when you get out, you can tell them where I am. I'm only going to slow you down."

Lily didn't hesitate. "No way, we're going out together. I guess we'll be safe here for a while. It's a low point. And by now, the aftershocks shouldn't be as big. We might as well rest a few hours and move out when your leg's better. Besides, with two of us, we should make good time if we're rested."

Lily leaned back and got as comfortable as she could.

A minute or so passed and Anna asked into the darkness, "So why are you so afraid of bridal shops?"

"Let's just say that walking down the aisle in a white dress has never been on my list of dreams."

"Wish I'd had that foresight," Anna muttered. "How did you get to be so wise?"

"Well, it isn't wisdom, exactly." Lily wavered. She was usually up front about her sexuality, but finding herself trapped with a homophobe would be the icing on the cake for a day like today. "It just isn't for me."

"Sorry, I didn't mean to get personal."

"No, it's okay . . . I just . . . I'm gay."

Silence. More silence.

As was often the case, Lily suddenly wished she had gone with her instincts and kept her mouth shut.

"Oh . . . so you really were feeling me up?"

From the sleep of the dead, Lily was jolted awake by a powerful aftershock. Without even thinking, she reached out for Anna and clasped her hand while the earth shook. The already buckled ceiling above them groaned under the weight of the collapsed building. She uttered a silent prayer that what was left of the walls and supports would hold. She could hear the sound of metal scraping and twisting and smelled the fresh dust and debris loosened by the rumble.

"You okay?" Anna asked when the tremors stopped.

"All things being equal, I'd prefer waking up to *Morning Edition*." Lily drew in a deep breath, and brushed against Anna as she stretched her arms. "We'd better get a move on. I don't know about you, but I'm ready to get out of here." She helped Anna to her feet. "How's the knee?"

"Better," she answered, but with enough hesitation to leave doubts.

"I guess we should get moving again then."

"How about you?"

Lily realized she didn't feel so hot herself. "Okay, I guess. I have a cut over my eye and it's making my head hurt."

"Are you bleeding?"

"I don't think so. Not anymore."

They repeated the drill from the bookstore. Anna crawled to the front of the bridal shop and checked along the top of the dirt wall for a draft, while Lily felt along the wall for a gap at either the ceiling or the floor.

"I think we're going to have to dig this time. There's a hole here but it isn't big enough to crawl through. We need to—"

"Listen!"

A faint whirring sound could be heard emanating from beyond the bookstore, but it stopped as suddenly as it had started. Someone was looking for them.

Lily sat frozen for several long minutes after the noise had stopped, straining desperately to hear the sound again.

"What do you think it was?" Anna asked.

"It sounded like a drill."

"Maybe we should go back the way you came. It sounds like they're looking back there for survivors."

"There is no back there, Anna. I think that first aftershock brought the ceiling down all the way in the shop where I started. Besides, I doubt we can get past the bookstore."

"Then maybe we should wait here for them to get to us."

"I don't know. Do you remember what the mall looked like from outside?"

"Sort of. I turned in from Endicott. I think the parking garage was on the left, and the—"

"That's right. The garage was on the flat part. But the mall was on a hill, and the main entrance was on the top floor at the far end," Lily said.

"That's right. I remember. I parked in the garage and came in on the ground floor . . . this floor, to be exact."

"And I parked on the upper level and came down the escalator. That means we're underground here, underneath that top floor. We have to keep moving toward the parking garage to get above ground level." The way Lily saw it, even if rescue workers had started to excavate the areas underground, they would be more likely to walk out in one piece if they reached the end of the mall.

"So we keep digging."

"Right."

"Right."

With their bare hands, they worked for what seemed like hours to chip away the rocky dirt from the bottom of the wall, Lily lost in thoughts of being trapped in an underground prison. Once the hole was big enough to crawl through, she tried it, but there wasn't enough room to maneuver on the other side. They had to scrape out a trench that would let them pull themselves all the way through.

Sweating profusely from the exertion, she pulled off her suit jacket and tossed it aside. "I picked a great day to wear my favorite suit, huh?"

"Yeah, me too. I had a meeting downtown, so I put on one of my best."

"What kind of work do you do?"

"I sell cars. What about you?"

Anna's response surprised her. From their brief conversations, this woman sounded well-educated and cultured, not like someone who told you a bunch of sleazy lies to separate you from your hard-earned money. "I'm a lawyer."

"I would have guessed that. You strike me as someone who could be pretty argumentative."

Since the darkness prevented either woman from seeing the other's expression, Lily was glad to get a jab from Anna's elbow to let her know she was only teasing. "Hey, watch it. You ever been sued for personal injury?"

"I guess I'd better move my ass . . . ets."

"Funny. Hey, I'm going to see if I can get through. That way I can dig faster on the other side."

"Sure you haven't changed your mind and decided to leave me here?"

"Don't be silly. I still need you for tall person things." She started for the hole but stopped. "Hey, I don't want you to take this personally, but before I go . . ."

"Yes?"

"I'm going back over by the other wall and take a leak. Cover your ears or something."

"I see. And then you're going to crawl through that hole and leave me in here. Do I have that right?"

"Right."

Anna squirmed on her back through the tight hole, glad to get an extra tug from Lily on the other side. Every time she pushed with her injured leg, pain radiated all the way to her ankle. To that, she added the tenderness across her upper chest, imagining she probably had a horrific bruise from where the bookcase had struck her and pinned her to the ground. "Where are we now?"

"It's another shoe store. Dress shoes and purses. Need anything?"

"Why couldn't it be one of those vitamin stores with all those energy drinks?"

"I know what you mean."

"How long do you think it's been, Lily? I'd guess at least twenty-four hours."

"Yeah, probably. If I'd known this was going to happen, I would have finished my lunch." Lily snorted. "I hate to think what my car smells like right now. I left an unwrapped cheeseburger on the front seat."

"Onions?"

"Probably. I only got one bite before this giant blob of ketchup fell out and landed in the middle of my chest. I was supposed to be back in court at one o'clock. That's why I had to run in here and buy a new top."

"You're kidding." Anna started to laugh. "I have to know. Are you still wearing that top?"

"Yeah, I'd just walked into the fitting room when the earthquake hit. Why?"

"I've been worrying that putrid smell was some kind of poisonous gas. Turns out it's just you."

"Stop it." Lily smacked her arm playfully. "I can't help it."

There was something almost surreal about the way they were laughing and teasing each other, Anna thought. It was as if both were only too aware of the danger they were in and unwilling to face it with anything but optimism. If she let herself think about it—which she usually did in those long quiet moments while she was blindly searching the cracks and corners—she knew there was no guarantee they would get out of here. Before long, they might be too weak or dehydrated to push ahead. But not talking about it was the only strategy that kept them going.

"What were you buying in the bookstore?" Lily asked.

She recalled the book she had been holding when the ground started to shake, but pushed it out of her mind. "I came to pick up a book for my brother-in-law. I had it right there beside me. I'd go back for it if you hadn't peed all over the floor right where we had to climb up."

"Me? What about you?" Lily shoved her shoulder. "I heard you going too after I crawled in here."

"You pervert. I should have known you were listening."

"I couldn't help it. I thought a water pipe had broken."

No matter how hard she tried to feign offense, Anna couldn't stifle a laugh. "If the rescuers came in right now and heard us laughing like this, they'd cart us off to a rubber room."

"Maybe," Lily said. "But if I have to be stuck in a place like this, I'm glad it's with someone who has a sense of humor. If you had been one of those hand-wringing wailers, I probably would have left you back in the bookstore."

"No, you wouldn't have. You talk a tough story, but you're a creampuff. I can tell."

"No, you can't. I'm a lawyer. I'm supposed to be tough as nails."

Anna's thoughts turned serious as she mentally clicked through the women she knew—her sister Kim, her business acquaintances or the privileged girls she had known growing up in Beverly Hills. She couldn't think who among them would have the strength or determination to take charge of this predicament the way Lily had. "You are tough. I'll give you that."

As in Foot Locker, shoes boxes were piled high in the middle of the sunken floor, making it difficult to walk without stumbling. But the crevasse in this store wasn't as deep as in the last, which Lily hoped meant they were nearing the way out.

At least that's what she kept telling herself. By her estimation they should already be above ground, but there still wasn't any light from the atrium. Given the strength of the quake, it was possible the collapse of the second floor had driven the entire lower level underground, especially since the ground had ruptured. She didn't want to think about it, but it was possible they would reach the end of the mall only to remain trapped.

What worried her most was how low the ceiling was in this store. Up to now, it had gotten progressively higher, suggesting they would eventually reach a room that was intact. But it was possible the end of the crevasse meant the total collapse of the second floor.

Those were thoughts she kept to herself. Nothing good could come from voicing her doubts, doubts that might make them give up and wait for help that might never come.

Just as she thought again about rescuers, the whirring sound they had heard before returned, sounding even farther away this time. "You hear that?"

"It sounds like a drill," Anna said.

"Or a saw. Maybe they're trying to cut through the concrete."

"Are you sure we shouldn't be heading in that direction?"

Lily slumped onto the floor in frustration. "I don't know, Anna. I thought we'd be safer here than back there, especially since I heard the ceiling fall behind me. Like I said, I'm not even sure we could get past the bookstore anymore."

"You're probably right."

"Or not. I'm just flying by the seat of my pants here." It was one thing to take responsibility for her own lot, but quite another to decide the fate of someone else. "If you really think we should try to go back, let's go."

"I don't know either. I hate to waste time chasing some noise when we don't even know where it's coming from. For all we know, they're up there trying to free people that they've already found on the second floor."

"Anna, they probably don't even know this hole is down here. If we can't see the atrium, they can't see through to us."

"Then we should keep going the way we're going."

"Are you sure? I'm willing to try going back."

"No, Lily. I think your instincts are right. But maybe we ought to try making some noise of our own."

As Anna yelled and screamed, Lily rummaged around on the floor for something heavy she could use to bang on the walls and ceiling. The only tool of substance was a metal shoe sizer, which made a pinging noise that she doubted would carry beyond the room. "This might make a good shovel," she said. "You keep yelling and I'll start digging."

Anna did, stopping on occasion to listen for a sign she had been heard. "I bet you're right. They're up there on the other end of the mall picking through whatever fell from the top floor. Are you having any luck?"

"Does bad luck count?" Lily dropped the shoe sizer and wiped the sweat from her face. "I've dug almost a foot down and it's nothing but concrete. This must have been a support wall or something."

"And there's nothing at the ceiling?"

"Not that I can find, but maybe you can feel a little higher." Lily didn't want to say it, but it was hanging in the air. "We might have to turn back after all."

She could hear Anna shuffling through the shoe boxes as she crossed the store to sit down on the dirt embankment. "We're going to get out of here, Lily. I'm sure of it."

"Oh yeah?"

"I just don't think you would have come along and pulled me out from under that bookshelf if I was meant to die in here."

"I hope you're right, Amazon."

Anna found a gap at the top of the wall, but determined it was only about two inches high and four inches across, and the wall was reinforced with immovable metal shanks. "We'll just have to think of something else," she said, trying her best to sound reassuring. She could tell Lily had grown discouraged.

"We could use a few minutes to rest anyway, right?"

Grateful for the temporary reprieve, Anna sank to the floor. She was about to doze off when it suddenly occurred to her to wonder what was going on outside their tomb. The sound from above had stopped, a likely sign that rescuers had given up. "Who's waiting for you if we make it out of here?"

"I'm not sure anyone is. I told our secretary I had to run an errand but I didn't say where."

"So no girlfriend?"

"No. I'm between heartbreaks."

"Yeah, I bet. I would guess you're the heartbreaker. You seem like somebody who can handle being in charge."

"It's a ruse." Lily was quiet for a moment. "Is anyone waiting for you?"

"My husband, I guess."

"You guess?"

"I told them at the dealership I was stopping in here to get the book. So I'm sure they told him and he's there by now." Anna grew pensive. She didn't want Lily to think she had married an ogre, but this dismal prison was depressing enough without adding to their misery by telling her sorry tale. "I don't want to give you the wrong impression. My husband's a good man. It's just that we may have rushed a bit in getting married." She paused and voiced her fear aloud for the first time. "I'm not sure we're going to make it."

"How long have you been married?"

"Not all that long . . . a little over a year."

Lily placed a hand on Anna's shoulder. "If you want to talk about it, I'm not going anywhere. Literally."

"No, that's okay." Anna shook her head in the dark. It was humiliating enough just to dwell on it. Sharing it with someone else would make it unbearable. "I've had a lot of trouble talking about it. It's just one of those things I'm going to have to work

43

out on my own. And with my husband."

"You rushed into it, huh? How long did you know him?"

"About four months before we got engaged . . . and another four before the wedding."

"That's a lifetime compared to lesbians. Haven't you heard what a lesbian brings along on a second date?"

"I have no idea."

"A U-Haul."

Anna didn't understand at first, unless it meant—"Are you saying lesbians move in with each other after only one date?"

"Not really, but it happens enough to be the stereotype. I think if lesbians could get married, most of us would. We're pretty big on instant commitment."

"Would you be married?"

"No, but that's no thanks to me. I seem to be most attracted to women who don't want commitment."

"But you want it?"

"I always thought I'd like that . . . spending my whole life with somebody. It would be nice to think someone would always be there for me."

Anna sighed. "I thought I wanted it too, but I'm not so sure anymore." Despite her stated reluctance to talk about the situation with Scott, here she was, saying things to a virtual stranger she hadn't told another soul. "I don't know. Maybe I don't have what it takes to be married."

"What does your husband do?"

"He's a professor at USC. I met him when I was getting my MBA. He was . . ." How much did she want to say? That Scott was different because he was interested in her business ideas? That he wasn't so focused on getting her between the sheets? "He's a very nice man."

"Just maybe not the man for you?"

Anna groaned and relaxed against the dirt wall.

"I know. You don't want to talk about it, but here we are all alone trying not to think about starvation and doom. You have a humanitarian obligation to keep me entertained," Lily said as she tapped the shoe sizer against the ceiling.

"Fine. So we started spending time together and talking about the things we had in common. At first, it wasn't even like we were dating. We just got to know each other as friends and he turned out to be the first man I'd met who had all the things I always thought I wanted in a husband. He was kind, interesting . . . good father material. And he didn't act like I was some kind of trophy." Nor did he seem interested in her family's money. "Then we sort of took things to a romantic level and I started thinking maybe he was the one. Eventually we got engaged and my parents planned this gigantic spectacle of a wedding."

In the dark, Lily handed her a jagged piece of tile, something she had chipped off the ceiling. "You must be an only child."

"No, but my sister eloped, so my wedding had to make up for her too." Anna shuddered inwardly at her memories of the elaborate affair. Over four hundred people had witnessed their vows—promises that now stood in shambles unless Anna could find it in herself to recommit to her marriage. Another piece of tile landed in her lap. "What is this stuff you keep handing me?"

"Get up, Amazon. We're going through the ceiling."

Chapter 4

"Damn, this thing is stubborn," Lily exclaimed. Once she discovered the false ceiling, she expected to be able just to tear it away and climb through the gap into the next store. But it was firmly affixed to the concrete above with a grid of metal braces. They had been working for what seemed like an hour to loosen just one panel so they could crawl up inside.

In the center of the room, the ceiling was low enough for Anna to stretch her arms up and reach it. Lily had located a plastic chair on which to stand, though it teetered precariously where she had it wedged between the fallen floor and the dirt wall. Each time they pushed, pulled or pounded, the ceiling gave a little but always returned snugly to its place. On one occasion, Lily reached through the opening when it was pushed upward and determined there was only about a foot of space between the ceiling tile and the actual ceiling of the shoe store. That would be barely enough room to maneuver, but first they needed access.

Trying valiantly to keep their spirits up, Lily had been jabbering on about how they could have picked up souvenirs along the way, emerging from the rubble in dirty white wedding gowns with tennis shoes and cheap earrings. One thing she recalled clearly was the red satin teddy in the window of the lingerie store. "Just imagine what we could pick up in Lacy Lady."

Anna was the one who was quiet now, probably mired in thoughts of her marriage problems, which she hadn't really explained other than to acknowledge their existence.

"Pardon me, am I keeping you awake?" Lily asked, still trying to inject levity into their predicament.

"Sorry. I was thinking about something. What were you saying?"

"I was saying why don't you finish telling me why you're so worried about things with your husband? Maybe it would help to talk it out." Lily continued to tug at the ceiling tile.

Anna sighed, and plopped down on the sloping floor. "It's humiliating enough without anyone else knowing about it. I haven't even talked to my sister about this, and I usually tell her everything."

Lily couldn't imagine what was so terrible that Anna felt she had to keep it all inside. "You don't have to be humiliated on my account. Just try getting it off your chest. Maybe you'll feel better. I'm not going to judge you."

"Well, it's . . . you see, I . . . I learned right before Christmas that my husband had fathered a child with another woman."

Lily had a feeling there might have been someone else in the picture, especially since Anna had been so reluctant to talk about it. A stepfamily didn't have to be an insurmountable problem, but Lily knew from her legal work with blended families that some people had trouble adjusting to new family members, especially when it meant having contact with former spouses or partners. "So all of a sudden you have a stepchild you didn't even know about."

"It's not the child. It's the circumstances."

"Is there an ex-wife in the picture?"

"Yes . . . no. Not an ex-wife—an ex-girlfriend. But this child was only a year old last July—which means he was conceived right after Scott and I got engaged . . . and after we had been intimate with each other."

"Oh, I get it now. No wonder you're upset." Lily stepped down off the stool to pat Anna's shoulder. "But you shouldn't be the one feeling humiliated. You didn't do anything wrong. And just for the record, I now disagree with what you said about your husband being a very nice man. Nice people don't pull shit like that."

"It's complicated." Now that the dam was broken, she seemed ready to talk. "The woman was his old girlfriend. He said they had been drinking, and he didn't know about this baby until we ran into them back in November. She never even told him she was pregnant." Anna sighed. "And I've been sleeping in the guest room ever since."

"Being drunk is no excuse. People have to be responsible for their actions."

"I know, Lily, but people make mistakes. He's really not a bad person."

"True. But screwing around is a deal breaker for most relationships."

"Yes, and it would have been for us if I had found out about it before the wedding. But I didn't. And since we got married, he hasn't done anything to break his vows, and he swears he never will. So I feel like I made a promise and I have to honor it. Maybe I should quit beating both of us up and get over it."

Lily was starting to understand Anna's dilemma. She was hurt by her husband's cheating, but bound by her own sense of commitment. "Those vows might have been spoken at your wedding, but they were implied the minute he asked you to marry him and you said yes. No one in their right mind would expect you to honor a commitment under these circumstances. The real question is whether or not you still love him enough to stay married."

"That is the question, isn't it?"

Lily climbed back up on the chair and started working on the ceiling again. "What does your husband want?"

"He wants me to pretend it never happened."

"Can you do that?"

"Of course not. And he can't pretend he doesn't have a son. He's excited about it, just as he should be, and he wants to be part of the boy's life. Even if he didn't, it's an obligation he can't ignore."

Flecks of dust and debris rained down from above and Lily brushed it off her hair. "But is that the issue? That he has a son? Or that he fooled around with somebody else when he was supposed to be committed to you?"

"The issue is that my husband now has a whole life that's separate from ours. I didn't plan to share the man I married with another family. And seeing Sara that night with the baby—he looked exactly like Scott—it was just . . . I don't know, bizarre. I felt like an outsider."

Lily's instincts said Anna should cut her losses, but Anna didn't need relationship advice from someone with her track record. With a strong jerk, she broke off a corner of the sturdy tile and reached above it. "Shit."

"What?"

"It's no wonder this ceiling is so hard to break through. It's held together with braces on every tile. We're going to have to break out three or four of them just to get up here."

"Can we do it?"

"Eventually. But I'm tired. You mind having a turn?" She put her hand on Anna's shoulder as she stepped down from the chair.

"Thanks for listening to my morbid story. I actually do feel a little better now that I've talked it out."

Lily heard bits of tile being snapped off. "Have you decided what you're going to do?"

"What do you think I should do?"

"You're asking the wrong person. I'd say it depends on how you feel about each other. Besides, you definitely don't want to be taking advice on your love life from someone like me."

"Oh, right. I forgot I was in here with The Heartbreak Kid."

"That isn't what I said. I make bad decisions. Repeatedly."

"So tell me your sordid tales."

"You'll think I'm pathetic," Lily groaned.

"Hold the chair. I think I can get a better angle up here. Maybe I'll feel even better if your luck's been worse than mine."

"Okay, but you're going to think I'm such a loser. And I'm only telling you the B-version. That's the one my mother gets."

Anna chuckled. "That's fine. I'll fill in the blanks."

"My first girlfriend . . ."

"No boyfriends ever?"

"Boys are icky," she said, enjoying Anna's laugh. "My first girlfriend was a young woman named Melanie. I met her my sophomore year at UCLA and fell in love immediately."

"Right, the U-Haul thing."

"Except Melanie wasn't a U-Haul kind of girl. She was one of those college lesbians, the ones who fooled around with women because it was cool. Eventually, they all find boyfriends."

"And Melanie found a boyfriend."

"Or two. Then my first year in law school, I met Becca Silby."

"I know that name."

"She was UCLA's All-American point guard."

"That's right. And she turned down the WNBA to go play in Europe."

"Who's telling this story?"

"So is that how your relationship ended?"

"Correct." A piece of tile hit Lily in the head. "Watch it."

"Sorry. Any more after that?"

"I saved the best for last. My darling Beverly." Lily didn't bother to hide her sarcasm. "I met Bev right after I got out of law school. She was ten years older, and had a five-year-old son who I just adored. So I thought, 'Great, someone mature for a change.' We lived together for about two years, until I suggested maybe we should have some sort of commitment ceremony. You would have thought I'd asked her to move with me to a straw hut in Zimbabwe."

"Not the marrying kind, huh?"

"Worse than that. As soon as I mentioned commitment, our relationship was over. But she couldn't just break up. No, she had to make me the bad guy, so she'd pick fights with me and then get mad whenever I lost my temper or walked away from her." Lily couldn't believe she was confessing to such a poor choice for a girlfriend. "And she told all of our friends that she asked me to move out because I was becoming a bad influence on Josh . . . which was a big fat lie."

"Why do people have to do things like that?"

"Because they can't ever admit they're wrong." Lily realized she was getting worked up, as she often did when she spent too much energy dwelling on her time with Beverly. Two years had passed since their awful parting, but the feelings were still raw. "So I'm a three-time loser," she finished. "If I ever do really fall in love, I seriously doubt I'll be able to tell if it's real. Now you see why I say you shouldn't ask me for love advice."

"You don't sound like a loser to me. You sound like somebody who opened up her heart and people just took advantage. Your turn again, okay? My arms feel like they're going to fall off." Anna had successfully removed another portion of the tile.

"Sure," Lily said, trading places with Anna on the chair. "Every now and then, I start feeling like I'm over that Beverly thing and then I hear all that anger in my voice when I talk about it."

"It's funny how some things get to us and we just can't let them go."

"I need to, though. Negative energy doesn't serve any purpose." She pulled down a large piece of the tile. "Except when I'm able to take out my anger on tile ceilings. I think this hole's big enough to crawl through."

"Ready when you are."

"Only two more stores to go, Anna."

"What if we're still underground?"

"We won't be."

Lying prone inside the false ceiling, Anna wanted nothing more than to close her eyes and go to sleep. She was exhausted, sore, hungry and thirsty, but Lily showed no signs of wanting to rest, so Anna couldn't bring herself to suggest it. Dehydration was their biggest worry now.

About an hour ago, they had climbed into the narrow crawlspace above the false ceiling. The support structure for the suspended tiles, a grid of metal frames and braces, was difficult to navigate, especially in total darkness. She was struggling with every move, her long legs constantly scraping against the bolts and sharp metal protruding from the frames. Progress was slow in the limited space.

"Damn it!" Lily said, slapping her hand against one of the braces. "We can't get to the middle part from here."

"Why not?"

"We can't move forward. All the braces run crossways."

"Can you tell if the wall sags enough for us to get through?"

"I think it does, but it's going to be close. I can squeeze my fingers through here"—she pushed them through a crack and slid them sideways—"but not here. So I'm hoping that means it slants more toward the middle of the store."

"I hope so too." Anna sighed and started to wiggle backward. "We'll have to go back to that row where the light fixtures were. It's the only one without the crossbars."

Lily groaned. "I'm so tired. Why don't you grab my ankles and drag me?"

Anna lent the request more serious consideration than Lily had probably intended, figuring it wouldn't be that hard to pull her backward. Her plan dissolved, however, when she discovered that touching Lily's feet made her giggle and jerk uncontrollably. "I can't believe you're ticklish. I thought we agreed lesbians were supposed to be tough."

"You're pretty tough. Are you a lesbian?"

The question came as a shock, not because it bore any trace of sincerity, but because it was a stinging rebuke of her stereotyping remark. "I never thought about it. Maybe that's my problem."

"I'd say that's definitely something you ought to share with your marriage counselor."

Anna was about to remark that her marriage counselor was her office at Premier Motors when Lily gasped.

"I can't believe I just said that. Anna, I'm so sorry."

"For what?"

"For . . . I don't know, making fun of your marital problems. I wasn't even thinking at all. It just—"

"It's not a big deal."

"It is. I was a jerk. An insensitive jerk."

"I knew that hours ago when you said I peed like a ruptured water pipe."

They both began to laugh.

"I can't believe you mentioned peeing again," Lily said, her voice a squeak.

"Me neither." Anna shifted when she reached the corridor that housed the light fixtures. "I'm going to back up some more and let you lead the way. You can do this faster than I can."

"Okay. Let me know when you think I should turn in toward

the wall again." On the second try, Lily found the widest part of the opening. "The wall's crumbling here, but it still isn't big enough for us to get through. I think we're going to have to break it away like we did with the tile."

Anna crawled along the adjacent corridor until they were side by side, chipping away at the drywall with their fingers. "I wish we still had that shoe thing we used to break the tiles."

"Maybe I should go back and get it," Lily said.

"You're going back to pee again, aren't you?"

"Whatever gave you that idea?" she asked, squeaking again. "Why don't you take a nap or something while I'm gone? It'll probably take me half an hour to get down there and back. Then I can rest a little while you use the shoe sizer."

"A nap would be nice."

"Try not to dream about your bladder."

"I really wish you hadn't said that."

Crawling out backward and finding the shoe sizer proved to be the easy part of Lily's task. Getting back up into the crawl-space without help was more of a challenge than she wanted to admit. It took her a half dozen tries to get enough leverage to pull herself up, and when she finally did, she was exhausted.

Worse than that, the crawl space was filled with dust, bugs and rodent droppings. The stagnant air and exertion combined to produce the tickling wheeze she had dreaded since discovering she was trapped. As she scooted closer to where Anna was waiting, she erupted in a violent coughing fit.

"Are you all right?" Anna asked, her soft voice a sign she had been asleep.

"I'll be fine." Lily rasped as she crawled into the narrow space beside Anna. "I'm having a little trouble with my asthma, but if I rest a little bit, it probably won't get any worse."

Anna took the shoe sizer from her and began pounding at the

edges of the crumbling drywall. Lily insisted on doing her part too, though her coughing spells were getting worse. As much as she needed to preserve her strength, she also needed to get out of this confined space.

"What can I do?" Anna asked.

"Nothing." She drew a shallow, raspy breath. "I just need to get out of here and get some fresh air."

Anna took the sizer and began to work feverishly on the wall. She refused Lily's further attempts to take a turn, banging away until the hole was large enough to pass through. "Okay, I'm going first."

Lily couldn't have moved if she had wanted to. Had it not been for Anna's hands hooking her forearms and pulling her through the opening, she might have drifted off in the crawl space. As she slid forward, she heard Anna groan in agony, presumably from bearing extra weight on her injured leg.

"It's okay, Lily. We're almost at the end. The air's better in here. You'll be okay."

Lily was taking rapid shallow breaths and coughing profusely. "I need to . . . prop up . . . breathe better."

She felt Anna scooting close behind her, and she leaned back against her chest. Soft hands smoothed the short strands of hair from her face, and Anna rocked her gently. For Lily, it was familiar relief. When she had severe asthma attacks as a child, her mom would hold her close and rock her while she wheezed. Lily knew she was in big trouble. Without her inhaler, the attack could get much worse. Anna needed to keep moving.

"You need to go on now," she rasped. "Send someone back."

"Not a chance, Pygmy. Like you said, we're going out together." Anna hugged her loosely. "Just get some rest and calm down. You'll feel better."

Lily closed her eyes and tried to relax, hoping Anna was right. She couldn't remember a time in her life when an attack this bad went away on its own.

Something was different. Anna awoke to Lily's vicious coughing spell. She helped her sit up and rubbed small circles on her back to comfort her as she gasped for breath. Anna looked around the gift store. A faint but definite glow was evident at the back edge of the wall going into the next store.

"Lily, I can see daylight. Look." Anna turned her in the direction of the patch of light. "Let's go."

Lily shook her head, apparently unable to move. "Go, Anna . . . I can't."

Anna was frozen with fear. She couldn't leave her. Lily had saved her life.

"You have to get help." She gasped for breath then coughed violently. "I need to . . . get . . . an inhaler," she stammered.

Anna squeezed Lily's hands and kissed her bloodied forehead. "I'll be back. It'll be okay, I promise." She stood stiffly and hobbled toward the faintly lit crack.

The dividing wall between the last two stores had separated from the concrete blocks that lined the back of the store, but the opening was too narrow to squeeze through. Anna rummaged in the darkness among merchandise that had fallen to the center of the room, feeling for something she could use to tear through the wall. Her hands wrapped around a wooden figure . . . a carved giraffe, she guessed, about three feet high. Holding onto its head, she pounded fiercely on the sheetrock until it began to crumble, her leg screaming in agony with every swing. With each clump of wallboard that fell away, the room grew brighter and brighter. Frantically she hammered, until finally she was able to squirm through the hole, elated to see a solid beam of light coming in from a quarter-sized opening at the apex of the room, about nine feet above the floor on the far wall.

"Help!" She screamed louder this time than she ever had. Looking about in the barely lit store, she spotted an extension rod used by clerks to reach items on the higher displays. Stretching it to its full length, Anna poked it through the hole to the outside. Up and down, side to side.

What if no one was there?

No, they had to be there. They had to be searching the building for survivors. It was too soon for them to give up.

After almost fifteen minutes, there was no response. She could hear Lily coughing in the next room and she yelled again.

But still no one heard. No one came.

Her eyes had grown accustomed to the dim light, and she spotted a mannequin at her feet, dressed in a red satin teddy. Anna pulled the extension rod back inside and tied the teddy to its end. Shoving it back through the tiny hole, she again waved it up and down, side to side, screaming for all she was worth.

The pole suddenly stopped moving as someone grabbed it from above. Anna pulled it back through, and yelled again. "Can you hear me?"

"We're here. We're going to get you out. Are you hurt?"

"I'm all right. My friend needs help. She's having an asthma attack. Please hurry."

"You need to stand back. We're going to make this hole bigger. Get as far away as you can. Tell us when you're ready."

Anna scrambled back to the passageway. "Go ahead! I'm ready."

The next ten minutes seemed like hours, but finally the searchers had widened the hole enough to illuminate the entire room. "It's going to be a few more minutes. We'll need to use some machinery to break through this cinder block," a man's voice assured.

"My friend can't wait," she pleaded. "She needs an inhaler now for her asthma. She can't breathe."

A few long seconds later, a head emerged through the hole. "Where is your friend?" the emergency medical technician asked.

"She's in the next store, back there." Anna pointed toward the hole through which she had previously climbed.

He disappeared, but soon the hole in the ceiling was filled by another man. "We want you to stay here. It's too dangerous for you to go back there. When we get the hole widened, we'll pull you out and send in one of the firefighters."

Anna was filled with a sudden rage. "Give me the goddamned medicine now! She's dying."

The man retreated and the EMT reappeared. "I'm going to pass it to you in a pouch. Do you know how to use it?"

"Yes," she lied. She figured Lily would know, and she didn't want to waste another second getting safety instruction from people who had no idea what either of them had been through.

Moments later, a red pouch dropped through the hole to the floor below. Anna hurried to pick it up and shouted upward. "I'm going back. You can do whatever you want. I won't be in the way."

With the hole now larger, the light extended dimly into the gift store, enough for Anna to make out Lily's form. By her lack of response, Anna feared she was on the brink of unconsciousness. She scooted again behind her and pulled Lily's head onto her lap. "Stay with me, girl. I've got the medicine, but I need your help." The EMT had assembled the inhaler for immediate use, and Anna held it to Lily's mouth.

Lily fumbled a bit then wrapped her hand around the instrument and pumped it once into her mouth, breathing deeply. The reprieve was instant. She took three or four deep breaths, and pumped the device again.

Anna almost cried with relief when she felt Lily push herself up. "We're about to get rescued. Are you ready?"

"You bet," Lily whispered.

Together, they ambled to the passageway. As they crawled into the lingerie store from the separated wall, Anna was overjoyed to see a firefighter descending a ladder, carrying blankets and first aid equipment.

"Anna!"

She squinted and held her hand above her brow to shield her eyes from the bright sun. Scott was shouting to her as she emerged from the hole the rescuers had made in the crumbling wall. He pushed past the security guard and broke into a run. Moments later, he was there, holding her to his chest, and she felt a convergence of emotions that threatened to overwhelm her completely.

"Thank god, Anna. Oh, thank god!" was all he could say as tears streamed down his cheeks.

Anna returned his hug, crying now as well. Over his shoulder, she spotted her sister Kim, who joined them seconds later in a group embrace. "I'm okay now. It's all okay."

Their joyful reunion was interrupted by the EMT, who was directing Anna to a waiting ambulance. Instead, she turned back to the rescuers as they brought Lily through the opening on a stretcher, an oxygen mask affixed to her mouth and nose. She was slender and blond, with small features that belied her toughness. A nasty gash crossed her forehead above her left eye, which was swollen and black, and her clothes were covered with blood.

"Scott, write my phone number down on something. Quick!" Anna hobbled over, crouching as low as she could to the stretcher, and took Lily's hand.

Lily reached for the mask and pulled it aside. "Thank you, Anna. I couldn't have made it without you."

"And I wouldn't have made it without you. You saved my life." Taking the paper scrap from Scott, she brought Lily's hand to her lips and kissed it. "Here's my number. Call me as soon as you're better. We're going to be great friends, Pygmy." She stuffed the paper into the pocket of Lily's skirt.

An EMT leaned over and swabbed a dirty patch of skin on Lily's forearm.

"Is she going to be okay?" Anna asked anxiously as he inserted a butterfly clip.

"I think so. We're just going to get some fluids into her as soon as possible. This is the best way to do it." His voice was reassuring. "You should probably have some too."

"Will I see her again at the hospital?" she asked as she staggered toward the waiting ambulance, still shaking from her ordeal.

"I doubt it. I think you're going to Cedars and she's going to St. George. We need to get her asthma treated right away."

"But she's going to be okay?"

"Yeah." He smiled as he guided her into the arms of another attendant. "She's going to be just great."

Anna turned back to watch Lily's departure. An older woman now crouched over her, crying and smiling, obviously joyous to have her loved one back. Anna liked knowing someone had been waiting for Lily after all, someone who clearly loved her very much.

Scott was still grinning at her and Kim was already on the phone sharing the good news. "Will you guys meet me at Cedars?" Anna stepped up gingerly into the back of the ambulance. She didn't want to go alone, but she didn't want to ride with Scott either.

"Of course!" they blurted, as they turned and ran for the car.

Anna peered through the window one last time as the rescue workers lifted Lily's stretcher into the ambulance. She couldn't wait to see her again, to hear her laugh and tease.

Lily had dreamed this earlier, just before Anna had come back with the medicine. They were both rescued and swept up by the people who loved them. But then she and Anna had climbed into a car and driven off together.

She had gotten only a fleeting glimpse of the woman who had

saved her life. Long dark hair . . . beautiful blue eyes. Her dirty cheeks had been stained with sweat and tears, but it was the kindest face Lily had ever seen.

Her eyes opened suddenly as something stung the cut on her brow. She was in an ambulance, where a strange woman was wiping her forehead.

"Stings a little, I bet."

Lily was too tired to answer. She just wanted to sleep. She could hear the radio crackle behind her head.

"Sounds like we just got a change of plans," the woman said. "St. George is full, so we'll be going to Valley."

"My mother . . ."

The woman looked out the back window. "She's still behind us."

Lily dozed until she heard the door open at her feet. The next few minutes were a blur, as her gurney was wheeled through glass doors and into a curtained room, where the EMTs hoisted her onto a bed. A nurse came in and gently removed her clothing, placing it in a plastic bag.

"What name do you want me to write on this?" she asked, her pen poised to scratch an ID into the white space on the bag.

"Just throw them away," Lily answered tiredly. Her bruises and scars were souvenirs enough.

Chapter 5

Seven Months Later

"I'm so proud of you Lionel. You were perfect. It was just the way we practiced." Lily drew the shy four-year-old into her arms and hugged him.

Then she turned to her best friend, Sandy Henke, at the courthouse today in her role as Lionel's social worker. "I think Judge Evans will come back with what we want. This kind of stuff really gets to him." What they had asked for was the boy's removal from a drug-infested and violent home. Lionel's grandmother had petitioned for custody, fearing he would suffer irreparable harm under her daughter's care.

"You did a great job, Lily. I'm in that courtroom for these hearings all the time, and I'm telling you, nobody goes into there better prepared than you. That's why ol' Rusty is putty in your hands."

Lily chuckled. "At least he's finally forgiven me for that bad check." Sandy's praise always meant a lot to her, especially in professional circles, where Sandy often introduced her to colleagues as a powerful ally for families in trouble. Lily hoped her late mentor, Katharine Fortier, could hear that from wherever she was. That's what she had always aspired to be, and seeing her work recognized by people she respected was far better than the money she might have earned for the partners of a fancy law firm.

She steered the boy to his grandmother's side. "You two should get some lunch at the café downstairs. We need to be back here by one. I think we'll get a decision then." She turned back to Sandy. "I've got to make a couple of calls. Any chance I could talk you into grabbing me a tuna sandwich and a bottle of water? I'll head outside to one of those benches." She indicated the exit.

"Sure, I'll be right there." Sandy and her clients turned for the stairs, leaving Lily standing near the wall as dozens of people milled about in the hallway.

Lily set her heavy briefcase on the floor and stooped to find her cell phone. She hated the unwritten rules of decorum that said she couldn't hike up her skirt and sit cross-legged on the floor. It would make things so much easier.

Finally she found her phone and pressed the buttons to retrieve her messages. Standing again, her attention was drawn to a woman moving among the crowd of people in the corridor. It had been seven months since the earthquake, and still, whenever she noticed tall women with long dark hair, it triggered her memory of the remarkable woman she had met on that fateful day. She studied each of them, hoping one day to see that kind face she remembered.

As the first message began to play, her eyes followed the figure, now walking in her direction, her face obscured by the people in the crowded hallway. Suddenly, the crowd parted and they were standing face to face, the unforgettable sapphire eyes staring back at her in surprise. It was Anna.

Both women stood frozen for a long moment as the recognition settled. Absently pocketing her cell phone, Lily was the first to find her voice. "Anna?"

"Lily?" Her face lit up with a broad grin.

They rushed the final few steps to come together in a joyous hug, neither saying a word. Lily found herself suddenly awash in memories of their ordeal. She relished the sensation of holding Anna close, amazed the moment was actually happening. She finally pulled back to take in Anna's smiling face, but wouldn't relinquish her grip. Tears of joy welled up in her eyes. "I'd almost given up hope of ever seeing you again."

Anna's eyes were shining too. "I waited for you to call. When you didn't, I figured you just wanted to put it all behind you."

Lily's heart broke to hear the hurt in Anna's words. "No, I would have called you. I tried, but I didn't know how."

Anna shook her head. "I put my number in your pocket when they were taking you away. Don't you remember?"

A vague memory of Anna leaning over her stretcher flashed in her head. She covered her open mouth. "Oh, my gosh. Now that I hear you say it, I do remember . . . at least vaguely. I was so out of it by then. And then when they asked me at the hospital if I wanted my clothes, I said no."

"No wonder . . . all that ketchup."

Lily laughed with surprise. "I can't believe you remember that."

"I remember everything."

Still gripping Anna in an embrace, Lily went on to explain how she had tried in vain to track her through the Red Cross and the hospital. "You never told me your last name. And the only Anna they had from the mall was some seventy-year-old they rescued on the first day. I know because I called her and talked to her for an hour."

"My full name is Christianna. That's probably why you

couldn't find me." Anna then recounted her own frustrations about trying to learn what she could. "They said you were going to St. George Hospital. I called them the next day and they had no record of a Lily or a Lilian, or even a Lilliputian."

"Stop it already with the short jokes. I didn't go to St. George. I went to Valley."

"I don't believe it," Sandy said as she joined them. "Is this who I think it is?"

Still beaming, Lily reached out and pulled her friend closer. "Sandy, I'd like to officially introduce you to Anna the Amazon. Anna, this is one of my dearest friends, Sandy Henke. Sandy's a social worker and we're here today to argue a custody case."

Anna finally broke their embrace to hold out her hand. "Hi, Sandy. I'm Anna Ru—" She stopped mid-word. "Kaklis. Anna Kaklis. Pleased to meet you."

Kaklis. Lily said the name in her head a half dozen times. She loved the sound of it. Strong. Distinctive.

"It's great to finally meet you too. Lily's been talking about you for months, and she described you perfectly. I think I would have known you anywhere."

Lily felt a blush creeping up her neck. How many times had she used the word gorgeous to describe the woman she saw when they brought her out on the stretcher? Anna was certainly that today, dressed smartly in a tailored navy suit, the cropped jacket accentuating her trim waist. A strand of ivory pearls with matching earrings finished the look. Stunning was more appropriate, she thought.

"I'm surprised she even remembered what I looked like, especially with all those other people around. Besides, we only saw each other for a minute after we came out of the mall, and she was kind of on the edge there."

Lily doubted she would ever forget what Anna looked like. "You made quite an impression, saving my life and all."

"Look who's talking."

"So what brings you to the courthouse?" Lily wouldn't have cared if she was on trial as a mass murderer. Anna would always be her hero.

"I came for my divorce hearing," Anna stated, drawing a deep breath as if waiting for judgment.

Lily could only stare back in astonishment, compassion welling inside her. Her instinct was to pull Anna into another hug, but Anna had withdrawn.

Sandy broke the extended silence. "Listen, I'm going to head outside and look for a bench. Come out whenever you're ready, Lily." Turning to Anna, she added, "It was very nice to meet you."

"Same here, Sandy. The pleasure was mine." Anna held her hand out again to Sandy, who took it in hers. "I hope to see you again."

Lily watched her friend leave and turned again to face Anna. She remembered how troubled Anna had been when they were trapped, how determined she was to work through her marital problems, and how she had vowed to stop beating up both her husband and herself. What could have gone wrong? Taking Anna's hands, she tried to find the right words to lend her support. "I'm so sorry things didn't work out."

"Who says they didn't?" Anna straightened to her full height and smiled. "I've always believed things happen as they should. This is better for everyone."

Lily admired her determination, but she knew from working with troubled families that divorce was a painful process for everyone. "I'm still sorry you had to go through this, but I hope you're feeling okay about it."

"I am. Better than okay."

Lily couldn't imagine what kind of fool would let a woman like Anna get away.

"I have an idea." Anna squeezed her hands. "I'm joining my sister and her husband tonight for dinner to sort of . . . well, to celebrate a fresh start. How about coming with us? I really want them to meet you."

"I'd love to," Lily answered, without a trace of hesitation. She would have said yes to anything Anna asked.

"That's wonderful. They can finally put a face on the woman I've been talking about since February."

Lily seriously doubted Anna had talked about her as much as she had talked about Anna. Sandy and her partner Suzanne had heard every detail of their underground adventure several times, as had her mother. The people at the law clinic were subjected to the story only twice, and practically everyone else she had talked to since the earthquake had heard of how she had beaten the odds—thanks to the mysterious Anna.

She noticed more details as Anna reached into her purse and retrieved a business card and a pen. She was the picture of elegance. The purse was Italian, probably costing more than what she paid in rent every month, and her watch was probably worth more than the entire contents of Lily's jewelry box. Her makeup was subtle, and her nails were short, but manicured and polished. From the looks of the things, selling cars was a lucrative business.

"Here's my number. Don't lose it this time," Anna said teasingly, as she scribbled on the back. "My cell phone's on the back. That's usually the best way to reach me."

Lily reached into her own briefcase and passed Anna a card, also scribbling her home number. "So what are the plans for dinner?"

"We have eight o'clock reservations at Empyre's in Beverly Hills. It's a Greek place, one of my favorite restaurants. I'll call and change it to four. If you want, we can pick you up."

"No, that's okay. It would probably be easier if I met you there."

"Are you sure?"

Lily nodded. Something told her Anna would be unimpressed by her small apartment in Sun Valley.

"The reservation is under Philips. That's my brother-in-law."

"Okay, then I'll see you at eight." She looked at Anna again, and without a trace of awkwardness, took her again in a mighty hug. "I've got to go. I'm supposed to be back in court soon, and I need to eat first or I'll get cranky and say something that gets me fined. That happens more than I like to admit."

Anna smiled back. "I can't believe we've finally found each other. You can't hide from me again. Remember, I told you we were going to be great friends."

Still smiling from her serendipitous encounter, Anna walked from the courthouse to the parking lot. She wasn't entirely surprised to find Scott leaning against the hood of her car.

"Anna." His hands buried in his pockets, he appeared nervous about seeing her.

"I looked for you afterward."

"I had to go over some things with my lawyer . . . namely, his bill."

Anna chuckled. Their divorce had been relatively straightforward, since most of the settlement questions were covered by a prenuptial. Thank goodness she had listened to Walter Mumford, her father's longtime attorney and friend.

"I didn't know when we might see each other again, and I wanted to say . . . I don't know. What is it civilized people say? Thanks for the memories?" His eyes misted with tears.

"Scott . . ." She wrapped her arms around his shoulders. Her anger about his indiscretion had passed as she lay recovering after the earthquake. But it was in the hospital she resolved to acknowledge her own mistake in choosing a partner. It wasn't that Scott had been unfaithful. It was the discovery that her feelings for him weren't strong enough to weather this troubled time.

"I'm so sorry for everything."

"You're forgiven. I swear." She wanted him to be happy, not to live his life shrouded in guilt about one mistake. "You have a beautiful son, and he deserves to have you around."

Shamelessly, Scott sobbed once against her shoulder and hugged her hard. "I'll always love you, Anna."

"I'll love you too."

After a few more seconds, they broke apart and he kissed her softly on the cheek. Then he was gone.

"I don't have anything to wear to a place like that!" Lily shrieked. "I'm going to make such a fool of myself. 'I'd like you to meet my friend Lily from Hooterville.'"

She had visited Empyre's Web site and explored the menu. Entrees started at forty bucks, and there was that condescending footnote, *Proper attire required.*

Sandy had accompanied her back to her downtown office for moral support. "You know, you're from San Jose, not Hooterville, and you're getting yourself worked up over nothing. It's just dinner with a friend. It's not like it's a date or anything." She cocked her head slightly. "Is it?"

"Of course not!" Lily plopped down in her leather armchair and sighed. "I just want to make a good impression." She fingered the embossed business card. "Anna Kaklis. Vice-President, Premier Motors." She was starting to get a grip on who Anna was. "All this time I thought she just sold cars. Hell, her family probably owns the place. BMWs, for crying out loud."

Lily wasn't a stranger to people with money. After all, she had grown up in Silicon Valley, where even teenagers drove expensive foreign cars. As the daughter of a schoolteacher, it was just another thing that had separated her from her peers. Still, she wouldn't have traded her comfortable life with her mom for all the money in the world.

Like other attorneys, she had opportunities for monetary success. But she had never been interested in that.

So why was she feeling so inadequate all of a sudden? "I'd like to think we could be friends some day. Really good friends. But I'm not sure we have all that much in common." Lily's friends didn't drive luxury cars. They were social workers, nurses and other young lawyers like herself.

"Look, it's just dinner, right?"

Lily nodded.

"So why don't you go out and splurge a little on a new dress? It's not like you're going to break the bank. It's just one dress. You can wear it the next time you go to a wedding reception. I say go for it."

Lily voiced her doubt, but she had already decided Sandy was right. She really wanted to look good tonight. "Come with me to Bloomingdale's so I don't buy anything ridiculous."

Several hours and nine hundred dollars later, she was slipping on the brand new black heels that matched her new black purse, that matched the simple black, sleeveless, shimmery dress that she wore under the lightweight black shawl. She withdrew from a box under her bed the small diamond earrings she had received from Katharine's estate upon her death.

She smiled wryly at the image that stared back from the full-length mirror in her walk-in closet, thinking she had never looked better. Anna probably wouldn't even notice. Or if she did, it would be because no one wore sequins with a shawl or closed-toed shoes. People like Anna got dressed without having to obsess about every single item.

On the way to the restaurant, she could hardly keep from laughing at the stark contrast between the way she looked tonight and the hunk of junk she was driving. When she spotted the parking valet at the restaurant, she decided to park the battered SUV in a public garage and walk the remaining two blocks.

It was two minutes after eight when she entered the restaurant. An attendant traded a small blue claim check for her wrap, and the maitre d' directed her to the bar where her companions were already waiting. Suddenly very nervous, she checked her reflection one last time in the foyer's mirror. Taking a deep breath, she gathered her confidence and walked tentatively through the entry. Sandy was right. This wasn't a date.

Sitting in a round booth against the far wall, Anna was impossible to miss. Lily had expected her to be beautiful in her evening attire, but she was dazzled by the sight. Anna was stunning in a deep burgundy strapless cocktail dress, the lines of her collarbone prominent against the creamy white skin. She had swept her thick black hair into a French twist, and her ears sparkled with diamonds that made Lily's earrings look like tiny chips.

The grain of confidence she had felt only moments earlier dissipated as she made her way to the table. The redheaded woman at the table—Anna's sister, she guessed—was striking as well.

"Sorry I'm a little late." Lily cringed as Anna stood and eyed her head to toe.

"I'm so glad you could come. I love that dress."

She loves the dress. Lily played those words twice in her head to be sure she heard right. That meant she didn't look like an idiot after all. At least her dress had passed muster. "Thank you. I'm glad I could make it too. I appreciate the invitation."

Anna held out an arm to draw her closer, and wrapped it around her shoulder. Turning to the others, she made the introductions. "Kim, Hal, I'd like for you to meet my dear friend, Lily Stewart. Lily, this is my sister Kim Philips, and her boring husband, Hal."

Hal stood to take Lily's outstretched hand, shooting an accusatory glare at Anna before breaking into a broad grin. "Nice to finally meet you, Lily. Anna's been talking about you ever since the earthquake."

Lily was thrilled to hear that, but doubted Anna's chatter had been anything like her own. She had talked non-stop about the woman from the earthquake to anyone who would listen.

"Indeed she has," Kim joined in. The attractive redhead surprised everyone by standing and drawing Lily into a fierce hug. "Thank you for saving my sister," she whispered, her voice filled with emotion.

Lily was almost overcome by the message, especially when she pulled back and noticed tears brimming in Kim's hazel eyes. "I can see I'm going to have to set the record straight on who saved whom. Your sister was the hero that day."

"Ha! I'd still be stuck under that bookcase if it weren't for you."

Lily gently jabbed Anna in the side. "That wasn't heroic. I knew I needed you for tall-person things."

"Didn't I tell you guys she called me Amazon the whole time?"

"And she called me Pygmy." Lily then turned to Kim, dropping the playful tone. "The real heroic part was Anna going for help when I got asthma and couldn't breathe. She could barely walk because of her leg, but she went anyway. I have no doubt I would have died if she hadn't hurried."

Anna chimed in. "Notice how she glossed over that bookcase bit? What she didn't tell you is the aftershocks were bringing the walls down on us, but she risked her life to stay behind and pull me out."

"You two are like the mutual admiration society," Hal said.

"I admire her more," Lily said matter-of-factly.

"No, I admire her more," Anna answered.

"Do not."

"Do too."

The maitre d' appeared and escorted them to their table in the dining room. Lily worked hard on her poker face as she opened the menu, deciding immediately her entire food budget for the week was going toward this meal. Following Anna's lead, she ordered the swordfish and a small Greek salad.

When the waiter left, Kim folded her arms on the table and

faced Anna. "So tell us how things went in court."

"Court." Anna sighed. "Well, I'm now officially divorced, so I guess it worked out the way it was supposed to."

"Did you see Scott?"

Anna nodded. "He was there. He waited for me at my car and we had a pretty good cry. I saved mine for the ride home, though."

Lily's heart went out at the sadness in Anna's voice. This was harder on her than she was letting on.

"I wish you would have let me kick his ass," Hal said.

Anna leaned over to explain. "My brother-in-law is very protective of me. So don't try anything."

Lily started to laugh, until it occurred to her to wonder what Anna thought she might try. Was she worried that—

"In other words, you can't be mean to me, especially not today." Anna said hurriedly, picking up her glass. "How about a toast? To a really nice guy . . . whom I never should have married in the first place."

Their glasses clinked and they took a sip of wine in unison.

"My turn," Kim said, shifting to aim her glass at Anna's. "To Anna, for knowing when to look forward instead of back."

Anna gave her sister an unmistakable look of love. "Thank you," she said quietly, touching her sister's glass and pressing against it for a long moment. Then tears trickled down her cheeks and she pushed them away. "Excuse me for a minute."

Lily wanted to follow, but Kim laid a hand on her arm. "She'll be okay."

"Are you sure?"

"Yeah, she doesn't want anyone to see her like this. She wants us all to think she's made of stone."

"She must be hurting a lot." Lily remembered how difficult it had been for Anna to talk about her marital problems. "It's nice of you guys to bring her out tonight for a celebration."

"Oh, this was Anna's idea," Hal said, looking at Kim as if for permission to continue. "But if you ask me, I think she just made up the celebration part because she didn't want to be alone."

"That's part of it," Kim said. "I think she really wanted this to be a celebration. She just feels guilty about it."

"Then I'm glad we're all here," Lily said.

"She's very glad you're here," Kim replied. "You should have heard how excited she was this afternoon. Honestly, she's been going nuts trying to find you for months."

"I've been doing the same thing." Lily related her version of events, all the while anxious about Anna's return. If Kim didn't soon go see about her sister, she would.

"You idiot," Anna mumbled into the mirror, shaking out the contents of her purse on the counter. She had dabbed a tissue around her eyes, smearing so much mascara that she now needed a touchup.

Why on earth was she crying over Scott? It wasn't as if her heart were broken. She was getting exactly what she wanted with this divorce, a chance to undo a humiliating mistake. They had to be sympathy tears, she decided. She hated how much this was hurting Scott, but there wasn't anything she could do to take that away. That die was cast before they were ever married, by him and his old girlfriend.

She also hated losing control of her emotions in front of Lily, especially on their first real chance to see each other since the earthquake. She should be celebrating their friendship, not wallowing in misery about something that was over.

She brushed her eyelashes one last time and freshened her lipstick before heading back to the dining room. As she approached their table, Lily looked up and smiled, and Anna felt a surge of excitement. How lucky she was to have Lily back in her life.

"Sorry. Did I miss anything?"

Hal jumped up to help Anna with her chair. "Lily was telling us about her work at the law clinic."

"I want to hear too. Start over." In truth, Anna already knew a good bit about the Braxton Street Legal Aid Clinic, because she had followed the URL on Lily's business card to the Web site. She was ten times more impressed than if her job had been with one of the high-powered downtown firms.

Lily talked about her job through dinner, and when a tuxedoed waiter began clearing their plates, she excused herself to the ladies' room.

"She's very nice, Anna," Kim gushed.

"Didn't I tell you? There's just something about her that . . . I don't know, shines. I know that sounds stupid, but she's an amazing person."

"She certainly doesn't look like any lesbian I know," Hal said, prompting his wife to smack him on the arm.

"I can't believe you just said that."

"Said what? She's cute."

"Like lesbians can't be cute?"

"You know what I mean."

"No, I don't."

Anna would have jumped on him too, but Kim was doing an adequate job on her own. It wasn't unusual for them to gang up on Hal when they were together, to tease him about his conservative demeanor or how he loved his boat more than his wife. Always good-natured, he took it in stride. Anna thought him the perfect foil for her sister's vivacious personality, and she loved him like a brother.

"Just because people can make you as an accountant from across the room doesn't mean everyone else should fit a stereotype," Kim continued.

Hal tossed his hands up in surrender. "Sorry. I obviously misspoke."

Anna didn't know many lesbians, but the ones she knew looked pretty much like everyone else. She didn't recall seeing any dressed as elegantly as Lily was tonight, but that didn't mean they didn't. "Where do you see all these lesbians, Hal?"

He shrugged. "There was a group at Berkeley . . . they didn't shave their legs."

Kim sighed indulgently and looked at Anna. "I can't take him anywhere."

"You need to get out more, Hal. Those stereotypes don't work anymore."

"Stereotypes?" Lily suddenly returned to her seat.

"Yeah, it happens to me all the time at work," Anna said quickly, hoping Lily hadn't heard too much. "I was just telling them about an incident on the lot yesterday. The sales staff came in at seven for training on next year's features. Right before we opened at eight, this guy drove up in a Mitsubishi Eclipse, Special Edition and started looking at the 535i with the Sport Package." She realized too late that she probably sounded like a nerd talking about cars in such detail to people not in the business. "I walked out and asked if he had any questions, and he said 'No, I've been doing my research. I already know probably as much as you do about this car.'" She deepened her voice and bobbed her head back and forth as she mocked him.

"Right, like he knows more than my sister with the mechanical engineering degree," Kim interjected.

"So then he said he wanted to make an offer on the car, and asked me to go get the manager. I explained to him that the manager was in a meeting, and I could handle the transaction. But no, he insisted, so I dragged Brad—he's our sales manager—out of the meeting to talk to him. They hammered out a price, but Brad said he needed the owner's okay—which wasn't true, but Brad wanted to jerk his chain—so he paged me to his office to look over the deal. You should have seen the look on that man's face when I walked back in."

"So what did you do?" Lily asked, her eyes wide.

"Oh, I approved it. Brad doesn't give cars away. And when

this guy came back to pick up his new car, I met him again and gave him the overview. I told him everything he never wanted to know about twin turbo technology and piezo fuel injection, and all he could do was nod and say, 'uh-huh.'"

"I bet that was priceless."

"Happens all the time."

"Because it's a stereotype that women don't know anything about cars," Lily said.

"Right."

The waiter returned at that moment to offer coffee and dessert. He was back soon with baklava and espresso.

"So what part of town do you live in, Lily?" Kim asked.

"Sun Valley."

"Do you have a house? A condo?"

"Uh-oh, Kim's putting on her real estate hat," Hal said.

"I am not. I just wanted to know."

"Actually, I live in an apartment. It's in a prime location, I'm told, convenient to public transportation. I learned after moving in that it means it's directly underneath the flight path for Burbank."

Anna smiled, remembering how Lily had kept her sense of humor when they were trapped in the mall.

"I've been saving for a down payment on a house, but every time I get ready to look, the prices jump again."

"Well, at the risk of being accused of doing business at dinner"—she shot a sidelong glance at her husband—"give me a call if you want some help finding what you want. I sometimes get a heads-up on new listings before they go on the market." She fished a business card from her purse and passed it across the table. "And I have hundreds of friends all over LA who can help out as well."

"Wow, thanks. I will. Hal, I don't suppose you have any ideas for making my modest savings account explode into a fortune in a few short weeks, do you?"

"I wish." Hal reached over and covered his wife's hand with his. "I hate to be a party pooper, but I'm about ready to call it a night."

"He has a date with his beloved boat in the morning," Kim whispered conspiratorially.

Anna wasn't ready for the evening to end, but she had to admit she was physically tired. She had been working long hours lately to get her mind off her personal problems, and today in particular had been especially stressful.

"Did our waiter bring the check?" Hal asked.

Kim leaned over and whispered loud enough for everyone to hear. "Yes, but Anna slipped him her credit card when he brought the dessert. Didn't you see that?"

"Apparently not."

"I didn't see it either," Lily said. "Thank you so much."

"You're so welcome," Anna answered. This was her celebration, and she didn't mind footing the bill.

While the women waited for their wraps, Hal exited to order their car. Anna helped Lily with her shawl, wishing they could talk longer. She thought about suggesting a drink, but she really was tired, and besides, she had ridden to the restaurant with Hal and Kim.

"Lily, you should give Hal your valet ticket too," Kim said. "He'll get your car while we wait."

"Mine's in the garage around the corner. There was a line for the valet, and I was worried about being late, so I just parked it myself."

"How would you feel about dropping me at home?" Anna asked suddenly. "I live pretty close. That way, you won't have to walk to the garage by yourself."

Lily seemed to hesitate, but answered, "Sure, I'd be happy to."

"If it's any trouble—"

"Not at all. I was just thinking about the mess in my car."

"Still leaving burgers on the front seat?"

"Oh, you're funny, Amazon." They said goodnight to Kim and Hal, and began the short walk to the garage. Lily gestured toward Anna's leg. "So is that limp a souvenir from the earthquake?"

"Yeah, I had a little crack in my femur. Can you believe that?"

"You're kidding. Well, I guess I'm not really surprised since it was so swollen."

"It's all right now. It just gets stiff when I sit for a long time. The doctor says it'll be fine eventually."

"You never let on that it hurt that much."

"You didn't strike me as the sympathetic sort."

"Now that hurts." Lily smiled, letting Anna know she wasn't serious. "You know, it's really amazing when you think about it . . . what we lived through."

"It is. I think about it a lot. I even had nightmares for a while."

"Me too."

"But I'm not the only one with a souvenir." Anna reached out and gently traced the small red scar above Lily's left eye. "I couldn't believe it when we came out of that hole and you were covered with all that blood."

"Some of it was ketchup, remember?"

Anna laughed. "All in all, we were both pretty lucky, I'd say."

"Definitely . . . and meeting you in there was the lucky part."

"I know exactly what you mean." It was gratifying for Anna to learn they felt the same way, especially after thinking for so long their shared experience hadn't made much of a lasting impression on Lily. "I hope we don't lose touch again."

"I don't intend to."

They climbed the stairs to the second floor of the garage, where Anna looked at the row of cars, wondering which one might be Lily's. As a car dealer, she had always felt she could tell a lot about people by what sort of car they drove.

Lily pulled her car keys from her purse and clicked the key

fob, causing the lights to flash on a RAV4 that had seen better days. "You know, when I was in the hospital after the earthquake, one of my comforts was when they told me the parking garage had collapsed. I was looking forward to collecting the insurance money and getting a new car."

Anna watched in amusement as Lily opened the driver's door and stretched across the front seat to roll down the passenger window.

"But as luck would have it, mine was the only car in the whole garage that came out without a single scratch that wasn't there to begin with."

Lily then walked around the car and reached through the window, giving the door handle a hard yank as she leaned back. Anna stepped up into the passenger seat, and Lily slammed the door.

"Well, at the risk of sounding a lot like my sister, I sell cars."

"You two are quite the tag-team. Are there others I should watch out for?"

"No, just the two of us. Kim's my stepsister actually. My mom died of breast cancer when I was ten, and my dad married her mom four years later. Kim's only a year younger, so we got to be friends right away. I can't imagine being closer to anyone."

"I can tell you're close to each other. And Hal is such a good sport to put up with you two."

"He is. My sister really lucked out." Despite Lily's arrival to liven up the evening, Anna's thoughts kept drifting back to Scott. Most of her close friends and associates knew by now that she and Scott were splitting up, but word of their divorce would likely prompt a fresh spate of fishing expeditions for details, which Anna had shared only with Kim, Hal and Lily. While she appreciated the calls and cards from well-meaning friends, each message was a humbling reminder of her failure. Finding Lily again was just the antidote she needed to remember that some things in her life had gone right.

Chapter 6

"I couldn't believe it either, Mom. I just looked up and there she was." Lily paced the floor of her bedroom while she talked on the phone, still flying high with excitement from her dinner with Anna the night before.

"I wish I could meet her. I'd give her a big hug for helping you out of there."

"Her sister did that to me last night. Anna told everybody I saved her."

"Well, you did."

"Not any more than she saved me." She smiled at the realization they were having the same conversation as the one from the night before. The truth was neither of them would be here if not for the other, and that's what made their bond special. "She's so nice. And her family owns the BMW dealership in Beverly Hills. I drove her home after dinner. Her house is like a mansion."

"When did you start being impressed by things like that?"

"I didn't say I was impressed. It's just that I had no idea she was so well-off. All she said was she sold cars." She thought back to their conversation at dinner. "I think she got a surprise too, because I told her back then I was a lawyer. She found out yesterday that I worked for a legal aid clinic instead of some big law firm. So she turned out to be a big shot, and I turned out to be a big nobody."

"Don't you even say such a thing. Katharine would spin in her grave."

"I don't mean it that way. I just thought it was funny we had such opposite views of each other."

"Maybe I'll meet her next time I come down."

Since the earthquake, she and her mother had seen each other at least once a month, no longer satisfied with the phone calls and fleeting visits. Life and love were more precious to them now.

"Yeah, that would be fun. You're about due for a visit. " Lily was already thinking ahead for excuses to call and plan another get-together with Anna. Since she had met Kim and Hal, it was only fair to have Anna meet her family.

"So . . . are you . . . is Anna . . . are you friends?"

It took a moment for her mother's real question to register. "Yes. I mean, that's what I hope we'll be. Anna's not a lesbian, Mom. She just got divorced."

"What does that prove? If I were a lesbian, I'd get divorced too."

Lily laughed. "You're a nut."

"I'm just looking out for you. If you aren't going to give me grandchildren, at least you can give me a daughter-in-law."

"Maybe one of these days, I will. But don't expect it to be this one." Lily knew she was lucky to have such an open relationship with her mother, but for some strange reason, talking about the women she dated was always awkward. The only one she had ever brought home was Beverly, and while her mother had been polite, she had not been particularly warm. Her mom said later—after Beverly had ended the relationship—it was a mother's intuition, that Beverly hadn't seemed a good fit.

Her mother sighed dramatically, causing Lily to laugh.

"But I still want you to meet her . . . as long as you behave yourself." She glanced at the bedside clock. "I have to go. Sandy and Suzanne are having a cookout."

"Tell them I said hi."

"I will. I love you."

"I love you too, sweetie."

Lily clicked the "end" button on her phone and stared at it as the line went dead. "And if Anna Kaklis turns out to be a lesbian, I promise you'll be the second to know."

Anna pressed the redial for what seemed like the twentieth time. She had waffled all day on whether or not to call Lily again so soon, but once she made the decision, she was determined to get through. It sure seemed as if they had hit it off, so why shouldn't they do things together when they had the chance?

"Hello."

She was startled to finally hear a real voice instead of the voicemail message telling her the party was on the phone. "Lily?"

"Yes. Anna?"

"I'm afraid so." Lily chuckled at her response, and Anna relaxed. She had no idea why she was so nervous about calling.

"What are you up to, Amazon? Six feet?"

"You little people are always clever." She tried to feign offense, but couldn't pull it off. "I'm still at work. What are you doing?"

"I'm heading for a cookout at Sandy's. You remember my friend from the courthouse?"

"Of course, the social worker. She seems like a nice person."

"She is. We've been good friends for about five years."

A thought suddenly occurred to Anna. "You and Sandy . . . are you . . . ?"

"Oh, gosh no!" Lily laughed.

"Sorry. That was probably nosy."

"Not at all. I just had a similar conversation with someone else and it struck me funny."

"If that's the case, maybe you and Sandy are the only ones without a clue."

"I really don't think Suzanne would appreciate my attraction to her wife, if you catch my drift."

"Ah, so Sandy and Suzanne are a couple, and you're . . . what? Chopped liver?"

"That's exactly right. Always on the outside looking in."

Anna could practically hear the smile on Lily's face, and she couldn't resist playing along. "So sad."

"I told you I was a loser."

"Yes, you did. But if you would allow me to put a little light in your lonely life, I have an invitation for you. I was calling to see if you had any interest in going to the Dodgers game tomorrow. My account manager at the *LA Times* sent me two tickets to their skybox."

"The skybox?"

"Yes, you know. Their corporate suite. We spend a lot of money on advertising, and they pass on tickets to things from time to time."

"Are you kidding? The Dodgers on a Sunday afternoon? I'd love to."

"Great. It starts at one. What if I come by and pick you up about twelve fifteen?"

"Are you sure you don't mind? I could meet you somewhere, or I could come by and get you."

"No, that's okay. Just give me your address. I have a GPS in the car. I'll punch it in."

"If you're sure." Lily gave her the address. "I've never been in a skybox before. What should I wear?"

"Well, they're a little stiff. I always try to dress like I think Hal would."

"That's not exactly the fashion advice I was looking for. And I don't own a brown tie."

"Neither should he. I usually wear slacks and a nice shirt. And bring a sweater, because they always run the air conditioner on full blast."

"Okay, that helps."

"Good. I'll see you tomorrow."

"I can't wait. Oh, and Anna?"

"Yes?"

"You shouldn't be at work at seven o'clock on Saturday night."

"I know, and I'm leaving now. Tell Sandy I said hello."

"I will. Thanks for calling."

Anna hung up and twirled in her desk chair. If she had more friends like Lily, maybe she would have better things to do on a Saturday night.

Lily couldn't wait to tell Sandy and Suzanne all about her evening out. In fact, it would probably take a concerted effort on her part to talk about anything else.

From their driveway, she could smell the burning charcoal as soon as she stepped from her car, so she followed the path around the garage to the redwood deck. Suzanne was tending the grill, and she could hear Sandy in the kitchen.

"I brought wine," she announced, holding up Sandy's favorite merlot.

Suzanne wiped her hands on her jeans before giving Lily a hug. Then Sandy burst through the back door and claimed her hug as well. Lily always loved the exuberance of their greetings, as if they hadn't seen each other in months.

Sandy took the bottle and began teasing the top with a corkscrew. "So tell us everything."

"It was so much fun. I had a great time. Anna was so nice, and so was her sister. Well, not really her sister. Kim's her stepsister. She sells real estate, and she even offered to help me look for a house whenever I got ready. Anna's dad married Kim's mom when Anna was fourteen. Kim says she's much, much younger than Anna, but I think it's only a year. Anna's almost thirty-two. And Kim's husband is Hal. He's really sweet. They made fun of him like you wouldn't believe, but it just rolled off his back."

She knew from their indulgent grins that she was barely making sense with the train of details, but she was too excited to rein herself in.

"They had the most delicious swordfish I've ever eaten. No wonder that's Anna's favorite restaurant. Oh, and you were right about the dress, Sandy. It was perfect. At first, I wasn't so sure, but then Anna said she loved it. I wore the earrings I got from Katharine. The diamonds, you remember?"

Sandy nodded, still grinning.

"They were like little specks next to the ones Anna had. And hers showed up even bigger because she had her hair up. God, she's beautiful."

Suzanne grabbed the nozzle of the hose and aimed it in Lily's direction. "Should I hose her down, honey?"

Sandy laughed and shook her head. "Let's give her a while longer, but only if she promises to breathe between sentences."

Lily laughed along, not caring about their teasing. She knew they were happy for her, and they were the kind of friends who enjoyed her excitement, no matter what they said. "I can't help it. I'm excited." She turned to Suzanne. "Did Sandy tell you Anna tried to track me down through St. George?"

"Yeah, but we were slammed. I didn't even get to leave the ER for almost three days."

"That was awful. I remember when you got home you just crashed for thirty-six hours," Sandy said. "Wouldn't you have freaked out if they'd brought Lily in?"

"Hell, yes. It was hard enough to concentrate on work when I didn't know where everybody was. If my friends had started coming through the door, I would have had a meltdown."

Lily knew better than to listen to Suzanne's ranting. From what Sandy said, Suzanne was an excellent nurse whose biggest problem was not being able to say no when asked to work double shifts. "It really was something to see people after the earthquake and realize what everyone had been through."

"Nobody came close to what you went through," Sandy said.

"Maybe not, but didn't you say a telephone pole fell right in front of your car? That could have been disastrous. And Tony's house came off the foundation, and—"

"We were all lucky," Suzanne said, tossing marinated chicken breasts onto the flames. "But I'll never forget how worried Sandy was when Tony called and said they'd found your car in the parking garage at the mall."

"And your mom, Lily. I felt so sorry for her."

"I was so glad to see her when I came out. You guys were good to take care of her back then."

Sandy poured three glasses of wine and distributed them. "I think we should drink to miracles."

They clinked their glasses together. "And to lifetime friends," Lily added.

"Do you think Anna will be in that category?" Sandy asked.

"I hope so." Lily was eager to share the rest of her news. "She called just a few minutes ago to invite me to the Dodgers game tomorrow. She has tickets to the skybox," she said snootily.

"Didn't you tell her you always went hiking on Sundays?" Suzanne asked.

Lily rolled her eyes. "It's the Dodgers. In a skybox." With

Anna Kaklis.

The subject of Anna dominated their dinner discussion. Sandy especially was eager for details of their dinner, and Lily loved reliving them, especially since new tidbits emerged in the retelling. She didn't say much about Anna's divorce, though, because that seemed too personal to share. When the dishes were done, they returned to the deck for a soak in the hot tub. In the darkness, all three shed their clothes and slipped into the warm, churning water.

Sandy leaned her head back against the pillow at the corner. "Lily, I sure wish you could meet a lesbian that would light your fire like Anna has."

"You and me both," Lily replied, realizing too late she had just admitted feeling sparks for Anna.

"She's straight, you know," Suzanne warned. "You need to be careful, or she'll cut your heart out."

Lily didn't want her evening ruined by a grim scolding from her friends. "We're just friends, Suzanne. I don't expect more than that. It's just that we went through something together that changed our lives. I feel a very special bond with her, and I think she feels it too. Does that automatically have to mean sexual attraction?"

"No, of course not," Sandy said. "You know how bossy Suzanne is."

Suzanne flinched, a sure sign her partner had pinched her beneath the bubbles. "I just don't want to see you hurt."

"Where do you want these?" Kim asked, carrying a stack of sweaters into Anna's master bedroom.

"On the bed is fine. I have to sort out where everything goes." Anna had finally gotten over her mental block about sleeping in the room she had shared with Scott. Now it had all-new furniture, since she had given Scott the other suite when he moved out.

"I can't believe you slept in that little room for so long. Scott should have been the one in the doghouse."

"It wasn't too bad. At least I had my own bathroom."

"But now you've got this one," Kim exclaimed. She had found the house and thought it perfect for Anna and Scott, with its dual sinks, steam shower and sunken tub.

"I don't know what I'm going to do with all this space." In actuality, Anna was thinking about selling the big house and finding something smaller.

"Who knows, Anna? Maybe you'll meet—"

Anna held up her hand. "Don't even say it."

"I know. You don't want to date anyone. You just want to be by yourself."

"Kim, I've been divorced all of two days. Do you mind if I take just a week or two before getting married again?"

"You didn't do anything wrong, Anna. You don't have any penance to pay over this." Kim sat at the foot of the king-sized bed while Anna folded lingerie and placed it in the dresser. "And I won't stand by and let you do what you did after that Vince guy."

Anna groaned, as she did every time she thought of the young man she dated for almost a year while in college at Cal Poly. Curiosity about sex had finally led her to experience it for herself, and it had left her disillusioned and embarrassed, and vowing never to share that again until she was sure it would be an expression of love. "Believe me, there will be no more Vince Marshalls."

"It isn't the Vince Marshalls I'm worried about, Anna. It's you. You didn't even go out on a date for over five years after that, all because you didn't trust yourself."

This was the price of sharing secrets with her sister. Kim never forgot anything, especially when it came to details about her sex life. "This isn't anything like that. I deserve some time to myself after what I've been through."

"That's fine, as long as it's not five years. Or even five months. What you've always wanted is someone who'll be your friend. That's what you said was so special about Scott. There are other men out there who can be your friend too, and believe it or not, some of them can keep their pecker in their pants."

Anna could always tell when her sister was trying to get a rise out of her, so she ignored the crass comment and went on folding her clothes.

"I know you feel raw right now, but you pulled yourself into a shell when all of this started, and it's time for you to come out again." Kim stood up and put both of her hands on Anna's shoulders. "You don't have anything to hang your head about. Just get out there and enjoy people again. Make friends. Go to parties . . . get laid."

Anna sighed heavily and shook her head. "You almost made it through a whole conversation without saying something ridiculous."

"I know, but then you would have asked who I was and what had I done with your sister."

"It just so happens I am going out with friends this afternoon. My account rep from the *Times* gave me two tickets to their skybox for the Dodgers game, and I'm picking up Lily at a quarter after twelve."

"That's perfect. Lily's fun and she won't let you sulk."

"I do not sulk."

"And she won't shove you out of the way when the cute guys come along."

"You're impossible."

"I know."

Despite her mother's admonishment, Lily was duly impressed with Anna's luxurious, brand new, black 650i coupe, especially the global positioning system. From her passenger seat, the multitude of gauges made it seem as if the car drove itself. "You'd have to be pretty smart to drive a car like this."

"Not a problem," Anna replied dryly. "It broke my heart to lose the 850 in the mall garage. I loved that car, and they don't make them anymore."

"What was so special about it?"

"They only sold about seven thousand here in the states. Mine was the rarest of all. It was called the CSi, and it had a six-speed manual transmission. You just can't get a driving experience like that with anything else."

Lily looked at the gearshift. "Isn't this one a six-speed?"

"Yeah, but it has a different feel. This one has a lot of the new technology, like the Dynamic Driving Control. It's well-made, but it's not the same."

It was obvious that cars were more than a business for Anna. They were a passion, and she seemed to love talking about them.

Anna showed her guest pass to the parking attendant and pulled into the VIP lot at Dodger Stadium. "Don't be surprised if my account rep fawns all over you. He's a nice guy, but this isn't about friendship. It's about how much money Premier spends on advertising."

"I'm not used to being fawned over, but I'll do my best to deal with it." She followed closely as Anna showed their tickets at the gate.

"The box is this way," Anna said, steering them toward the escalator that would take them to the concourse for the lower level suites. She was dressed casually but sharply, in black tailored slacks and a light blue sleeveless silk shirt. Her hair was pulled back and gathered in a black scrunchie, and a lightweight cream-colored sweater hung loosely around her shoulders.

Taking her cue from what Anna had said, Lily had pressed her khakis and donned a lightweight forest green sweater. It wasn't that this was the best outfit she could find. Rather it was the one she was trying on when her doorbell rang.

When they entered the suite, they were greeted by a handsome man in gray slacks and a starched white shirt. "Anna. It's great to see you. Glad you could make it."

"Thank you. Steve, I'd like you to meet my friend, Lily Stewart. Lily, this is Steve French. Steve is my account manager at the *Times* and our host for today."

"I'm really pleased to meet you. Thanks so much for the invitation." Lily couldn't help but notice that Steve hardly glanced her way, his eyes glued to Anna.

"So Anna, where is Scott today?"

"That I wouldn't know. Scott and I have divorced."

"I'm so sorry to hear that, Anna."

Lily was almost agape at the phoniness in his voice. Either Anna hadn't noticed, or she had expected his response.

"Thank you. I appreciate that."

Steve led them to their seats in the front row of the suite just in time for the National Anthem. Lily resisted the urge to pinch herself. She couldn't believe she was in a luxury suite at Dodger Stadium, sitting beside the most beautiful woman in LA.

"Play ball!"

"I like the Dodgers' chances this year," Anna said. "They finally got some middle relief."

"That only helps when their bats are going," Lily said. She was pleasantly surprised to find Anna knew her stuff when it came to baseball. They talked about players, trades, strategies and statistics, all to the consternation of Steve French, who kept trying to get Anna's attention.

"I think someone has his eye on you," Lily whispered.

"Oh yeah?" Anna glanced back at Steve, who had been looking at her and smiling all afternoon. "He's a handsome man, don't you think?"

"Yeah, I guess," Lily shrugged, feigning exaggerated boredom. "If you go for that trim and muscular, square jaw with deep-set eyes thing. Not really my type, though."

"So what is your type, Ms. Stewart?"

"You mean apart from my gender specifications?"

"Well, I was assuming that, of course . . . unless you like to leave all your options open."

"Oh, no. Some options are always closed. Let's see, I go for smart first, then a sense of humor. Outer beauty means little to me," Lily said haughtily.

"Right, and I like ugly cars too."

Anna pulled away from the apartment complex, glad Lily had accepted her invitation on such short notice. She couldn't count the number of times she had gotten the urge to go to the ballpark or theater and passed on it because she couldn't find anyone to go. Lily was up for things anytime, she said.

Lily's favorite pastime was hiking, not something Anna knew much about. But she had promised to give it a try sometime, though she had teased her about not being able to see the appeal of dragging one's ass up a mountain when there were perfectly good off-road vehicles to get you there.

Though they were miles apart when it came to their social circles, Anna found that a refreshing change of pace from the girls she had grown up with in Beverly Hills, the ones she counted now as her casual friends. Lily had an interesting job, and what she did with struggling families made a real difference in the world.

All in all, she was delighted to have Lily back in her life, especially now, when it would be easier just to wallow in the loneliness of her empty house. Kim was right that she needed to get out and have fun. The biggest problem she anticipated with this new friendship was wearing it out by calling too often.

❧

"Lilian Stewart," she said, picking up the phone on her desk.

"So how did you know he was going to call?"

Lily had been expecting a call from a client, and it took her a moment to recognize the voice. "Anna?"

"Seriously. How did you know that?"

It amused her that Anna was so obviously surprised. "I'm fine. Thank you so much for asking."

"Sorry. How are you?"

"What are you going on about?"

"Steve French just invited me to San Diego next Saturday for the first game of the Dodgers' road trip."

Lily knew this was going to happen, and she had to admit it annoyed her. When she had gotten up to get a drink at the game, she had overheard French bragging to his buddy that he could get Anna to go out with him. His arrogant manner had pissed her off, especially since he probably had more than just a date in mind. "So what was your reply? I suppose you fell for that line about having the chance to get to know each other better on the drive down." Despite her attempt at nonchalance, the words came out with a bite.

"Wow, it sounds like you don't like Steve much."

Knowing she was busted, Lily considered coming clean about what she had overheard, but it then occurred to her Anna might actually be interested in whatever Steve had in mind. If that were the case, her objections would sound silly. "No, Steve is very nice. I was just teasing. Welcome back to the world of dating. I always keep my ears open to hear what lines work best on women."

"I'd let you know, but I don't have a clue either. That stuff just flies right over my head. I really was surprised when he called."

"That's because you were too busy thinking about twin-cam . . . overdrive, turbo-charged"—her brain worked to come up with car-related words—"anti-braking lock systems."

"You're hilarious."

Lily smiled to herself, glad that Anna appreciated her sense of humor. "Want to have dinner tomorrow night?"

"I can't. It's my dad's birthday. What about later in the week?"

Lily thumbed through her calendar. "Sorry. I just found out my friend Suzanne is having surgery on Wednesday, and I promised Sandy I'd help sit with her for the rest of the week."

"I hope it's nothing serious."

"It's back surgery. She's spent too many hours on her feet in ER."

"Is she a doctor?"

"A nurse." Of course, Anna's friends were probably doctors, she thought.

"If there's anything I can do, let me know."

"That's very sweet. I'm sure we have it covered, but I'll let Sandy know you offered."

"Thank you. So let's try again next week, okay?"

"Sure. What if I give you a call on Sunday? You can tell me all about the game in San Diego." And what a wonderful time she had with the handsome, square-jawed Steve French, Lily thought dismally.

For his sixty-first birthday, Anna's father had asked to have his celebration dinner outside on the patio. He always said his best memories were of barbecues around the pool in the backyard.

Anna's stepmother, Martine, stood in the kitchen, garnishing the serving plates for the Turkish pilaf and stuffed baked tomatoes. Five porterhouse steaks marinated on the counter, next to the large, elaborately decorated cake.

"Can I help with anything?" Anna asked, dropping her wrapped present on the dining room table with the others.

"You can tell Hal the steaks are ready for the grill."

She called out the back door to her brother-in-law, and then turned back to her stepmother. "So did Kim tell you who we had dinner with the other night?"

"She said you ran into that woman from the earthquake. That's so amazing."

"It was. After all this time I was looking for her, she just shows up out of the blue. And get this. It turns out she was looking for me too. She lost my number at the hospital and we never told each other our last names."

"Kim said she was very nice."

"She is. And she went with me to the Dodgers game on Sunday."

"I bet you had a lot to talk about," Martine said.

"We did." Anna pinched a cucumber from the salad, thinking back to her conversations with Lily. "It's funny. We talked all about the earthquake the other night with Kim and Hal, but I don't think we mentioned it once on Sunday."

"Maybe you both got closure about it."

"Yeah, maybe so." Anna knew she was lucky to have a good relationship with her stepmother, so good that she felt perfectly comfortable thinking of Martine as her mother. She owed most of that to Martine's easygoing manner and her determination to take on Anna as a daughter when they all became a family, the same way her father had taken on Kim. "That's really an interesting observation. I'll have to ask Lily about that."

"I should warn you, by the way, your father is feeling a little emotional today. Don't be surprised if he hugs you and starts to cry."

"What's that about?"

"I'm not sure, but I think he's trying to decide if this was his worst year or his best."

"Why?"

"Because he almost lost you in the earthquake, but then you got out. It was both horrible and miraculous. Then his friend Morty died. And I think he's still upset about Scott."

Anna sighed. Kim and Hal knew about Scott's infidelity, but

96

she had asked them not to say anything to anyone else. It served no purpose to make Scott a bad guy, especially when she realized there were other things wrong with their relationship for which she bore responsibility. "Would it make him feel better if I told him how great I felt?"

"I don't know. It might make him feel worse. He thinks you and Scott acted too hastily."

They had—when they had gotten married in the first place. "How do you think I should handle him?"

"I don't know, Anna. I just thought you should know how he's feeling just in case he gets emotional."

"Thanks."

Dinner was a lively affair after all, Anna thought. Her father's mood was better than she had expected, given what Martine had said. She had deliberately avoided the subject of Scott, talking instead about running into Lily.

" . . . and she was trying to find me, but she didn't know my last name. She was asking about Anna, and all the records had Christianna."

"But you said she wasn't at the hospital when you checked. Had she been discharged?" Martine asked.

"No, she went to a different hospital from the one they told me. And she stayed there four days, just like I did."

"I liked her a lot," Kim said. "And so did Hal. She's very nice."

"Then you should invite her over the next time we have a party," Martine said. "We'd all love to meet her. Wouldn't we, George?"

For the last several minutes, Anna had noticed from the corner of her eye that her father was watching her pensively. She had been careful not to speak of Scott, and her only reference to the earthquake was the joyous discovery of her lost savior.

"So what is everyone doing this weekend?" her father asked, ignoring Martine's question.

"Going out on the boat," said Hal cheerfully.

"Going out on the boat," Kim echoed with a groan, turning to Anna with a pleading voice. "Come with us?"

"Sorry. I'm going to the Dodgers game in San Diego."

"With whom?" her father asked.

"Steve French," she said hesitantly, knowing it might be a sore spot because of Scott. She was merely taking her sister's advice and doing more things with friends. And since making up her mind not to think of this outing as a date, she was actually looking forward to it.

"Steve French?" her father asked, obviously surprised. "Isn't it awfully soon for that sort of thing?"

"What sort of thing? We're just friends. I went to their skybox last week for the Reds game, and he knows what a Dodgers fan I am."

"I don't know, darling. He's our account manager. You know what they say about mixing business and pleasure."

Kim stood up to help clear the plates. "Oh, for goodness sakes, Dad. Anna's not going to run off and elope."

Anna seized on the opening and followed suit, grabbing a stack of dishes and following her sister into the kitchen. "You had to go and mention eloping. Now he won't sleep all night."

Kim giggled. "I know. But it drives me nuts when he butts in like that. You should go and have a good time."

"I intend to. But you heard what I said to him. This isn't a date."

"Fine."

Anna felt compelled to make her case anyway. "Steve's a nice guy, and he likes the Dodgers as much as I do. I'm just taking your advice on making friends."

"And it doesn't hurt at all if they happen to be handsome friends."

∾

Lily stretched across the couch to grab the phone, not taking her eyes off UCLA's gridiron battle with the Stanford Cardinals. Fresh from her shower after cleaning her apartment and washing her car, she now wore an oversized blue and yellow jersey that boasted her alma mater. Her beloved Bruins were already up 7-0 in the first quarter.

"Hello?"

"So how did you know Steve French was a creep?"

Football flew right out of her head as she recognized the voice and smiled. "Anna, I'm fine. Thanks for asking."

"Let me be your tour guide for the landmark Hotel del Coronado in San Diego. We're here in the mahogany trimmed ladies' room off the Del's main lobby, admiring the polished brass fixtures that adorn the ornately carved marble sinks."

"What on earth are you doing in the bathroom at the Del?"

"Such a personal question!" Anna said with mock indignation. "Steve suggested the Del for dinner, and I stopped in here to wash up."

"And you thought you'd call to tell me your date was a creep? I already knew that."

"It's worse than you thought. You aren't going to believe this. We came here for dinner, right? Just a nice meal to finish off our day. So I stepped into the ladies' room, and when I went out, he was at the desk, putting his wallet away and picking up a key card."

"You're kidding."

"I'm not. I couldn't believe it, so I waited for him to walk out to the veranda. Then I went up to the desk and asked if he'd just gotten a room. At first, the woman wouldn't tell me, but I told her I was here for dinner with him, and thought I deserved to know his intentions."

"That sleazebag!"

"That's not the worst of it. She said he'd asked for a king-sized bed with an ocean view and a bottle of champagne on ice."

Though already jaded regarding Steve French, Lily couldn't believe how pompous the guy actually was. "What an arrogant jerk!"

"Yeah. I was going to fake a migraine, but it looks like I might not have to fake it after all. It's already started. I'm thinking about renting a car and driving home."

"You get migraines?"

"Sometimes."

"What if I drive down and pick you up? I could be there in about two and a half hours." She started upstairs to change into her jeans.

"I couldn't ask you to do that."

"What if your headache gets worse? What will you do?"

"I guess I'd just pull over and find a place to stay the night."

"Forget it, then. Tell Steve French to piss off. I'll be there at"—she spun around to find a clock—"nine o'clock." Then she pulled on a V-neck sweater and slipped her feet into a pair of clogs.

"Well, I can't stay in the restroom till then. Maybe I'll have dinner and take a walk along the beach. Are you sure, Lily? San Diego and back is a lot of driving in one night."

"I'm heading out the door now." Katharine used to have migraines, so Lily knew how bad they could be. No way would she let Anna drive herself home with one.

She made good time on the San Diego Freeway, and pulled into the valet circle at the Del at ten till nine. "I'm just here to pick someone up," she told the young man in the pith helmet who had moved to take her keys.

"Lily."

She turned toward the voice and immediately smiled. "Hey! How's your headache?"

"It's lurking. If I can get home and get into bed before it erupts, it might not be so bad."

"Let's go, then." Feeling protective all of a sudden, she took

100

Anna by the elbow and guided her out to the car, where she reached through the open window and yanked on the passenger door.

"Did I mention that I know where you can get a great deal on a new car?" Anna said with a smirk.

Lily headed back out to the 5, pressing for details about how Anna had dumped Steve French.

"I told him I didn't appreciate him being so presumptuous, and he tried to tell me he thought I might like to freshen up or something."

"Oh, sure. What's that, like four hundred dollars for a powder room?"

"Yeah, and then I asked him about the champagne and he just turned into a blob of Jell-O. I think that's when it occurred to him he'd just pissed off one of his biggest clients."

"I would have given anything to have seen that."

"It was a sight." Anna suddenly grimaced and pressed the heel of her hand to her forehead.

"Are you all right?"

"I think so. I just need to close my eyes."

"Hit that lever on the side and recline the seat. I can stop and get something if you think it would help."

Anna leaned the seat back. "This is good. Why don't you tell me about yourself so I don't have to talk? What's your family like? How come you decided to be a lawyer?"

Most of Lily's friends knew she was adopted, but only Sandy and Suzanne were aware that her biological mother had neglected and abused her. She never wanted people to feel sorry for her or worse, to think she might be maladjusted from her early life. But she trusted Anna with the truth, and started the story as Anna relaxed in the front seat with her eyes closed.

"Okay, let's see. I was born in Oakland. My biological mother was sixteen years old and living mostly on the streets or wherever she could find a bed for the night." She glanced over at Anna,

101

who had turned to watch her talk. "You sure you want to hear this?"

"Of course."

"Most of what I know about my early childhood comes from social service records. I have no idea who my father is, but apparently, I got passed around a lot when I was a baby so my mother could go do whatever it was she did . . . drugs and alcohol . . . and probably prostitution. Every time she went to jail, I went to foster care. I lived in a bunch of different foster homes while she was piling up a criminal record." She looked again at Anna, who had closed her eyes. "Do you want me to save this for later so you can sleep?"

"No, this is interesting. Keep talking."

"Okay, I'll jump ahead to the good part. The luckiest day of my life came when I was seven. That's when social services put me at a school in San Jose where a nice young woman named Eleanor Stewart was my first grade teacher. I don't know what it was about her, but I just loved her, and I'd never had that feeling before. So I worked hard and behaved myself for a change because she would always tell me how proud she was. I would have done anything for her approval. I started getting good grades, but then they tried to move me again and I hid in the cloak room so I wouldn't have to go home. Miss Stewart found me and asked social services if I could stay with her. They said yes, and that's why I was so lucky."

"This is just the most amazing story. I can't believe you didn't tell me this when we were in the earthquake."

"I don't tell everybody where I come from, Anna. I don't want people to feel sorry for me. I had a rough start, but my mom—and whenever I say Mom, I mean Eleanor Stewart—she gave me everything I needed to get my life on track and keep it there. When she filed the papers to adopt me, my biological mother suddenly showed up and wanted me back because she found out the state would give her money to take care of a child. That's when Mom found Katharine Fortier. She was a family services lawyer like I am now, and she helped us win in court."

"Your mother sounds remarkable. You say her name's Eleanor?"

"Yes," Lily answered. "And we got to be good friends with Katharine. She's the one who talked me into going to law school, and then when I graduated and took the job at Braxton Street, she was excited because I was mostly doing family law like she did."

"I bet she's proud of you."

"She was. She died a couple of years ago in a plane crash in Alaska. We really miss her."

"I'm sorry. That's so sad."

"It is. I don't know what I would have done without her when I was growing up. When I was in high school, I told one of my friends I might be gay. I thought I could trust her, but she told everybody and turned my life into a living hell."

"You came out in high school?"

"Not by choice. I freaked out and told Mom, and she said it wasn't a problem, that Katharine was a lesbian and she turned out all right. And just to show you there's no such thing as gaydar, I didn't have a clue about Katharine. But they both said they pretty much knew about me, and that was kind of embarrassing."

Anna chuckled. "I can see that. It would be embarrassing to have people know you better than you know yourself. But you were lucky to have that kind of support."

"Believe me, I know. I wouldn't be here today if it weren't for them, especially Mom."

Anna was silent for so long, Lily thought she had drifted off to sleep. Then she stirred and spoke. "You know what I just figured out?"

"What?"

"This is going to sound hokey, but I think what you had to go through when you were little is what got you through the earthquake."

Lily was taken aback by the depth of Anna's assessment. There was probably a lot of truth to it, she realized, and it filled her with pride to have Anna say so.

"Seriously, Lily, I had to reach deep inside myself to find the courage and strength to keep going. But I think those things are just an integral part of who you are."

Lily blew out a breath and shook her head. "That's probably the nicest thing anyone has ever said to me."

"I bet a lot of people think that about you. You don't have any pretense at all."

"You don't either, Anna. And I think you're selling yourself short when it comes to courage and strength. I see plenty."

Anna returned her hand to her forehead and whimpered. "Uh-oh, I think I just went from little headache to big migraine."

"Just rest. I'll have you home in forty minutes."

The last part of their ride was logged in companionable silence, with Anna dozing and Lily lost in thought about the feelings she knew were growing for the woman beside her. Each time she realized where her thoughts were headed, she mentally cautioned herself. Suzanne was right that falling in love with a straight woman would bring nothing but heartache.

She found her way to Anna's house and pulled into the driveway. Her companion was sound asleep. "Anna? We're here." She gently shook her arm, which felt clammy. "Are you okay? What can I do?"

Anna sat up and pressed two fingers onto her right eyebrow. "It's a big one. I think I'm going to be sick."

Lily jumped out and helped her into the big house, sticking close by all the way to her upstairs bedroom. As Anna had predicted, she was sick as soon as entered the adjoining bathroom. Lily wet a cloth and tenderly wiped her face as she slumped on the cool tile floor.

"Sorry to be so disgusting. At least I waited until I was out of your car."

Lily smiled softly. "It's no big deal. Do you have medicine?"

Anna nodded slowly. "There's a plastic jar in the door of the refrigerator. Can you bring it?"

"Of course." Lily found the medicine and returned to the bathroom with a small glass of water. "Here you go."

Anna unscrewed the cap and removed one of the yellow capsules. Inexplicably, she smiled when she saw the offered glass. "Um . . . these are suppositories. They work faster, and I don't throw them up."

"Oh." Lily could feel the heat rush up her chest to her face, and she knew she was bright red with embarrassment. "I'll just . . . uh, I'll wait out here." She left the bathroom, closing the door behind her.

When Anna emerged a few minutes later, she sat on the king-sized bed. "I need to lie down now. The medicine will knock me out cold in about ten minutes."

"Do you want me to stay awhile, until you're asleep?"

"No, I'll be okay." Anna withdrew a blue silk nightshirt from the bottom drawer of the nightstand. "There's an extra key in the kitchen drawer under the phone. Take it, and lock up for me, okay?"

Lily nodded. "Can I give you a call tomorrow?"

"Sure."

Anna began to unbutton her blouse, revealing a lacy bra. Lily felt her face go red again. "I hope you feel better." Nervously, she leaned forward and lightly kissed Anna's forehead.

"Thank you, Lily. Thank you for everything."

Anna finished the last of her chips and wiped her greasy fingers on a napkin. "I love it that you ignore me when I tell you to bring me a salad."

Kim laughed, shoving the last of a meatball sub into her mouth. "I knew you'd just sit there and covet mine if I didn't bring you the same thing."

They were in Anna's office, which was piled high with print-outs. "I'm thinking of stealing your husband."

"That would make Sunday dinners interesting at the big house." That's what they called their parents' majestic home in Beverly Hills.

Anna smirked. "I mean stealing him from his accounting firm. What do you think he'd say?"

"He'd probably entertain the idea, especially if you caught him on the right day. Some of his clients make him nuts."

"Maybe you can give me a heads-up when he comes home complaining, and I'll ask him then."

"What would George say? He's always liked Morty Schneider's firm."

Anna thought they needed a financial expert in-house, but her father disagreed. "Yeah, but he might not care as much now that Morty's gone."

"So how did your date go in San Diego? Are you married again?"

Anna rolled her eyes. "I think it's safe to say Steve and I have decided to see other people."

"That bad, huh?"

Anna related the fiasco, finishing with Lily's rescue and her migraine.

"That was nice of her," Kim said with a seriousness Anna knew wouldn't last. "You should definitely try to keep her as a friend, because I sure wouldn't have driven all the way to San Diego and back for you."

"Lily's a better person than you are."

"I tend to agree." She wadded up the paper from her sand-wich and tossed it toward the trashcan, missing by a good six feet. "Oops. I've got a new listing off Rosewood you might like.

Five bedrooms, three-car garage, media room, guest cottage. Want to see it this afternoon?"

"What would I do with all those rooms?"

"You're right. You should just get a motor home and park it out back."

Anna sneered, trying not to smile. "What kind of engines do those things have?"

"Lilian Stewart," the familiar voice barked.

Anna was startled. This didn't sound at all like the easy-going Lily she had come to expect. "Sounds like somebody's having a bad day."

Lily sighed. "Yes, I'm having a shitty day."

"Oh, I'm fine, and thanks for asking." The line went quiet and Anna wondered if her joke had come at the wrong time.

"Sorry," Lily finally said. "I just got some unpleasant news, and I forgot my manners."

"What's wrong?"

"Oh, it's just a funding cut. In our line of work you get used to it. I didn't mean to snap at you."

"It's okay. I was calling to see if you might be interested in an early lunch. I'm downtown for a meeting, and it looks like we'll be wrapping up a little after eleven."

"Getting out of this office would be a good thing, especially for a friendly face."

Anna arrived and the usual excitement ensued. Lily introduced her as her fellow earthquake survivor and everyone in the office came out to say hello and ask questions about how they had managed to escape. Then Anna gave all the credit to Lily, and Lily bounced it right back.

"You ready to go?"

"Sure," Anna answered, bidding farewell to the office staff.

They picked up sandwiches at a nearby deli before settling on a park bench.

"So what's with your funding problem?" Anna asked.

"There's this program called Kidz Kamp that sponsors camping trips for kids in foster care. My boss, Tony, the guy you met at the office, is the executive director, and all of us at the office take turns with people from social services or juvenile justice to take these kids out. We've been doing it for almost four years, but now the funding's been cut."

"Who was your funder?"

"We had a grant from the Chamber of Commerce, but they're switching their priorities to afterschool programs. I'm sure that's a worthy cause, but we had a good thing going. The kids love it, the foster parents get a break, and all the volunteers get a chance to build trust with the kids we see on the job."

Anna thought back to the Chamber presentation she had seen on the day of the earthquake, and the subsequent discussions among the membership to back the afterschool programs. "I wish I'd known more about your program. I would have tried to keep it up and running."

"You're in the Chamber?"

Anna winced. "I'm the treasurer."

Lily's shoulders slumped. "I don't suppose there's anything you can do at this point?"

Anna shook her head. "No, we finalized our budget a couple of months ago. Are there any other agencies that might be willing to help out?"

"Maybe, but it looks like we'll have a gap. Tony said he was going to see about getting a little corporate support to cover our next three trips. That might buy us enough time to write a new grant."

"I'm sure it'll be easy to get a new sponsor. It sounds like a great program." Except for the camping part, she thought to herself.

"Hmm . . . I'm getting a great idea."

"Oh, no. I don't sleep on the ground."

"But I'm the only female chaperone for the next trip and we have three girls on the list to go. Please, please, please!"

"No, no, no! I don't do bugs. Or snakes."

"But it's fun."

"Not for me. Now if you ever need help taking them to a play or to a museum, sign me up. I'm just not . . ."

"You're prissy."

"I'm not prissy, I'm refined."

"You're prissy."

Anna pulled into Lily's complex just before eight on Sunday morning to find Lily already waiting on the steps to her apartment. Camping wasn't Anna's thing, but she enjoyed an occasional outing with Kim and Hal on the boat, and she would enjoy it even more today because Lily was coming along.

"I can't wait. This is going to be so much fun," Lily said, tossing her backpack into the backseat as she got in.

"Do you go boating a lot?"

"No, just once with some friends from law school. But I loved it."

"What all did you bring?"

"Just the stuff you said . . . sunscreen, a jacket . . . and dry clothes in case you push me in."

"Good thinking. I'm feeling feisty."

Hal was ready to launch when they reached the marina. It was on the cool side as they set out, but it warmed up quickly as the sun climbed higher. Anna sat with her sister on the cushions at the back of the boat—or the stern, as Hal always corrected her—while Lily rode shotgun, getting a lesson from Hal on the boat's features.

"She's a lot of fun," Kim said, gesturing at Lily. "And she's making Hal's day, asking all those questions. Do you think she's just being nice, or is my husband really all that fascinating?"

"Are you actually suggesting we might have misjudged the guy all these years?"

"Nah, couldn't be. I think Lily's just easily entertained."

"Well, I'd worry about anyone who found Hal entertaining."

Lily chose that moment to glance their way. When she realized she and Hal were the subject of their amusement, she stuck out her tongue and turned her back haughtily. Fifteen minutes later, she was proudly driving the boat on her own.

"So what was so funny?" Hal demanded as he slid onto the cushion beside Kim.

"We were trying to decide if Lily was really interested in your boat lesson or if she was just being nice," Kim said.

"I don't suppose it occurred to you that she is nice and I'm interesting?"

Anna chuckled, leaving them to debate the merits of Hal's delusion as she stripped down to a plum-colored one-piece bathing suit. Then she took the tall co-pilot seat alongside Lily, who was standing on her tiptoes with her chin up, peering out over the shimmering blue plane.

"Having a little trouble seeing over the bow, Pygmy?"

"Will you still think you're funny when we run a sail up your neck, Amazon?" Lily turned to face her and her jaw went slack.

Accustomed to being admired, Anna recognized the look. Apparently, Lily hadn't expected to see her in a bathing suit. By her open stare, she certainly seemed to approve. "Did you wear your suit?"

"Uh, yeah."

Anna had never marveled at her own features until she began working with Nikki, the personal trainer who took over after the physical therapy for her leg. She was proud of her hard work, and if Lily was admiring her physique, that was fine by her. In fact, she wasn't sure why it mattered, but it pleased her to think Lily found her attractive.

"You look like you work out."

Suddenly shy, Anna could only smile and look away. "I did for a while, but I've fallen out of it."

"If fallen out looks like that, you can give me a push."

Anna laughed. Behind her sunglasses, she stole a glance as Lily discarded her shirt and shorts, revealing an aquamarine tankini. Suddenly, it was Anna's turn to stare. Lily had muscular legs, tapering at her hips to a tiny waist. Her shoulders and arms looked strong and lithe, and her breasts seemed larger than they appeared in her suits and casual clothes. Anna almost laughed as she wondered what Lily would think if she knew her breasts were being scrutinized.

How was it possible someone like Lily could not have a girl-friend? Not only was she lovely to look at, she was smart, funny and compassionate, and she had shown herself to be a great friend. So why weren't all of LA's single lesbians throwing themselves at her? Anna didn't care much about the answer. She liked that Lily was spending time with her instead.

They cruised north along California's picturesque coastline, turning back at mid-afternoon. As the sun began to fade, they donned their clothes and jackets and Anna wrapped herself in a blanket from the cabin below. Seeing Lily shiver as the wind blew through her lightweight fleece, she held her arms open and invited her to huddle inside. When Lily stepped in front, Anna closed the blanket around them both, instantly sparking a memory of pulling her close as she struggled for breath in the collapsed mall. A sense of panic suddenly invaded her, and she squeezed Lily tightly to her chest.

Lily shifted her shoulders, sinking deeper into the plush leather of Anna's passenger seat. She was tired from their outing, but it was a happy tired. As far as she was concerned, the day could not have gone better. She and Anna were closer now, though it was hard to say exactly why. Something subtle had passed between them as they huddled beneath the blanket, something warm and familiar. Whatever it was, it vanquished the lingering insecurity Lily had harbored about their differences. Anna was right. They would be great friends.

"I'm glad you came with us," Anna said. "Kim and Hal were, too . . . especially Hal, because you actually cared about his bilge pump."

"Poor Hal. He's no worse about his boat than someone I know is about her car."

"I know, but cars are fascinating."

Anna turned into the parking lot at her complex, drawing their day to an end unless Lily came up with an idea for extending it. "You want to come in? I could order a pizza."

"That sounds like so much more fun than tallying second quarter sales figures with my dad. Unfortunately, we need that report first thing tomorrow morning."

"You have to work on a Sunday night?"

"Not usually. We were supposed to do it on Thursday morning, but I had that Chamber meeting." Anna surprised her by turning off the engine and getting out of the car. "Let me help you with your stuff."

All Lily had was her backpack and a damp towel, but she didn't mind that Anna was walking her in. "Thanks for inviting me along today. I had a great time."

"Good. We'll do it again if you want. They invite me practically every week, so let me know."

Lily sighed dramatically. "You'll have to go without me next week. I'm going camping . . . all alone."

"So you are."

So much for sympathy, Lily thought. But she got something far better than that when Anna wrapped her in a hug and planted a kiss on her temple before heading back to her car. It was all Lily could do to stand as she waved good-bye.

Chapter 7

"Lilian Stewart," Lily answered enthusiastically, recognizing the number on her display.

"Good morning, Lily. How are you?" Anna's voice was syrupy sweet.

"Hey, good for you, Amazon! Your social skills are really coming along."

"Don't let it get out. Others might raise their expectations."

"I'll keep it just between us. What's up? By the way, I really had a great time yesterday. I know I said that already, but I'm still thinking about it."

"Yeah, me too. And Kim called just a few minutes ago to make it an open invitation whenever you want, so all you have to do is speak up."

Lily looked at her calendar. After Kidz Kamp, she was due a trip to San Jose. "Maybe we can do it again in a few weeks. I need to go up and see Mom soon."

"Which brings me to another question . . . I was wondering if—hypothetically speaking, of course—a person were to decide to go, say . . . camping, what sorts of camping equipment that person might require? Hypothetically, of course."

Lily sat up, very excited at where this conversation seemed to be headed. "I don't think one would need a lot. Perhaps only a sleeping bag, a day pack, some good hiking boots and a few odds and ends to enhance one's comfort." She paused and added, "Hypothetically, of course."

"Of course. So if one were to—hypothetically—decide she needed such equipment, where might she find help in selecting the right things?"

"Oh, I think someone might be available on Wednesday night to escort such a person to an outfitter store for said items."

"Six thirty?"

"Six thirty it is."

Lily hung up the phone and twirled all the way around in her chair. Then she jumped up and walked briskly down the hall to Tony's office. Sailing through his open door, she delivered the good news. "I've got another woman for Silverwood Lake."

"Who is it?"

"You remember my friend from the earthquake, the woman who stopped in last week to go to lunch with me?"

"Anna? Believe me, no guy is going to forget somebody like her."

She didn't like the sound of that. Tony wasn't particularly handsome, but he had a charming way about him that ladies loved. "She'll be riding up with me, and I need to ask you a big favor."

"Sure. Name it."

"I want you to . . . lay off."

He gave her a confused look. "You mean lay off Anna? As in don't ask her out?"

"Exactly. She's just been through a tough divorce and guys

have been giving her a hard time." Anna had proven she could take care of herself, but Lily didn't want her to feel uncomfortable, especially with someone from her office. "I want her to just have a nice, relaxing weekend."

He nodded. "No problem. I'll be a perfect gentleman."

She softened, hoping she hadn't sounded too bossy. "I'm sure you're always a perfect gentleman. I just don't want her to feel any pressure."

"She won't, Lily. And I'm glad she's going."

"Me too."

She returned to her office, glad for the way the conversation had gone. What a mess it would have been if Tony had hit on her. Anna needed a break from pushy guys.

The RAV4 picked its way along the wooded road until they reached the campsite. Anna counted three men and six boys already at work unloading tents and setting up the cooking supplies. One of the men was Tony, Lily's boss, whom she had met the other day.

"We have to hustle," Lily said. "It'll be dark soon, but getting a hot meal on the first night in camp gets the weekend off to a good start."

"That makes sense," Anna said. The trip to Silverwood Lake, north of San Bernardino, had taken nearly three hours, most of that spent navigating LA traffic to exit the city. Lily said this was their favorite campsite, because it had everything the kids liked to do—fishing, swimming, hiking and canoeing. Anna decided she liked it too when she spotted the restrooms nearby.

She had grown increasingly uneasy as they drove farther from the city. After the shopping trip with Lily, she had come to terms with leaving behind the comforts of home. What had her on edge today were the three girls in the backseat. Rosa and Carlotta were eleven-year-old twins who giggled and whispered to each other in Spanish. Lateisha, a nine-year-old African-American girl, kept to herself, staring out the window lost in thought. Lily engaged the twins in occasional dialogue, asking about school, their friends and things they liked to do. But Anna held back. She doubted anyone on this trip besides Lily had any interest in hearing from a mechanical engineer who lived in Bel Air and sold luxury cars. So like Lateisha, she too retreated in silence.

"I'll get the twins to help me set up the tent," Lily said. "Why don't you and Lateisha get the supplies out of the back? You can stack the food stuff by that big picnic table, and everything else over by the tent."

"Okay." Though apprehensive about being alone with this quiet child, Anna was glad to be doing something other than just sitting. Staying busy would make the weekend pass more quickly.

She opened the hatchback and tried to make sense of what belonged where. When Lateisha walked closer, Anna broke the ice. "Have you ever been camping before?"

The girl simply shook her head.

"Well, this is my first time too. I guess we both have a lot to learn this weekend." When Lateisha didn't reply, Anna knew she would have to think of something more engaging. "How about giving me a hand with this cooler? It's pretty heavy for just one person." Together, they hauled their load to where Tony had stacked the cooking supplies.

"Anna, good to see you again," Tony said, holding out his hand for a shake. "Who's your helper there?"

"This is Lateisha. She's pretty strong for a nine-year-old. It's a good thing, too, because I couldn't have carried this cooler by myself." The small girl finally gave a shy smile, the first sign to Anna that she was breaking through.

"I can see how strong she is. If you need any extra help from me, just let me know."

"Oh, I think we'll manage." They headed back to the RAV4

to finish their task.

While she worked to organize the cooking gear, Tony introduced her to the other leaders, Jack and Matthew. Jack was an intake officer from the juvenile detention facility. Four of the boys on this trip were his charges, he explained, because they had gotten into trouble over shoplifting, vandalism or fighting in school. The other man, Matthew, was Jack's brother-in-law. Lily said she loved it when these two came along, because they brought their two canoes.

Tony's two boys, like Lateisha and the twins, were in foster placement. Most of the kids were from troubled backgrounds, he explained, often with behavior problems. No wonder Lily had wanted another woman to come along.

Two hours after reaching the campsite, everyone was relaxing around an open fire.

"Excellent spaghetti, Tony," Lily said, patting her tummy.

"Thank you, thank you. Hold your applause."

One of the boys stood to toss his paper plate into the fire. "How come you had to cook? They should have cooked," he said, gesturing toward Anna and Lily.

Tony laughed. "For one thing, I like to cook. And for another, we all take turns doing different jobs. It doesn't matter if you're a man or a woman."

"But it's women's work."

"If I thought that way, I'd starve to death, because I live by myself."

"Then you need a wife," the boy argued.

"You're right. I need one to make my family photos prettier, but I don't need one to cook."

Anna's respect for Tony was skyrocketing.

Lily leaned over and whispered in her ear. "Sandy threw a fit a couple of years ago because the men all acted like the women should wait on them. She refused to go again unless everyone rotated jobs."

"Good for her."

"Good for everybody. It won't hurt these boys to gain a little respect for what their mothers have to do. By the way, we're in charge of breakfast for the next two days."

"Is there a drive-thru around here?"

Lily chucked her rib with an elbow. "Does this mean you don't cook?"

"You're about to find out. You and a dozen other unfortunate people."

Shortly after ten, the children were sent into the tents to settle in, while the five adults planned the next day. Jack and Matthew wanted to take their boys fishing first thing then hiking in the afternoon. The others opted to explore the nature trail in the morning, and swim in the afternoon if it warmed up.

Crawling into their tent, Lily and Anna discovered the twins had moved their sleeping bags to the right side, while Lateisha had moved hers all the way to the left. That left them to squeeze into the middle, side by side.

As they settled in, Carlotta spilled her sister's secret. "Rosa's afraid of the dark."

"We know what it's like to be in the dark, don't we?" Lily asked, nudging Anna.

"I think you should tell the girls that story."

"Good idea." Minus a few gruesome details, Lily related their story of being trapped together in the mall, and finding their way out in the darkness. "I used to sleep with a light on at night, but since the earthquake, I haven't needed it anymore."

Getting no reply, Anna realized all three girls had fallen asleep. "Well, I certainly enjoyed hearing the story again."

"Me too."

In the night, a small hand shook Anna awake. "I have to go the bathroom," Lateisha squeaked.

"I'll go with you." Anna fumbled with the zipper, trying to make as little noise as possible.

They found the flashlight and their shoes, and walked quietly to the nearby restroom. Without a word, they took care of their business and made their way along the path back to the tent, where the others were still asleep. "Goodnight, Lateisha," she whispered.

Several moments passed, leaving Anna to wonder why the girl was so shy. Finally, she heard a quiet reply of "goodnight."

Lily twisted and jerked, frustrated that her feet were trapped under the covers. It took her a few seconds to remember she was in a sleeping bag, and to recognize the sound of voices outside the tent. She sat up to discover she was alone, and the light streaming in through the flapping zipper told her it was morning. She tugged on her boots and crawled to the opening, not believing the sight. Nine children and three grown men were lined up with their mess kits, each getting a heaping dose of oatmeal and brown sugar from the Amazon Chef. She hurriedly grabbed her kit and scrambled to the back of the line.

"Wow! Who does your hair?" Anna said with a broad smile.

"I suppose you crawl out of bed looking like Cinderella every morning." Suddenly self-conscious, she reached up to flatten her locks as Anna filled her plate and presented her with a piping hot cup of coffee.

"Hardly . . . more like Sleeping Beauty." Anna filled her own plate last and followed Lily in search of a seat. "I think I'll sit with Lateisha," she said, indicating a spot next to the girl on a fallen log near the edge of the campsite.

Lily had to hand it to Anna for her continued efforts to reach out. Sullen children like Lateisha were tough nuts to crack, but every now and then, a special person came along and broke through. From what she knew about Lateisha, the girl didn't need saving, like Eleanor Stewart had saved her. Lateisha's father was eager to take care of her, as soon as his overseas tour in the army ended.

Everyone looked up suddenly as Lateisha began to sob. Anna quickly took the girl in her arms, stroking her braided hair as she rocked her back and forth. Lily started toward them, but Anna held up a hand. Whatever the problem was, she had it under control. Five minutes later, the girl had calmed and was talking freely with Anna.

"What was that all about?" Lily whispered as they stowed their trash in preparation for a hike.

"Her mother just died. That's why she's so sad."

Lily couldn't believe she was hearing this for the first time. "I knew she was waiting for her dad to get out of the service, but social services didn't say anything about her mother. No wonder she's been so quiet."

"Yeah, I told her my mother died too when I was a little girl. I know exactly how she feels. At least I had my father."

"Poor girl."

"Maybe she'll loosen up a little now that she told somebody. I'll stick close to her."

"You're good with her, Anna. She's lucky she met you this weekend." Lily was glad Lateisha had found a friend, but she knew Anna too would be richly rewarded for reaching this troubled child. These were the treasures Lily pursued when she worked with children and families in trouble. No amount of monetary compensation was worth the feeling she got when she knew she was making a difference in someone's life.

When the group set out on their nature hike, the sight of Anna holding the small child's hand triggered in Lily an emotional groundswell. She had never met anyone like Anna Kaklis.

Lunch that day was hotdogs, chips and cookies, always a hit with the kids. If Lily had worried Anna might not like the outdoor cuisine, she needn't have bothered. She and Lateisha piled their plates high and retreated to their fallen log. In fact, Anna was coming off like an old hand with this camping stuff.

In the afternoon, the boys decided to brave the cold water and go swimming. Lily and Anna commandeered the two canoes for a trip across the lake.

"This isn't as easy as it looks," Anna called. She and Lateisha were struggling to avoid several low branches that hung over the water directly in their path. Anna paddled one way while Lateisha paddled the other, and now they were hopelessly trapped.

"Maybe not, but you're certainly entertaining," Lily answered smugly. From the other canoe, she and the twins were howling with laughter at their predicament, and that seemed to make Anna even more determined to get out of the mess. She stood unsteadily, reaching for a branch to push them away from the shoreline. Unfortunately, Lateisha chose that instant to drop her oar in the water and push off from the sandy bottom. With a scream, Anna toppled head first into the freezing water.

Lily's first instinct was to laugh, but she fought it, rowing quickly to her fallen friend. Barely containing a grin, she watched Anna splash around to find her footing. "Are you hurt?"

"N-n-n-no!" Anna shivered as she stood waist-deep in the water.

Lily rowed closer and leaned over the side, asking in a voice so low only Anna could hear, "Is the water cold, or are you just glad to see me?"

In a lightning quick moment, Anna lunged toward her and grabbed her by her waistband and collar. "Oh, I'm glad to see you all right!" Lily found herself upside down in a somersault into the lake.

When she came up, Rosa and Carlotta were looking at her in shock.

Anna had pulled her canoe from the overhanging trees and aimed it toward the campsite. With a push, she climbed in and grabbed a paddle. "Row for your life, Lateisha!"

"You better paddle faster, Amazon! When I catch you, you're

going to be sorry you were ever born."

All three little girls shrieked with laughter as her threats continued. Anna and Lateisha reached the shore and dragged their canoe from the water, and Anna ran into the women's tent.

"Where is that Amazon?" Lily bellowed, feigning anger for the girls' benefit. Rushing into the tent, she found Anna kneeling topless with her back to the zippered entry. Oddly speechless, Lily stopped dead in her tracks.

"Gotcha," Anna said without turning, pulling a sweatshirt over her head.

The game momentarily forgotten, Lily blushed as she recognized the lustful sensations that overwhelmed her as she glimpsed the muscled expanse of Anna's back. Without a word, she moved to her bag to find some dry clothes.

"You're not angry, are you?" Anna asked.

"Are you kidding? I bet those girls haven't had that much fun in years." And Lily couldn't remember the last time she had forgotten how to speak.

Anna walked with Lateisha to the door of her apartment and knocked. "You have my number?"

The little girl patted her pocket.

Remembering how Lily lost her number, Anna said sternly, "Put it in a safe place when you get to your room, okay? And I want you to call me every Sunday until your father gets home. Deal?"

An elderly woman came to the door. "Did you have a good time?"

Lateisha nodded and started into the apartment.

"Hey, wait a minute." Anna squatted and opened her arms. Lateisha rushed back and gave her a powerful hug. "You be sweet. And don't lose my phone number."

"Thank you for taking her," the woman said.

"We were glad to have her." Anna returned to the SUV to find Lily beaming. "What?"

"Nothing." Lily wiped her eyes.

"Are those tears?"

"That was so sweet."

Anna rolled her eyes. "What? You thought I was made of stone?"

"I know you didn't really want to come, but your being with us on this trip was the best thing that could have happened to her."

"I liked her. She's a sweetheart, and I understand what she's going through."

"I'll bet you make a great mother one of these days. If that's what you want, that is."

"Funny you should say that. I got a call from my ex-husband on Friday before I left work. He wanted to let me know he's getting married again."

"He sure didn't waste any time."

"He's marrying the mother of his child, whom he probably should have married in the first place."

"Are you okay with it?"

Anna kept most of her feelings about Scott to herself because she didn't want people to judge him harshly, but she felt comfortable talking with Lily about anything. "To be honest, I was sort of perturbed when he first told me. I don't really know why, though. I don't have those kinds of feelings for him anymore."

"What do you think it was?"

"I think maybe I was a little bit jealous. He's getting a whole family, like the one I thought he'd have with me."

"I can see how that would bother you."

"Yeah, but I'll get over it. I suppose I'll have kids one of these days. I just hate the whole trial and error thing about marrying a suitable father."

"Who says you have to? There are lots of ways to have kids."

123

Anna had thought about alternatives a few years ago when she worried about missing the best of her childbearing years. "I wouldn't rule that out. What about you? You're good with kids."

"I'm particularly fond of other people's kids," Lily said. "I wouldn't mind raising one, but I don't have any burning desire to give birth."

"Lucky you're a lesbian then. I'd have a hell of a time finding a husband who was willing to go through that."

Lily was in trouble and she knew it. What she now felt for Anna was well past simple friendship, and she was on her way to having her heart broken. It was only a matter of time.

On Saturday night, she picked up Chinese food and headed to Sherman Oaks to have dinner with Sandy and Suzanne. She had reluctantly turned down a movie offer with Anna because she had been neglecting her friends for weeks. Suzanne was almost fully recovered from her back surgery, and eager to get back to work.

"Are you insane?" Suzanne erupted when Lily confessed she was falling for Anna.

"It's not like I can help it, Suzanne. She's smart and interesting. She makes me laugh. She's kind and generous." Lily wanted to add beautiful to the list, but knew that would make Suzanne's tirade even worse. "You should have seen her last week with one of our foster children. That girl had hardly said a word in three months, and by the time we dropped her off at home, they were best friends. Anna even gave the kid her phone number."

Sandy put the last of the dishes in the dishwasher and sat down next to her at the kitchen table. "Suzanne's right, Lily. Anna's going to break your heart all to pieces. It's not that she can't be a good friend to you. She obviously already is, and the two of you shared an incredible experience in that mall. But you know she can't return the feelings you have for her. You're only going to hurt yourself by pursuing this."

"I'm not pursuing anything," Lily argued. They were right, but she couldn't bear to think of backing away from the first woman in ages whose companionship she really enjoyed.

She managed to listen politely as Suzanne explained her plans for renovating the downstairs bathroom, all the while thinking miserable thoughts about Anna breaking off their friendship because she crossed the line. After an almost somber good-bye, she grabbed her jacket and headed for home.

Anna adjusted the entries in her spreadsheet and re-charted the figures. Third quarter sales were up eleven percent over last year, thanks to the early appearance of next year's models. At this rate, Premier would have its best year ever.

Her father appeared in the doorway to her office. "Are you planning on staying all night?"

"I could ask you the same question. How come you're still here?"

"I was talking with Brad about the sales force. He thinks we ought to . . . what was it he said . . . add a little diversity. I think if we've got sales openings, they should go to whoever is most qualified. Anything else seems like discrimination to me."

Anna was glad to hear Brad had broached the topic with her father, who had been out of the hiring loop for quite some time. It was her idea to bring in more diversity, especially since two of her top three salespeople were minorities, and the third was a woman. "It makes good business sense to have a diverse sales force, Dad. People want to feel like their dealer is a part of their community."

"I understand that. But this is Beverly Hills, not Chinatown." He took a seat in one of the wingback chairs across from her desk.

"We're more than Beverly Hills, though. We're the top

BMW dealer in Southern California. People come from all over the region to shop here. How would you feel if you went into a dealership and everyone working there was Mexican?"

"I'd turn around and walk out."

"Why?"

"Because I'd figure those cars were for Mexicans, not fat, old, cranky Greek guys."

"You're not that fat."

"This is all your doing, isn't it?"

"Yes," she said, grinning with satisfaction. "We're spending a lot of money on advertising to get people in here to look at our cars. I want everyone who walks in that door—man, woman, white, Asian, Hispanic—to feel like the BMW is for people like them."

His face was twisted in a smirk. "What's next? We're going to have child care?"

"Maybe. If it helps our business, why not?"

"So how come you're not out with Hal and Kim tonight?"

"They're spending the night on the boat. Three's a crowd. I wanted to catch a movie with Lily, but she's having dinner with friends tonight."

"Lily . . . you're seeing a good bit of her since you ran into each other."

"We've done a few things together. She's really quite a fascinating person. Of course, I knew that the first time we met."

"And you said . . . she was gay?"

"That's right." Anna knew her father struggled a bit when it came to issues of tolerance, but she and others had been bringing him along over the years, even getting him to sign off on domestic partner benefits at Premier. "Maybe you and Mom can meet her soon. I know you'll like her. Everyone does."

He grunted and pushed up from the chair. "I'm calling it a night. I have to rest up to get my not-that-fat-but-old Greek self to the golf course tomorrow."

Anna chuckled. "You forgot cranky."

From her office on the second floor, Lily watched with delight as Anna exited her car at the curb and walked briskly toward the entrance of her building. The idea that Anna felt comfortable enough with their friendship to surprise her by dropping in for lunch filled her with amused satisfaction. Lily quickly reached into her top drawer for her compact mirror and checked her appearance. Then, so she wouldn't spoil Anna's surprise, she picked up her pen and shuffled her papers to give the impression of being absorbed in her work.

She heard voices in the reception area, one of them Anna's, but she couldn't understand what was being said. Moments later, all went quiet and she readied herself for a buzz from her phone intercom or a head in her doorway.

Neither happened.

When she could stand it no longer, she looked out the window again, convinced she must have been mistaken about the identity of the visitor. But it was definitely Anna, and she was getting back into her car—with Tony.

"How could he do that?" She hadn't meant to shout, but it was too late. Lauren and Pauline were already rushing into her office.

"What's wrong?" Lauren asked.

Lily took in their curious faces, scrambling for a way to spin her outburst into something reasonable. "I just saw Tony leave. I needed to ask him something."

"He just went to lunch. I doubt he'll be gone long."

"Was that . . . who was . . . ?"

"It was Anna Ka- something," Pauline said. "That friend of yours who came in a couple of weeks ago."

"Anna Kaklis. She went with us on Kidz Kamp," Lily said, slumping into her chair.

"What's wrong, Lily? Is there a problem?" Lauren asked.

Lily could fool Pauline, but Lauren knew her better and could tell when something was bugging her. "Not really, I guess. It's just that I asked Tony not to hit on her. She's recently been through a bad divorce."

"It wasn't Tony," Pauline said. "She's the one that called and asked him to go."

Lily thought she was going to be sick. She had always thought Tony was the kind of guy women ought to choose, a guy who cared about people less fortunate, a guy who loved kids. But the idea of Anna hooking up with her boss was more than she could take.

Lauren and Pauline went back to their desks, leaving her to her misery. An hour later, Anna's BMW returned, and Tony got out alone. Lily fumed at the satisfied smirk on his face.

To make matters worse, he soon brought his gloating grin to her doorway. "It's a beautiful day, Lily."

"I told you Anna was going through a tough time. I can't believe you took advantage of her that way."

His smile faded. "But she . . . you think I shouldn't have . . . oh, wait." Suddenly, he grinned again, this one broader and, for Lily, more infuriating, than the first. "Lily, that wasn't a lunch date. It was a business meeting." He drew an envelope from his pocket and laid it on her desk.

Lily picked it up, noting the return label for Premier Motors. Inside was a check from the dealership, made out to Kidz Kamp, enough to cover its annual budget.

Lily gasped as she pulled through the open gate at the Kaklis home, the big house, Kim had called it. It was. In her worn out SUV, she felt woefully out of place. Kim's invitation to Anna's thirty-second birthday dinner had come as a delightful surprise, but as she parked among the BMWs, she couldn't help but feel self-conscious.

Anna answered the door with a startled look.

"Surprise!" Lily stepped into a light hug.

"I can't believe my sister's this good at keeping secrets."

"She told me not to say a word."

"And she told me her car wouldn't start. So of course I rushed right over."

Lily laughed, thinking Anna was the only woman in LA who would fall for a trick like that just because she really wanted to check out the car.

"Let me introduce you to everyone."

As Anna walked her through the majestic house, Lily took in the splendor of the fine home, lavishly decorated with art and antiques. Once outside on the backyard patio, she was dragged by the hand to the umbrella table, where Kim and Hal sat with an older couple she presumed to be Anna's parents.

"How's my favorite first mate?" Hal asked enthusiastically.

"Hey, fella! I'm supposed to be your favorite first mate," whined Kim, backhanding her husband playfully across his stomach. She pushed in front to hug Lily. "I'm glad you could come."

"Me too. Thanks for inviting me."

Anna moved beside her stepmother. "Lily, I'd like you to meet my mother, Martine."

"I'm pleased to meet you, Mrs. Kaklis."

"And I'm happy to meet you, as long as you call me Martine."

"And this is my father, George."

Lily would have known him anywhere, as Anna had his height, his coloring and especially his gorgeous blue eyes. "Mr. Kaklis."

"It's George."

Anna finished by circling the group to stand beside her. "Mom, Dad, this is my dear friend, Lily Stewart."

George Kaklis's reaction reminded her of her first meeting

with Kim. He stepped forward to embrace her, then stood back to eye her up and down. "I can't tell you how happy I am to meet the woman who saved my daughter's life."

"You know, she always says that, but I've learned she usually leaves out the part where she saved mine. I wouldn't be here if you hadn't raised such a courageous daughter."

Kim leaned over and butted in. "Hal and I call them the mutual admiration society. Isn't it nauseating?"

Dinner was lively, with lots of conversation and laughter. Lily was peppered with questions throughout.

"So Lily, I take it you aren't married," Martine said.

"That's right."

Hal gave her a wink. "Anna told us about something funny you said when you guys were in that bridal store at the mall. What was that again?"

Anna repeated Lily's quip about her worst fear, and while everyone else laughed, Martine obviously didn't get it.

Kim's whisper was loud enough for everyone at the table to hear. "Lily's a lesbian, Mother."

Martine's face turned bright pink. She too whispered loudly, "Oh, I'm sorry."

Lily just laughed and whispered back, "Don't worry. I'm cool with it."

"I mean . . . I just . . . why am I whispering?"

All through dinner, Lily enjoyed herself thoroughly. The Kaklis family was fun, and they obviously were extremely devoted to one another. Having been raised by a single mother, she had never experienced this type of family life. Not that she was complaining—life with Eleanor Stewart had been perfect as far as she was concerned—but it was interesting to see the sibling dynamics, as well as the familial interchange between George and Martine. This was the life Lily wanted for all of the children she worked with in the foster care system.

Of everyone at the table, George was the enigma. Lily

thought him genuinely kind, but something ran beneath the surface, as if he were withholding judgment until he learned all he could about her. "Lily, I'm curious. Do you ever encounter discrimination in your work?"

"You mean because of my height?" She guessed he was talking about her sexual orientation, and the question surprised her.

"No, I was just wondering if prejudice is as bad in the court system as it is in the business world. I don't consider myself prejudiced, but I have to confess I've always shied away from hiring people who were open about their sexual preferences. Anna and I were talking about this just the other day. We want our customers to feel like they're doing business with someone they can relate to."

Lily bristled slightly, trying her best to figure out how George Kaklis could feel that way and not consider himself prejudiced. For some reason, it wasn't taboo to be open about your sexual preferences if you were straight. But she didn't want to offend Anna's father, so she tried not to take it personally. "Don't you sell BMWs to gays and lesbians too?"

She glanced at Anna to see if she was stepping over any lines with her response. To her displeasure, Anna was looking at her father pensively, as if considering his argument.

"Yes, I'm sure we do. But they don't usually announce their sexuality. I don't think it would be appropriate if one of our salespeople did either."

"Unless he or she was straight, is that right?"

"You don't have to announce that. It's the norm. I just think customers want to walk into the showroom and see people like themselves."

"It's the 'don't ask, don't tell' of the business world."

He nodded seriously, clearly assuming she was buying his argument.

For Lily, the worst part of this was the apparent agreement by Anna to this Neanderthal point of view. Furthermore, that

George had mentioned it at all seemed purposive to Lily, as though he had intended to insult her.

She stood and looked around the table at the frozen faces. "I should be going. I've got three cases scheduled for court next week, and I need to prepare. I hope you've had a nice birthday, Anna." Turning to Kim and Hal, she added, "Thanks for including me in your plans. I can find my way out." Abruptly, she turned and left.

"Dad, that's not what we talked about."

"But Anna—"

"In fact, it was just the opposite," she said, jumping to her feet in pursuit of Lily. But she had underestimated Lily's eagerness to leave, and was surprised when she reached the front door to see the RAV4 already disappearing beyond the hedge. Livid, she stormed back to the patio where her father met her angry glare with a look of pure innocence.

"What was all that about?" she demanded. "You know we have gay people at the dealership. You even signed off on their benefits." In all her life, she had never spoken to her father in such a scolding tone, and the shock was clearly registered on all the faces of the Kaklis family.

"Anna, I'm sorry. I didn't mean to say anything offensive. I was just thinking about our conversation and wondering if she had any problems where she worked."

Her father seemed truly contrite, but she didn't like his recent showing of narrow-mindedness, whether it was about minorities at work or a lesbian who happened to be a guest in his home. "You and I are going to finish this conversation, but right now, I have to go apologize to my friend for your rudeness." She started to leave, but stopped at the sliding glass door. "Thank you all for the party. I'm sorry . . . but I have to go."

"Wait up, Anna." Kim rose to follow her to the door. "Are

you okay?"

"I can't believe I just sat there, Kim. I had no idea she was taking Dad's words to heart, and I should have stuck up for her."

"I don't know what's up with Dad, but Lily surely knows you don't feel that way." She took Anna's shoulders and looked her squarely in the eye. "You and Lily care about each other, and you need to see what that's about. Don't let Dad decide this."

Anna was struck dumb by her sister's words. *See what that's about?* She finally found her voice. "I . . . it isn't like that, Kim."

"Whatever it is, don't let Dad push you one way or the other. He already did that with Scott."

With her sister's words weighing on her mind, she headed out to find Lily.

Lily spun onto the freeway, furious with herself for not keeping her mouth shut. She had acted like a spoiled child. "I ruined dinner. I ruined Anna's party. I've ruined everything. Way to go, shithead," she said aloud, pounding on the steering wheel.

The RAV4 responded with a sputter, and slowed dramatically. Lily slid one lane to the right and exited the freeway. To her relief, she spotted a Chevron station ahead as the car continued to slow, but it was clear she wasn't going to make it. "Damn it! What else could—" She stopped herself suddenly, remembering the last time she had asked a question like that, the ground had disappeared beneath her feet. The RAV4 finally died against the curb, about thirty feet shy of the busy station.

She had plenty of gas, plenty of oil . . . the temperature gauge was right in the middle. That was the sum of her car knowledge.

Her purse slung over her shoulder, she got out and walked to the gas station, thrilled to see it had both a garage and a mechanic on duty. She explained her problem to the station owner, and a young man named Chuck was sent to see about it. There was nowhere inside to sit, so she walked back out and waited by the door for the verdict.

Chuck returned and spoke to the owner, who followed him back to the car. Another ten minutes passed before they returned.

"Your alternator's shot and two of the mounts are rusted out. I'm surprised it didn't fall off going down the road."

Lily sighed. "What's it going to cost to fix it?"

"To tell you the truth, I don't think it's worth fixing. The distributor's going to go next, and who knows what after that."

She followed him back inside where he thumbed through a catalog.

"I'll give you seven hundred dollars for it," he finally said.

"What?"

"I have a friend who can strip it down for parts, but he's not going to get much out of that one."

"Seven hundred dollars!" She knew her car was old and worn out, but she had no idea she was driving around in a junkyard reject. "The tires alone are worth a hundred and fifty apiece."

The man shrugged. "That's the best I can do. It'll probably cost you a couple of hundred just to tow it somewhere."

Lily groped for her phone when she heard the familiar chime, the special one she had programmed for when Anna called. She needed to face the music for her rash behavior. Then she would deal with her car.

"Anna, I'm so sorry I stormed out. I lost my head."

"No, Lily. You did nothing wrong. What Dad said was wrong, and I should have spoken up. I do all the hiring at the dealership, and I couldn't figure out what the hell he was talking about. I'm the one who needs to be forgiven."

"No, you're not. I was at a party in his house. He has a right to his opinions. I should have just controlled my temper. And I ruined your party. I'm so sorry."

"It wasn't your fault. And he doesn't have a right to that opinion."

Lily felt better about Anna, but still awful about the scene she had made.

"Where are you? I drove to your apartment."

"I'm on Henderson Avenue . . . at a Chevron station . . . with a dead car."

"I see you've learned the magic words to get me to come running."

"Yes, it's a great vehicle," Lily said. "I have no doubt at all it's the best SUV on the road, by far. It's just that it's a little out of my price range. A lot, actually."

It was after hours on a Saturday night at Premier Motors, but Lily was getting the VIP treatment, looking over the brand new X3 in the showroom. It was sweet—leather appointed, powerful, and loaded with bells and whistles. When she tacked on taxes and dealer fees, the price of even the lower end model was over forty thousand dollars.

"I can get you a good deal. I know the owner."

"I'm sure you can. But even with a good deal, it's more than I've saved for my house. I need to be looking at the Suzuki or the Kia."

Anna frowned and shook her head with obvious disapproval. "Look, Lily. What if you could get the X3 for the same price as one of those other cars? Say, twenty-five thousand. Which would you rather have?"

"The X3, of course. I'm not an idiot. But I can't let you drop the price on this car that much. This is business."

"It's more than business, though." Lily turned to interrupt, but Anna held up her hand. "Hear me out. I still have a little trouble with my leg when I can't stretch it out all the way. If I'm going to spend as much time in your new car as I did in your old car, then I want you to have something that's comfortable to me. I'm in a position to help you get something nice, since I do own the place, after all. I have demos . . . I have pre-owned . . ."

Lily was almost sold, especially if Anna could advise her on a used vehicle. She gestured at Anna's knee. "It still bothers you?"

"Sometimes."

Lily thought about the long trips from San Diego, and to and from Silverwood Lake. She felt awful to realize Anna had probably been in agony the whole time, but was too nice to say anything. "Okay, what can I get for thirty thousand?"

Anna smiled triumphantly. Then she grabbed Lily by the hand and dragged her through the glass door to the back lot. "You like silver?"

Chapter 8

"You should probably slow down a little bit," Anna said gently.

"Holy shit! I'm doing ninety-five." Lily eased up on the accelerator and dropped her speed to a respectable eighty miles per hour. She was still speeding, but no longer leading the pack on the Grapevine, that infamous twisting, climbing stretch of Interstate 5 north of LA. "I can't believe how powerful this thing is. I love it."

A driver had delivered the silver X3, a demonstrator model with over ten thousand miles, to Lily's apartment on Sunday afternoon. Anna had ignored her offer of thirty thousand, fixing the final price at twenty-five, financed over four years at a rock-bottom percentage rate. It was the same deal she would have given Kim or Hal, and she was glad to do it for Lily.

"I'm not carrying enough cash to get you out of jail," Anna

warned. "You'll have to spend the night."

Traffic was pretty light for a Friday night. They had both left work early to get a head start north to San Jose. Anna was glad for the chance to come along on Lily's visit with her mother. She had heard a lot about Eleanor and couldn't wait to meet the woman Lily credited with rescuing her from a dire future.

"Do you think I can persuade your mom to tell me stories about little Lily Stewart?"

"I'm sure she will. Did you get in touch with your friend?"

"Yeah, I'm meeting her in San Francisco for dinner tomorrow night. You're welcome to come."

"Thanks, but you guys have a lot to catch up on."

"No kidding. The last time I saw Liz was at my wedding almost two years ago. She couldn't believe it when I told her we had already gotten a divorce."

"Does she know the whole story?"

Anna shook her head. "The only people who know are you, Kim and Hal."

"Oh." Lily glanced at her and then back at the road. "I think I might have said something to Sandy and Suzanne. I'm sorry."

"It's okay. They don't know Scott. I just don't want people who know him to think he's a terrible person. He's not. He just screwed up. We all do that."

"I still can't believe you took that so well. Everyone else in the human race would have gone ballistic."

Anna was well aware others were more bothered by Scott's behavior than she was. "You know what I think it was? I think . . . I've never told anybody this, so please don't say anything, okay?"

"Of course I won't."

"I think at a subconscious level I saw it as a way out. I felt justified in leaving him, especially since I thought he might actually rather be with Sara than me. I felt like I could end it without hurting him."

"You were that unhappy?"

"Not exactly." Anna had been sorting through her feelings even more since her talk with Kim about where to go from here. "I just realized I wasn't as happy as I wanted to be. And that was my fault, because I should never have agreed to get married in the first place."

"So why did you?"

"Good question. I guess I thought it was time. I was thirty years old and had everything else worked out already. I'd been thinking about whether or not I was going to have kids. When I met Scott, it just seemed like things were falling into place. He liked who I was. He wanted the same things."

"Did you love him, Anna?"

"I thought so. I just . . . it's embarrassing to say this."

"You don't have to be embarrassed, but if you don't want to talk about it, it's okay."

"I thought being married would be more than just adding sex to a friendship. But it wasn't. I loved Scott, just not like I wanted to. When we ran into Sara and the baby, what bothered me most was that it didn't bother me enough."

Though the dashboard lights shone on Lily's face, Anna couldn't make out her expression. Still, she knew Lily well enough by now to know there wouldn't be a trace of judgment.

Lily reached over the console and patted her arm. "I hate to think about you going through all of that by yourself. I wish I'd been around for you to talk to."

Anna closed her hand over Lily's. It was nice having such a close friend, someone she felt free to touch, whether through a hug or a kiss on the cheek, or just holding hands as they did now. "You were. If you hadn't gotten me to talk this out in the mall, I might have gone back home to Scott and just given in. Instead, I called my lawyer from the hospital and had him draw up the papers."

"I'm glad it's behind you, Anna. You deserve to be happy."

"We all do."

Just before ten o'clock, Lily pulled to the curb in front of a small, two-story Victorian. Anna grabbed her overnight bag and followed Lily along the sidewalk to the lighted porch. The front door opened, and an unassuming woman of about sixty stepped out. From somewhere in the corner of her mind, Anna remembered the image of this woman standing over Lily's stretcher as she was loaded into the ambulance at the Endicott Mall.

"Hi, baby! I'm so glad you're here." The two embraced and hugged fiercely, their devotion unmistakable. A long moment passed before they broke apart.

"Mom, I want you to meet someone very special. This is Anna Kaklis. Anna, this is my mom, Eleanor Stewart."

Anna reached out her hand to the older woman, but Eleanor was having none of that. She pulled Anna close and hugged her tightly. "Thank you for saving my daughter."

In a now familiar scene, Anna answered in their usual way. "You're welcome. But I couldn't have done that if she hadn't saved me first."

They entered the cozy house and were met at once by a handsome basset hound. "This is my boy Chester. He's never met a stranger, so he'll probably follow you around the house. If he gets on your nerves, just push him away."

Taking her cue from Lily, Anna set her bag beside the staircase before following Eleanor into the small living room. The comfortable room held a stuffed swivel rocker and loveseat for the house's human occupants, and a sprawling flannel beanbag for the adorable hound. Chester took his place in the center of the room as she and Lily got comfortable on the loveseat, but changed his mind and came to sit at Anna's feet, following her every move with his droopy brown eyes.

"Hi there, fella. I hear you're easy," she said, reaching out to scratch behind his ears.

"Did you have a nice trip in that new car?" Eleanor asked.

"It was great," Lily answered. "I'll take you for a ride tomorrow and Anna can show you all the features. I haven't even learned where everything is yet."

Eleanor addressed Anna. "You should have seen Lily when she got the Toyota. For the whole first week, she parked it out there under the streetlight and slept with her curtains open so she could get up and look at it."

"I was seventeen, Mom."

Anna smiled at Lily, who was blushing. "If there's anyone who understands what it is to love a car, it's me."

For the next hour, Anna and Eleanor talked about Lily as though she weren't in the room, including Eleanor's version of how Lily had come to live with her first grade teacher. Factually, it was the same as Lily's, but included details about Lily's childhood scuffles and the legal hoops Eleanor had to jump through to finalize the adoption.

Anna's eyes wandered about the room as they talked, taking in the pictures and trinkets. When they later toured the house room by room, her thoughts drifted to what it must have been like for Lily growing up here. The house was warm, homey and filled with love.

Anna's lifelong love affair with San Francisco was fading as she cruised Guerrero Street for the fourth time looking for a place to park. Liz had suggested Stella's, a trendy neighborhood place in the Mission District only a few blocks from where she lived.

Finally, she caught someone leaving and maneuvered the X3 into the tiny space. In minutes, she arrived at the restaurant, where she was greeted by her beaming friend.

"You look fabulous. Do you mind me saying that divorce agrees with you?"

"I'm finding it pretty agreeable," Anna said.

"No, really. I talked to Janice last Christmas and she said she ran into you."

Like Liz, Janice Ripley was a friend from Cal Poly. "I remember. She brought her boyfriend to look at cars."

"I don't think he's her boyfriend anymore."

"Good. The twit ended up buying a Grand Marquis."

Liz laughed. "You judge everyone by their car, don't you?"

"It's what I know."

"Then let's not talk about my minivan."

"There aren't many people who look good in a minivan, but you're definitely one of them." Liz had always been a little on the heavy side, but her Italian features were striking. The olive complexion, the large brown eyes, and jet black hair always earned her a second look.

"I know you're blowing smoke up my ass, but I love you anyway. Janice said you were thin as a rail."

That was about a month after she learned of Scott's tryst. "Yeah, I was going through some hard times. But my appetite's returned with a vengeance," she said, grasping the menu in hopes of diverting their conversation. "How are Rick and Chloe?"

"They're fine. They wanted to see you, but I wanted you all to myself."

Through dinner, they caught up with one another, Anna glossing over details of her divorce, and Liz leaving out nothing with regard to her husband and daughter. Eventually, they got around to talking about the earthquake and Anna's serendipitous encounter with Lily in the courthouse.

"Do you ever hear from Carolyn?" Liz asked casually when the story was finished.

Anna always warmed when she thought of Carolyn Bunting, one of her closest friends at Cal Poly. As sophomores, they were practically inseparable. But when they returned for their junior year, Carolyn was distant, always busy with other things, other people. Anna had been deeply hurt, the ache taking months to subside.

"Not recently. But I saw her last year at the reunion. You and Rick were in Europe, I think."

"How was she?"

"Great. It was really nice to see her again. We talked a long time. She's living in Seattle working for one of those big software developers. She introduced me to her partner, a woman who works in the Seahawks' front office." Anna let the words settle a moment to see how Liz would react. "Did you know back in college that Carolyn was gay?"

"Yes, I did. Did you know she was in love with you?"

Anna felt her stomach drop. A flood of emotions long buried crept into her consciousness. "Why do you say that?"

"She told me. She called me in Sacramento after sophomore year. She asked me if I thought it was possible you felt the same way about her." Liz took a deep breath, as if nervous about what she was about to say. "I told her I knew for a fact you didn't think about women that way. Then I said it wasn't right for her to feel like that and pretend to just be your friend."

Anna sighed heavily and leaned back in her chair. "Well, that explains a lot. I never really understood why she didn't want to be friends anymore when we came back in the fall."

Liz reached across the table and took Anna's hand. "The problem is that I didn't know anything for a fact. I answered her that way because I didn't want the two of you to be like that. It took moving to San Francisco to realize how ignorant and narrow-minded I was. And I've always regretted what I said to Carolyn."

So many things made sense now, and not just with regard to how Carolyn had acted. For the first time, Anna entertained the fleeting possibility that her heartache at being abandoned was rooted in feelings of romantic love. "I'm sure you did what you thought was best at the time."

"No, you're not letting me off the hook that easily. I've wondered if Carolyn wasn't just what you really needed, especially after—don't kill me—after I saw you with Scott at your wedding."

"What do you mean after you saw me with Scott?" Anna waved the waiter away as he tried to refill her water glass.

"I told Rick you looked like you did when you turned in your senior thesis."

"What's that supposed to mean?"

"That you'd just checked off something else on your to-do list, not like you'd married the man of your dreams."

Anna's objections died in her throat. Liz had just put into words the very doubts she had harbored since the moment she decided to marry, the doubts she was just beginning to understand.

"I'm sorry, Anna."

"No, it's okay." She realized she was staring at her napkin, and forced herself to look at Liz. "I sometimes felt that way . . . like getting married was an end unto itself."

"And maybe with Scott, it was. But the reason I'm telling you this isn't because of Scott, or even Carolyn. It's because of your friend Lily."

"What does Lily have to do with any of this?"

"You should hear yourself talk about her. And the look on your face, I swear, Anna. It's the one I should have seen with Scott."

Anna was stunned, not just by Liz's observation, but by the realization she was indeed drawn to Lily in such a powerful way. "Lily is important to me."

"Important like me? Or important like Scott?"

"Do you think I'm gay?"

"I can't answer that for you, but maybe you should ask yourself if you could accept it if you were."

Anna huffed and shook her head, sure the look on her face

was giving away her anxiety at having this topic on the table. It was the same reaction she'd had last weekend when Kim urged her to follow Lily and set things right. "It's hardly how I've thought about myself for the last thirty-two years."

"That wasn't the question." Liz pinned her in place with a pointed stare. "Maybe you've let yourself get too focused on the wrong to-do list. If Lily turned out to be the one who made you happy, would you let her?"

"I don't . . . if . . . what . . ." Anna couldn't even form a rational thought.

"Seriously, how do you feel about her being a lesbian, Anna? Does that aspect of her interest you?"

"Yes," she answered quietly, feeling a sudden pressure on her chest as she confessed the secret she hadn't allowed herself to entertain. "Yes, it does."

"It sounds to me like you ought to play it out and see where it goes. At least give yourself permission to consider it. If it isn't right for you, you'll know it. But if it is right, it might be your only chance to be really happy."

"Have you told her?" Lily's mother joined her on the loveseat to watch for Anna's return.

"Told her what?"

"That you're in love with her."

Lily sighed and turned toward the window. "No, I haven't. I'm afraid it would freak her out."

"She doesn't strike me as the sort of person who would rattle easily."

"No, but I don't want to make things weird for her. Can you imagine what it would be like to know your friend has sexual feelings you can't reciprocate?"

"I don't have to imagine it, Lily. I lived it for more than twenty years."

Lily was sure she had misheard. "What are you saying?"

"I'm saying that, for twenty years, my best friend was in love with me. She told me that when you were eight years old, and again just a few weeks before she died."

"Katharine?"

"Of course. And I loved her . . . as much as I ever loved anyone, just not the way she wanted."

"Why didn't you ever tell me this?"

Her mother shrugged. "It was one of those private things, Lily. Especially when Brenda came along."

"That must have been awkward," she said, remembering the woman Katharine dated for several years.

"Not really. As far as I know, Katharine never told her."

"But . . ." Lily couldn't understand how their friendship had weathered such a strain. "Didn't it ever bother you to know she felt that way?"

"No, why would it? She never forced the issue. She just laid it out there and said if I ever decided to take a walk on the wild side, she'd like to be my escort."

It was exactly the sort of thing Lily would have expected from Katharine. "What a corny line! I love it."

"I loved it too. It was just so . . ."

"Katharine." It was fascinating to see her mom in a new light. "So you never had any problems with it?"

Eleanor shook her head. "None at all. We were honest with each other, and we both accepted the way things were. I never asked her to give me up, and she never pressed me for anything more than friendship."

Lily sighed and looked back out the window, her eyes misting. "I don't know, Mom. I think it would kill me if it drove her away."

Eleanor placed her palm on the side of Lily's face. With her thumb, she touched the tear that hovered. "She's a very special lady, sweetheart. Some things might be worth the risk."

From behind her sunglasses, Anna stole glances at Lily as they drove south toward LA. After sleeping on her revealing conversation with Liz, it was impossible not to see Lily in a new light. And it wasn't at all the unnatural feeling she might have expected. On the contrary, it felt familiar. She had acknowledged that day on the boat that she found Lily physically attractive . . .

Anna shook her head slightly. Even the word attractive meant something different today. There was undeniably something about Lily that attracted her, that made her want to have Lily physically close. Holding her as she had beneath the blanket on the boat had been soothing, and now, the thought of more intimate touching stirred her in a surprising way.

Totally absorbed in the mental recounting of her talk with Liz, Anna realized neither she nor Lily had spoken for quite some time. She wondered if Lily had a hint of her musings, or if she had ever entertained similar thoughts.

As if in answer, Lily suddenly grasped her hand, which was draped over the console. "Thanks for coming with me this weekend. It really meant a lot to Mom . . . and to me."

Anna intertwined their fingers and squeezed gently. They rode in silence like that for many miles, Anna acutely aware of their connection. She concentrated hard on the sensations, the simple touch and the warmth it rendered. She never held hands with her other friends. Why did this feel so natural?

And did she have the nerve to do something about it?

Recognizing the number on the display, Lily kicked her office door shut before answering. "Greetings."

"It snowed last night in the Sierras."

Lily smirked, but didn't answer.

"I know. You're fine. Thanks for asking."

"Hello to you, too. What's with the weather report?" Lily had begun to accept Anna's habit of starting her conversations in the middle. It was part of her charm.

Anna cleared her throat and enunciated formally. "I'm calling to request the pleasure of your company for Thanksgiving in Tahoe with the Kaklis clan."

Normally, an invitation like this would have been a no-brainer for Lily. An opportunity to spend a holiday with Anna was not something to be trifled with. But Lily was a strong believer in family traditions. She hadn't missed Thanksgiving with Eleanor since she was seven years old. "As tempting as that sounds, I always spend Thanksgiving with Mom."

"So how far is Tahoe from San Jose?"

"Mmmmm . . . about four hours. Why? You want to come down and have turkey with us?"

"No, this is called arm-twisting. I was hoping if you had a few days off you could drive up and spend at least a day or two with us. We could ski, or maybe go to a show at one of the casinos in Reno."

"That sounds like so much fun." Anything with Anna would be fun, but Lily didn't want to make a fool of herself on the slopes. "But I'm really not much of a skier."

"That doesn't matter. We'll find something to do."

"Tell you what. I'll talk it over with Mom. I don't want to hurt her feelings if she's got something planned. When do you need to know?"

"No deadline really. We're all going anyway, and there should be plenty of room. We can play it by ear. But I'd love to have you there. Especially when I'm thinking about things I'm thankful for."

Anna probably had no idea that everything she said or did made Lily fall in love with her more.

≈≈

The Lincoln Navigator's ride was impressive, but Anna couldn't imagine driving something that large as an everyday vehicle. "I wonder why Dad was so anxious about getting back home. He usually hates going back after Thanksgiving because Christmas is so busy."

"My guess is he didn't want to be here when Lily got here," said Kim, who had come along on the ride to drop their parents at the airport in Reno.

"Lily?" Anna had talked it out with her father after the birthday incident and was satisfied the incident was behind them. "I told him she was okay with everything."

"I think it's him who isn't okay."

"What the hell is going on with him? He's never been like this before."

"Yes, he was. You just didn't hear about it. The rest of us did, though."

Anna's irritation grew as her sister dragged out her cryptic explanation. "Spill it, Kim."

"It was back when you were in college and you brought your friend home. What was her name? Carolyn?"

"Carolyn Bunting," she said brusquely.

"I remember Dad going on and on about how he just knew she was a lesbian, and he wished you'd make different friends."

"What could he possibly have against lesbians?"

"It isn't about them, Anna. It's about you. He's scared to death you're going to be led astray." The last words were said with obvious sarcasm.

Anna slammed both hands on the steering wheel angrily. "Does everybody in the world think I'm gay?"

Kim blew out a deep breath and looked away.

"Talk to me, Kim."

"If you tell me you aren't, I'll believe you. But what I see between you and Lily looks like more than just friendship."

"But it isn't." With every word, this conversation was sound-

149

ing more like the one she had with Liz. "What is it you see?"

"You talk about her all the time. And when she's there, you can't take your eyes off her. You're different when you're with her . . . like you're happy just because she's there. I know that isn't exactly down and dirty sex, but you never did that with Scott."

Yes, this was shaping up exactly like the conversation with Liz, Anna thought. "Something's happening, Kim. I don't know what it is, but yes, I'm attracted to Lily."

"Good, because for what it's worth—and brace yourself, because I'm actually about to be serious—I like Lily better than anyone you've ever brought home, and I like you with Lily."

Anna still hadn't given herself permission to go forward. "I haven't said anything to her, so please try not to propose on my behalf."

"Are you going to talk to her this weekend?"

Anna shook her head. "I wouldn't have a clue what to say."

"Just don't say no. Not without being sure it isn't what you want. And whatever you do, don't let Dad intimidate you. Remember how he tried to do the same thing to me when I started seeing Hal? That's why we eloped."

It was undeniable their father was a notorious meddler when it came to their personal affairs. But she had to admit, his approval of Scott had been an important factor in her decision to get married. That made her an accomplice to her father's interference, because she bent to his wishes. But not this time. Kim was right—she had to follow her feelings with Lily wherever they led.

The drive had taken almost five hours, as fresh snow had narrowed Interstate 80 traffic to one lane at the higher elevations, but Lily was fearless in her four-wheel drive X3. She arrived at the rental cabin just after one in the afternoon. The surrounding woods were a beautiful white, and the smell of wood smoke filled her nostrils when she stepped from the SUV. Two other four-wheel drive vehicles, a Lincoln Navigator that looked like a rental and a Jeep Wrangler with a Cal-Berkeley alumni sticker, were already parked alongside the cabin.

A grinning Anna opened the door and pulled her inside. "Get in here and shut the door before all the heat gets out!"

"I had a lovely trip. Thanks for asking." Lily fell into a warm embrace.

"Shhhhh! What did I tell you about raising people's expectations?"

"Where is everybody?"

"Kim and Hal are on the slopes with Todd. He's a friend from their Berkeley days. I took Mom and Dad to the airport in Reno this morning."

If Lily had to bet, George Kaklis left town to avoid having to spend time with her. "Does your father hate me?"

"No, of course not. He got the silent treatment from all of us for a few days, so I think he's learned his lesson. I was going to put you in the room they had, but I didn't know Todd was coming up today. He was Hal's fraternity brother and best man when they snuck off and got married." She led the way up the staircase. "You'll be stuck with me, if that's okay."

Lily followed Anna into a small room, smiling to herself with anticipation until she saw the twin beds. "Hey, you put up with me in a tent. I guess I can suffer sharing a room."

The others returned just before dark, and they settled in for a relaxing evening by the fire. Hal and Todd traded memories of fraternity pranks as the women simply shook their heads in disbelief.

"You guys are so crude," Kim said in disgust. "Lily's got the right idea. I'm surprised more women aren't lesbians."

"There's still time," Anna joked.

"You know what they say," Lily said in agreement. "Better latent than never!"

151

⚜

On Saturday morning, Lily trudged behind the others along the path to the lift. Compared to the stylish sisters, she felt like a ragamuffin. The snow pants she wore were from pudgier days, and they bagged around her hips. Struggling clumsily with her rented boots and skis, she more than once considered taking a pass before she made a complete fool of herself. But with Anna's encouragement, she gamely plowed on.

She did fine on her first two runs, picking her way slowly down the center of the trail as Anna and Todd crisscrossed one another playfully. On the third trip, just when she felt she had the hang of it, a boy of about ten clipped her elbow as he raced past. Flailing desperately to keep her balance, she teetered first one way then the next, finally ending up sprawled face down in the snowbank at the side of the trail.

As if being knocked down by a kid wasn't humiliating enough, she was acutely aware that Anna, who had been skiing behind her, had seen the whole thing. The idea that she had just made a fool of herself in front of the one person she was trying to impress struck her as ridiculously funny. What else could she do but laugh?

"Lily, are you all right?" The panic in Anna's voice was unmistakable.

"I'm fine," she said, laughing as Anna grasped her shoulders and rolled her over.

Her laughter stopped abruptly when she met Anna's gaze, a frantic look that faded instantly to relief. In the next several seconds, something sparked between them—something unmistakably ardent—and her heart began to race. Their faces were mere inches apart, and Lily was almost certain they were closing for a kiss.

"Is everything okay here?" Todd threw a spray of powder as he appeared out of nowhere, shattering the moment.

"Yeah, I'm okay. Injured pride is all." Lily glanced back at Anna, who had looked away and was now intent on helping her to her feet. "I told you I wasn't much of a skier."

The three started slowly down the mountain.

"That was hardly your fault, Lily." Anna took her elbow to lend her support. "That kid wasn't paying attention to what he was doing. Are you sure you're all right?"

Lily wasn't hurt, but the familiar tickle in her chest signaled an impending asthma attack. "Actually, I'm fine, but I think my asthma is kicking up. I get this way sometimes when I exercise in the cold. Laughing so much probably pushed me over the edge."

Anna stopped suddenly and grabbed her shoulders, clearly panicked. "Did you remember your medicine? Do you need a doctor? What should I do?"

"Don't worry about me." Lily loosened her clips to remove her skis. "It isn't bad, and I have my medicine in my locker. As long as I don't do anything to make it worse, I should be fine."

"We should stop for the day. We'll go back to the cabin and you can rest."

"Or maybe you can sit in there and watch us come down," Todd suggested, pointing to the lodge with its two-story glass view of the slopes.

The idea of heading back to the cabin to explore whatever it was Todd had interrupted certainly had its appeal. But Lily didn't want to come off like a baby, especially with Todd clearly antsy about heading back up the slope with Anna.

She turned to Anna and smiled. "You missed a whole day of skiing yesterday because you were waiting for me. Todd's right. I'll can sit in there and watch you guys."

"I don't want to leave you by yourself," Anna said, obviously worried.

"I'll be fine. I promise. I'll feel bad if you miss out on your fun, so please go on."

"Come on, Anna. We'll be the entertainment committee,"

Todd said.

Anna looked at her. "Are you sure?"

"Go!" She gave both of them a playful shove. "Just don't leave without me. You know how I'd hate to miss dinner."

When they left, she turned in her boots and gathered her belongings from the rented locker. As usual, the medicine took effect right away and she felt better at once. She laughed out loud when she spotted Anna, Todd, Kim and Hal skiing toward the bottom in a makeshift conga line.

"We're gonna kick your ass!" Hal hissed to Lily.

"Aw, you sissies couldn't score if our whole team laid down on the field." The football wars were underway, as the Cal Bears took the field in Berkeley against the UCLA Bruins for the final game of the season. Hal and Todd had dragged the television to the center of the vaulted living room, arranging the sofa and loveseat close enough for all to see the action.

Kim and Hal staked their claim to the couch, and snuggled together affectionately. Todd took a seat opposite the pair on the loveseat. When she and Anna entered the room, he looked directly at Anna and gestured to the open space beside him.

"Hey, not fair." Lily said. The only empty seat was at the end of the couch with Kim and Hal. "You three Berkeley Bozos should have to sit together."

"That's right," Kim said. "We should sit together and do cheers."

"Nice try," said Todd. "I'm not getting near you two. The whole couch might spontaneously combust at any moment."

And he wasn't giving up Anna either, Lily thought cynically.

The game was one of the most exciting contests Lily could remember. Her Bruins scored first, which was good. The Bears answered back, which was bad. The Bruins intercepted, which was good again. Then the Bears recovered a fumble, which was bad. But the Bruins blocked a punt, which was great, because they ran it back to midfield.

Then something awful happened. Todd put his arm around Anna's shoulder. And it was all Lily could do not to go over there and knock it off.

Anna suddenly stood, leaving Todd's grasp. "Does anyone want anything to drink?" She disappeared into the kitchen as Kim and Hal called out their orders.

"Go help her, Lily," Kim suggested.

"I'll do it," Todd said, jumping to his feet and padding behind her.

An eternity passed in the next five minutes, and Lily could stand it no longer. "I'll go see if they need a hand." Full of apprehension, she walked quietly toward the kitchen.

The sight of Anna kissing the young man was like a blow to the gut.

Anna placed her hand firmly against Todd's chest and pushed him away. "I don't know where that came from, but if I've been sending you those signals, I apologize."

Todd looked at her sheepishly. "I, uh . . . just wishful thinking on my part, I guess."

"You're a nice guy, Todd. But I don't think of you that way."

"Noted," he said, looking every bit the school kid who was getting scolded by his teacher.

They both burst out laughing, breaking the tension.

"I think this would be a really good time for a beer run," he said. "I could use the fresh air."

Anna shook her head as she watched him leave through the side door. That could have gone a lot worse. At least both of them were laughing about it. She couldn't wait to tell Lily.

As she turned to finish fixing the drinks, she was struck by an irony. If Lily had followed her into the kitchen, Anna probably would have initiated the kiss. Smiling at that thought, she returned to the TV room juggling three drinks. "Where's Lily?"

Kim sat up and took her glass. "She said something about her asthma bothering her again."

Anna clambered up the stairs to the small room they shared, alarmed to find Lily already in bed, facing the wall. "Are you okay?" She sat on the edge of the bed and gently rubbed Lily's back.

"Yeah, I took some more medicine. I need to go to sleep, but I'll be fine."

Lily's reassurances did little to calm her fears, especially since this attack had come on so quickly. "Is there anything I can get you?"

"No, I just need to be alone so I can rest."

"Okay." Anna didn't want to leave, but she had to do what was best for Lily. Before leaving, she placed a light kiss on her temple. "Please feel better."

When Anna awoke, her first thought was of Lily and how she had fared through the night. Sitting up, she was pleased to see the empty bed, a sign she was up and about. Then she realized the folded paper on the pillow was a note.

Anna,
Thank you so much for the invitation this weekend. I had a wonderful time. Sorry I missed the end of the game last night. My asthma usually doesn't act up like that, but sometimes it happens when I'm in a place I'm not used to. Anyway, I'm fine now. I woke up early and thought I'd hit the road. I've got a busy week in court, so I could use a head start on getting my cases ready. Things are always busy at the office around the holidays, but maybe we'll have a chance to get together once things calm down. Have a safe trip home. Thanks again.
Lily

"You're a stupid fucking idiot!" Lily yelled to herself as she barreled south on the Golden State Freeway. "What the fuck did you think you were doing? What part of married to a man did you not fucking understand?" Only one word came close to expressing her frustration, and she couldn't seem to use it enough.

She had lain awake practically all night, fighting back tears as she tried to recall anything careless she had done to tip her hand. Her worst fear was not even that Anna was interested in Todd. It was that she wasn't interested in Lily, and felt she needed to send that message because she was picking up vibes that made her uncomfortable.

It was okay to fucking kiss a guy you barely knew. But god help you if you felt something for another woman—a woman who had been through an earthquake with you, for fuck's sake.

Either way, Lily was humiliated for even thinking she had a chance to be more than just Anna's friend. Everyone could see the futility of her stupid fucking dreams but her. And she would never hear the end of it from Suzanne.

After last night's little show, Anna probably figured she had Lily's advances under control now, and things would go back to normal when they returned to LA. But nothing could be normal again, as far as Lily was concerned. The idea of seeing Anna with Todd—or anyone else—was more than she could deal with. The best thing she could do was back off completely. Then Anna could do whatever the fuck she wanted.

The sudden appearance of red and blue lights in her rearview mirror caused her to look down at her speedometer. "Oh, fuck."

Chapter 9

Anna spun by Carmen's desk and picked up her messages. Thumbing through them quickly, she finally found the one she had been looking for since Tahoe. It was simple, just a checked box that said Lily had returned her call.

Which call? Anna had left no fewer than five messages in the past week. Lily had said in her note she would be busy through the holidays, but this was ridiculous. How did two people go from talking two or three times a day to not at all?

Turning to go upstairs to her office, she caught sight of two of her salesmen jostling each other for position near the door. "What's going on with them?"

Carmen laughed. "They've been working the phones all day and realized they both have customers coming to look at the last 650 ragtop."

"Are we already down to one?"

"Brad said we sold six this week, four of them right off the truck."

December was their busiest month, thanks to the steep discounts they offered to clear the lot of inventory before the end of the year. With the added incentives for the sales force, they were closing over fifteen deals a day.

So it was just as well Lily was busy. Anna was busy too.

Lily reached for her cell phone but stopped short when she recognized the special ring. The office calls and e-mails had stopped when she told Anna that Tony was cracking down on personal communications at work because of their heavy workload. It was a white lie, but it tied in nicely with her excuse of being swamped at work.

Anna had done nothing wrong, certainly nothing that deserved a cold shoulder, but Lily had to get some distance between them, enough to let her feelings die down a bit. Someday she would be ready to hear all about Anna's new relationship with Todd or Steve or whoever. But not while her heart was still on her sleeve.

At least the charade of having so much work to do around the holidays was paying dividends. Her cases were prepped all the way through January, and Lauren now owed her the farm, since Lily was covering her court appearances the week after Christmas. By the time New Year's rolled around, she might feel like socializing a little.

Her desk phone rang, the display indicating a pay phone in Pasadena. She couldn't recall having any clients out that way, but it wasn't unusual for them to call on pay phones in emergencies.

"Lilian Stewart."

"Should I be hurt that my cell phone's getting bounced?"

Lily shuddered hard at the familiar voice. "I, uh . . . I was down in the conference room. Did you just call?"

Anna mumbled something that sounded like "only about a hundred times."

"I've been slammed here. A lot of our clients have a hard time around the holidays. That's why I'm having to work so late."

"What is it about the holidays? I would think people would be in better moods."

"We see a lot of stress because nobody has enough money."

"I guess we take things for granted, don't we?" It wasn't really a question. "So other than working your tail off, how are you? I've missed you since Tahoe."

"I'm doing all right," she lied. "I'll be better in January when I can come up for air."

"You sound like you could use a break. Want to meet me for bite? I'm in Pasadena now, but I could be in your neighborhood in half an hour."

"I was just getting ready to leave. I—"

"I can meet you somewhere else then. Just name it."

In her heart, Lily knew Anna was just trying to be accommodating, but it felt more like a hard sell. "I can't tonight. I have too much to do."

"You poor creature. I thought I was busy, but I'm practically on vacation next to you. Why don't you pick a day next week and we'll meet? Any day's good for me. I have some great news to tell you about—"

"I can't commit, Anna. I'm sorry." And she didn't want to hear the great news about Todd.

"Please, Lily. I'll bring a pizza to your office if that's all you have time for. I just want to see you before Christmas."

Her defenses evaporated when Anna said please. Seeing her again so soon would turn her insides upside down, but she needed to get it over with, especially since Anna wasn't going to take no for an answer. The more Anna pressed, the harder it would be to say no without coming clean about why she left Tahoe.

"Okay, what about Wednesday?"

"Wednesday's great. How about the Starfish in Marina del Rey?"

"Fine, but I have court on Thursday, so I can't stay long."

"Can you get there by seven?"

Lily couldn't believe she had given in. She was already dreading it. "Yeah, seven."

"I can't wait to see you. Between your caseload and my end-of-year retail madness, we just have to work harder to make time for the people that matter. And you matter to me."

A lump hardened in Lily's throat. "You matter to me too."

The week passed all too quickly for Lily, and before she knew it, Wednesday arrived. None of her feelings for Anna had settled, at least not where she wanted them to settle. If anything, she ached even more for the loss of their friendship, and for that little sliver of hope that had let her dream about more.

Over the weekend, she had tried to clear her head with a long solo hike, choosing the trail up Mount Disappointment because it fit her mood. The question that plagued her was whether or not she could set aside the feelings that had grown and be the friend Anna wanted.

She had decided to try. People like Anna Kaklis—people who mattered—didn't come along often, and having the chance to share at least a part of her life would be worth the pain of unrequited love. Besides, the moment she entered the restaurant and spotted Anna at a table near the window, Lily tingled uncontrollably with happiness.

"Hi, stranger," she said, all of her defenses falling as Anna leapt from her chair to envelop her in a hug.

"Look who's talking. I was beginning to wonder if I'd ever see you again. You must be going crazy with all that work."

Lily had decided on the way to the restaurant to stick with

her original story as much as possible, that she would be busy at work at least until after the New Year. That would buy her some time to cool down a bit more, and to get used to the idea that Anna would be nothing more than a friend. "It's a madhouse right now, but things should get back to normal when the holidays are over . . . and Tony will chill about everyone's"—she made quote marks in the air with her fingers—"unnecessary personal communications."

Anna shook her head. "He just doesn't strike me as the kind of boss who'd clamp down on that sort of thing."

"You don't know Tony. He can get on the warpath when he wants to."

The waitress came and took their order, giving Lily time to study Anna a bit closer. She looked unusually ragged, with slumped shoulders and tired eyes, but still she was the most beautiful woman in the room.

"You'll never guess who I'm having dinner with on Friday," Anna said, smiling broadly.

Lily's stomach churned with dread. She wasn't a good enough actress to feign excitement over an idiot like Todd. "I have no idea."

"Leon Newhouse."

Wonderful. Anna's list of suitors was growing. "I don't think I know him."

"Staff Sergeant Leon Newhouse."

Lily still had no idea who he was.

"Lateisha's father is home. She called me and we're all going to dinner on Friday night."

Lily almost laughed with relief. "Anna, that's fantastic." It was more than fantastic. It was a perfect reminder of what kind of person Anna was, and why she mattered. "I'm so proud of you for being there for her. That really was a terrific thing to do."

"I've had such fun. We went Christmas shopping last week. I managed to talk her into getting a few new outfits, but mostly she was focused on getting something nice for her dad. It was really sweet."

Lily would have given anything to have been a fly on the wall for that shopping trip. As they ate, she heard the whole story in animated detail, including the hilarious account of Anna trying on a purple dress Lateisha thought she should wear.

"I'm just so lucky it didn't fit."

It felt good to laugh again, especially with Anna. How on earth had Lily thought she could live without this in her life? "It sounds like so much fun."

"It was. Especially since Lateisha got the best present of all when her dad came home."

They passed on dessert, but got coffee. Lily hated to leave, but she couldn't let Anna know her work story had been a cover for dodging her company.

"I can't believe another Christmas is here already," Anna said.

"Me neither. Where did the year go?"

"There's never enough time to get everything done. We're running this sales contest at work, and the cars are flying out of there as soon as we can get them processed off the truck."

"You must be working like crazy too."

"I am. I can't wait to relax this weekend. Hal's friend Todd is down for a few days and we're all going out on the boat Sunday. Can I tempt you to join us?"

To Lily, the sudden image of Todd and Anna huddling against the wind on Hal's boat was like a kick in the chest. There was no way she could be this close to Anna if it meant getting her nose rubbed in their romance.

"No, I have to work."

"Even on Sunday? Come on. Take a day off and join us."

"I can't," she said, unable to keep the sharpness from her voice. She wanted nothing to do with their flirtatious antics. "My work is important. If you slack up on the car lot, that's a few thousand dollars less in your pocket at the end of the month. If I do, women get slapped around, and kids get molested by their mother's boyfriends. That's why I have to work my ass off."

Anna looked as if she had been struck.

"I'm sorry. I didn't—" Lily couldn't believe the words had come from her mouth.

"Look, I know what I do doesn't hold a candle to your work. In fact, it shames me sometimes to think about how decadent our fancy cars are when some people don't even have a way to get to work."

"That's not your fault."

"I've always wanted to tell you"—Anna's crystal blue eyes seared her—"that you're a hero to me for the kind of work you do."

Lily had never felt so ashamed of herself. If the earth had opened again and swallowed her, it would have been a fitting ending to the moment. She insisted on paying the check this time, and they parted with no plans to see each other again.

"What did I tell you? Gorgeous, isn't it?" Kim held her arms wide in the foyer of the luxury condominium.

According to the sell sheet, it was twenty-two hundred square feet, two bedrooms and a loft, a private patio and a garage.

"It's gated, so you won't have to worry about unwelcome guests. And the maintenance fees are only eight hundred a month. That's a steal in this neighborhood."

"I don't know. It's okay, I guess." Anna couldn't seem to get enthused about any of the properties on Kim's list. She knew it was time to give up the big house. She had never been comfortable there.

"I wonder what Lily would think about it. She's got a pretty good sense of things."

Anna saw through her sister's suggestion. On Christmas Day, she had overheard Kim telling Martine she was back to working long hours and avoiding her family again, just as she had done when the trouble started in her marriage. And Kim was sure it had to do with Lily.

"Why don't we call her and see if she'll swing by?"

Anna walked away into the living room. "Does this fireplace work?"

"Yes. Did you just ignore me?"

Anna sighed and slumped on the low hearth. It had been a long five weeks since the restaurant, where they had left things on an awkward note. "Lily and I aren't seeing each other much these days. She's been really busy at work."

"Busy at work, huh? Did you two have a fight or something?"

Anna shook her head, not meeting her sister's eye. "No, nothing like that. I honestly don't know what happened." She related the circumstances as best she could. "I was ready to talk to her at Tahoe, and I would have. But then she got asthma that night and left without even saying good-bye. When we got back, I called, but she was never in. We finally got together for dinner the week before Christmas and things just sort of blew up." She sighed again. "I must have done something, but I don't know what it was."

"What happened when you all were in the kitchen?"

"What do you mean?"

"At Tahoe, when you and Todd went to get drinks for everybody." Kim cocked her head, as if straining to visualize the details. "Lily went in to help. Then she came back and said she was sick. Come to think of it, that's the last time I saw her."

Anna stood and started to pace the empty room. Clutching her head in her hands, the moment came back. "Shit! She came into the kitchen? Are you sure?"

"Positive."

"Damn it!"

"What?"

"Todd kissed me."

165

"He kissed you? Just out of the blue?"

"Yeah. But I stopped him. I told him I didn't think of him that way. He said he was sorry, and everything was okay after that."

"Except that Lily must have seen you."

Anna shook her head with disbelief. Why hadn't she thought of that? Of course that's what happened. "So she thought . . . Todd . . ." She scrunched her face as she tried to imagine being interested in Hal's friend. "And then I said that at the restaurant about Todd going with us on the boat. No wonder she got so upset all of a sudden. She thinks I'm seeing Todd."

"So can't you just tell her?"

"Tell her what? That I'm still available?" It was almost surreal to hear herself talking about Lily this way with her sister.

"Tell her everything. You can't let her slip away without knowing how you feel."

Anna was overwhelmed, not just at finally realizing what had gone wrong, but that she was talking about these feelings aloud again. Everyone saw it in her. She had fallen in love with Lily.

"Thanks, Kimmie." She reached out both arms to hug her sister, then picked up her purse and started for the door. "You're right. I have to fix this. I'm not even sure Lily feels the same way, especially after I've been so clueless."

Lily stumbled to the door to stop the incessant ringing and pounding, the effects of which were exacerbated by an entire bottle of cabernet sauvignon. "Lay off, already. I'm not fucking deaf!" Fumbling with the dead bolt, she flung the door back without checking through the peephole. There in her doorway stood two very angry women.

"What the hell's going on with you?" Suzanne demanded. "You don't return our phone calls. You ignore our invitations."

"Who the fuck do you think you are coming into my house and yelling at me like this?" She grabbed the door handle to steady herself. "Get the fuck out of here!"

"Lily," Sandy said gently, glancing about at her filthy apartment. She stepped forward and folded Lily into an embrace.

Lily resisted at first, trying to turn away, but Sandy was bigger and held on tight. She finally relaxed. She wanted to cry, but the tears were gone.

"What's this about, Lily? Is it Anna?"

She nodded. "You were right about her. And about me. I should have left her alone. I wanted her to fall in love with me. But she didn't."

"We told you that would happen," Suzanne said. "We could see it coming a mile away."

Lily sneered over Sandy's shoulder, thinking Suzanne would rather be right than president.

"Shut up, Suzanne," Sandy barked.

Even in her drunken state, Lily thought hearing that was worth letting them in.

"This is our fault," Sandy continued.

"What do you mean our fault?"

"Yeah, what do you mean your fault?" Lily asked, annoyed to hear her words slurred.

"I mean Lily has been ignoring us since Thanksgiving because she didn't want to hear us say I told you so." She lifted Lily's chin and looked her squarely in the eye. "We never meant for you to think we wouldn't be here for you."

"Even if I decided to wreck my own life?"

"Especially then."

The revelation that Lily had pulled away from her because of Todd was just the first step in reconciling all that had transpired. The most straightforward solution—the one Anna had mulled for three days—was to call and say it was all a misunderstanding. However, there were several problems with that approach, Anna realized, not the least of which was the fact that Lily wasn't taking her calls. And telling someone a kiss was uninvited wasn't exactly the sort of message to leave on a voicemail.

Besides, if Lily had already moved on—or never felt that way about her in the first place—she was going to feel pretty foolish when this all came out. But the main thing that stopped her from picking up the phone was realizing she wasn't prepared for Lily's response, no matter what it was.

"Are you getting excited about our trip?" Her father's sudden appearance in the doorway to her office startled her. On Monday morning, the two of them would leave for Germany where they would tour the BMW design center and meet with the engineers. It was something she and her father had done every three years since Anna was seventeen years old.

"Of course," she replied, but without her usual enthusiasm. "How about you?"

"I always look forward to these trips. Not so much because we're going to hear about the cars, but because I get to spend time with one of my favorite people."

They hadn't seen much of each other lately, since she had been spending so much time behind a closed door. More than once, she had considered asking for a couple of weeks away, time to get down to a beach in Mexico by herself and clear her head. But that would have raised questions she didn't want to answer.

"Sweetheart, I can usually tell when something's bothering you. If you want to talk, I'll listen. Who knows? Maybe your old man can help."

"Thanks. I appreciate that, Dad. I look forward to being with you too." She hated that he could read her so well, but dumping this melodrama on him wasn't an option. When he retreated, she stood and closed the door to her office. Pulling from her wallet the business card she had located last night, she dialed the Seattle number. It was time to take a step.

"Carolyn Bunting, please." Anna drummed her fingers nervously as she waited on the line for the familiar voice.

"This is Carolyn."

"Hi, stranger. It's Anna Kaklis. How are you?" She smiled to think of Lily's gentle admonitions about leaping headlong into phone conversations.

"Anna? Wow, isn't this a nice surprise? I'm fine. How are you?"

"I'm fine too. And Vicki?" Anna was glad she was in the habit of writing things down. When they had traded business cards at the reunion, she had scribbled Vicki's name on the back of Carolyn's so she wouldn't forget to ask about the woman with her.

"She's fine. I hope you're calling because you're in Seattle."

"No, I'm in LA. And I know this comes out of the blue, but I wonder if we could talk about something. It's personal, though, and I know you're at work. Could we maybe set a time to talk later tonight?"

"Anna, are you all right?"

She should have known her bizarre request would have caused alarm. "I really am fine, Carolyn. I just need some help getting my head screwed on right, and you might be the only one who can help."

"I'm here for you, whatever you need."

"I don't want to bother you at work."

"That's okay. We're pretty flexible here. Why don't I give you my cell number and you can call me back? I'll take a walk outside while we talk."

"That would be great." She scribbled the number on the card, and waited five minutes before dialing again.

"I can't believe you're calling. It's so nice to hear your voice again."

"I should apologize," Anna said. "It was good to see you at the reunion, and it's ridiculous I've waited so long to call."

"That's okay. It goes both ways. I'm glad you're calling now.

What's on your mind?"

Anna didn't know where to start. "I've met somebody, Carolyn." She took a deep breath. Once this left her lips, it wasn't coming back. "Her name is Lily. She's smart, funny and sweet, and one of the finest, most decent people I've ever known. She just . . . I don't know, it makes my heart race just to think about her."

Carolyn was silent so long Anna considered hitting the redial.

"Congratulations, Ms. Kaklis. I think you've actually surprised me."

"You think you're surprised, you should be inside my head."

"What about . . . Anna, didn't you get married?"

"I'm divorced. And it had nothing to do with Lily."

"So what's the problem?"

Anna was nearing the end of what she could articulate without going back a dozen years to their time in college. But that's why she had turned to Carolyn and not Liz or Kim. "I don't know where to go from here. There was only one other time in my life where I felt anything close to what I feel for Lily . . . and that was what I felt for you."

"Wow." Carolyn let out a deep breath. "I don't know what to say, Anna. I don't know if you know this or not, but I was in love with you back then."

"I had dinner with Liz in San Francisco a couple of months ago. She told me about talking to you that summer. Looking back on it now, I think she wishes she hadn't warned you away."

"We can't do much about the past, can we?"

"Not usually."

"That was a tough time for me, not just because of you, but because of the whole coming out thing. I guess you're finding that out for yourself."

"Sort of . . . I don't know if it's even the right thing to do. I just have so many questions, some about me, some about Lily. We're in a mess right now, and I need to fix it before I lose my sanity."

"Why don't you come up to Seattle for a couple of days? I'd love to see you, and so would Vicki. We'll talk. I promise you won't leave more confused than you are now."

It was already late Friday afternoon. "I can't. I have to leave Monday morning for Germany. And I'll be gone nine days." That seemed like an eternity to Anna. She wasn't sure how much longer she could take the uncertainty.

"Are you going to last nine days like this?"

"No, probably not."

"Then catch a plane tonight or first thing tomorrow. Go make the arrangements and call me back. I'll pick you up at the airport. You can go home on Sunday, in plenty of time for your trip."

Carolyn was right. She would find her answers in Seattle.

There was always something instinctively frightening about the phone ringing in the middle of the night. The digital clock read 1:31. Lily grabbed the receiver as she groped for the lamp on the nightstand. "Hello."

"Miss Stewart! Help me! He's outside and he says he's coming in. I think he has a gun." The frantic woman spoke with a heavy Spanish accent.

"Whoa, slow down. Is this Maria?"

"Yes, it's Miguel. He's been drinking. He called me and said he wanted to see his kids."

"Maria, hang up and call the police. I'm coming over right now, but you need to call the police. Can you do that?" Lily tumbled from the bed and started to dress. "I'll be there soon. Call the police now, and whatever you do, don't let him in."

Thirty minutes later, she stopped her X3 in front of a small white house in East LA. Two police cruisers were already on the scene, lights flashing and radios blaring. Neighbors watched the action from their yards. Lily ran toward the house to see Maria Esperanza being led away in handcuffs. The front door was torn from its frame.

"What's going on here? Where are you taking her?"

"Who are you?" the officer said with a scowl, pushing Maria roughly into the backseat of the cruiser.

"I'm Lilian Stewart, Mrs. Esperanza's attorney. And I'm advising you that I don't like the way you just shoved my client into the car." At that point, another officer emerged from the house with a handcuffed Miguel, whose face was bloodied badly.

"Look, lady, we have our rules. If they're both fighting, we haul them both in. The judge can sort it out in the morning."

"This is her home! She didn't just rip her own door off. She has a right to defend herself." It was all she could do to control her temper.

"Like I said, it isn't for me to sort out. If you want to help your client, you should come to the station with her."

A familiar sedan pulled in behind her car, and Sandy got out, flashing her credentials at one of the officers. "Where are the children?"

He tossed his thumb over his shoulder in the direction of the house and she charged ahead. Lily joined her at the door.

"What's going on?" Sandy asked.

"Miguel showed up drunk and broke the door down. Looks like Maria met his face with a two by four."

"Couldn't happen to a nicer guy," Sandy muttered.

They reached the back bedroom, where a boy and a girl sat with a female officer. Sandy introduced herself and Lily, and the officer left.

"Are you both okay?" Sandy asked.

The children nodded. It was obvious they had been crying. "They're taking Mommy," the girl said, holding tightly to her younger brother's hand.

"She'll be all right. This is Lily, and she's going to go help your mommy. I need you to come with me tonight, and we'll get everything fixed real soon."

Lily tried to smile for the children's sake. She was angry enough to tear off a door herself. Right now, she needed ammunition to keep Miguel locked up until she could guarantee the family's safety. "Did your father hurt you?"

"No," the girl said.

"Did he scare you?"

They didn't answer.

"Were you scared when he broke the door?"

Both nodded their heads.

That was probably enough for a restraining order, Lily thought. She patted Sandy on the shoulder. "Okay, I'm going downtown. I'll call you tomorrow."

"Good luck."

Central Booking was the social hub of LA at three in the morning. Prostitutes and their johns, drug dealers, burglars, barroom brawlers and all their lawyers filled the hallways awaiting their turn. It was going to be a very long night.

Lily and her client were called in at four fifteen, along with Miguel and his lawyer, Pete Simpkins.

"I don't want my client spending the night here," Lily said firmly to the booking officer.

"It's out of my hands," the man said calmly. "The statutes are there to cool everyone off. You can get her out in the morning."

Lily knew the statutes well. "This is an open-and-shut case of self defense. That lunatic broke down the front door. Mrs. Esperanza had a right to defend herself against someone entering her home." Her voice rose, but she was not yet shouting. However, all she was getting from the officer was a blank look. It was infuriating. "You know as well as I do the officers had discretion here. They only brought her in because they were too goddamned lazy to do the work on the scene to settle it."

"Lily, can we go somewhere and talk?" Simpkins motioned

173

toward the door.

"I'm not making any deals with you. Your client's a bully." Angrily, she snatched up her briefcase and jacket and stormed back into the busy hallway.

"Wait, Lily. We need to talk or this is going to happen again, and next time, somebody's really going to get hurt."

She turned and poked a finger into Simpkins's chest. "Then you need to explain to your client that he blew it big time. He lost custody in the first place because he can't control his goddamned temper. Now he shows up drunk and breaks the door down. What does he expect?" She stepped back and glared at him. "Talk to me when you've gotten him into an anger management class. I'm getting a fucking restraining order first thing in the morning, and if he shows up again within a hundred yards of their house, he's going to jail."

Pete stood calmly as she issued her threats. They had always enjoyed a respectful working relationship, but she was fed up with his client.

"Lily, I don't know what's gotten into you, but it wouldn't hurt if you sat in on a couple of those anger management seminars too."

Lily suddenly felt a wave of shame. "I'm sorry, Pete," she said, almost too low to hear. "I . . . What can we do? I'm listening."

Simpkins led her to a bench in the hallway. "Miguel tells me that Maria hasn't been letting him have visitation. She leaves and takes the kids when it's time for him to come over. He hasn't seen them since before Christmas."

"Why didn't he come to the court?"

"He didn't understand that he could. He thought since she was granted custody, it was up to her. That's my fault for not making it clear."

"I'll talk to her tomorrow. Can you see about getting him into a class? I really think it will help."

"Sure."

Lily turned to walk away, but Pete stopped her. "Whatever it is, Lily, good luck with it."

"Thanks, Pete. I'm sorry for being such a jerk."

"I still can't believe you're really here," Carolyn said. Her face had been plastered with a permanent smile since the airport.

Anna couldn't believe it herself. No one's life should be so complicated they had to fly a thousand miles for therapy from a friend. "It's so good to see you. I wish I wasn't here to dump on you this way."

"When you talk to a real friend, it isn't called dumping. I can't believe I still feel so close to you after all these years, but I do."

"I know what you mean." Indeed, the years had melted away as they got reacquainted over lunch at the harbor. Other than adding a few pounds, Carolyn had changed very little since college.

"We won't get those years back, Anna. But let's make a pact right now not to lose each other again."

"It's a deal." Anna stretched both hands across the table, palms up, and Carolyn grasped them and squeezed. "I'm so glad you let me come. I didn't know who else to turn to."

"So why don't you tell me all about this woman you've met?" Carolyn led her outside to walk along the waterfront.

Anna went all the way back to the beginning, through the dramatic story of the earthquake, and of finding Lily after her divorce. She recounted the baseball game and the ride from San Diego, and finally, the boat trip. "That's the first time I ever consciously realized I was looking at another woman's breasts. Now I think I probably always have, but the sight of hers in that bathing suit just pushed a button in me or something."

"I used to look at your breasts all the time."

Anna knew she was blushing, but took the comment in stride.

"Maybe if I had known that at the time I would have stood up straighter and worn something skimpier. Who knows?"

"It's just as well. I probably couldn't have handled it." Her broad smile was still in place. "So go on. What else?"

Anna told her of the camping trip.

"You actually went camping? I don't believe you. You're making this up."

Ignoring Carolyn's sarcasm, Anna continued with the story of her father's rude remarks, the trip to San Jose and Thanksgiving in Tahoe, emphasizing the looks they exchanged on the slope when Lily fell. "I swear, if Todd hadn't come over right at that moment, I think I might have just kissed her." She finished with the story of Todd in the kitchen. "And now, she won't take my calls. The few times I actually did talk to her, she said she was too busy to get together. I need to talk to her, to tell her what happened. But now I'm starting to think maybe she doesn't see me that way."

"Oh, I think she does."

"Why?" Anna needed to hear some good news.

"Because you're irresistible."

"Be serious."

"Okay, what it sounds like to me is you two kept getting closer and closer, right up until she saw you kissing Todd."

"I wasn't kissing Todd. He was kissing me."

Carolyn waved as if swatting a fly. "Lily has no way of knowing that. What she probably saw was the two of you kissing. As long as she had even the tiniest glimmer of hope of you being interested in her, she was going to stay close and be your best friend. As soon as that possibility disappeared, she needed to run away to protect herself."

"But that doesn't make sense. If we were so close, why wouldn't she talk to me about it?"

"Because Lily is a lesbian. Lesbians run the risk all the time of falling in love with straight women. It's not something we can help, especially when the women are as beautiful and charming as you."

Anna groaned.

"But once we see the handwriting on the wall, that self-preservation thing kicks in and there's nothing to do but run."

"She doesn't have to run from me. I'm not going to hurt her. And I'm not all that certain anymore that I'm straight," she added, almost inaudibly. "But that's an issue for another day. Right now, I just need to fix things with Lily so we can play it all out."

"Whether or not you're straight is more important than you think. If you're still anything like the Anna Kaklis I used to know, this isn't something you're going to do on a whim. It's a big deal, right?"

Anna nodded.

"It would be devastating for Lily if you were to wake up someday and decide you needed something else she can't give you. If she has to live with that possibility every day, it isn't going to be healthy for either of you. There's nothing but pain in that."

"But how do I know that isn't going to happen?"

"You probably don't. But you have to go into this with your eyes wide open. Lily's are open already. You need to think about whether or not you're ready for a relationship with Lily on her terms. She wants to hold you and kiss you and touch you. If you're going to go forward with her, you're going to have to want that too."

Anna processed Carolyn's words. She understood what Lily needed, but she hadn't let herself dwell on those thoughts. It was just too overwhelming. "You know, I really loved you a lot back in college, Carolyn. I might even have been in love with you too, but I was pretty naïve about things like that."

"I know I was in love with you."

"I probably would have done anything you asked, just to please you."

"Now you tell me," she chided. "But is that how you feel about Lily? That you'd have sex with her just to please her? Just so she'll do things with you again?"

"No, Carolyn. I want it for me too," she admitted it for the first time. "I don't think I've ever wanted anyone like this in my whole life." The words were some of the heaviest she had ever uttered, but saying them aloud seemed to lift the weight from her shoulders.

"Then you need to tell her."

"What if she doesn't feel the same way? I mean, if she wanted me that way, wouldn't she have said something by now?"

"Trust me. She feels the same way. But everything has to come from you. Lily won't act on her feelings. There's too much at risk for her. She's worried you'll reject her, and despise her for having those feelings about you. She can't bear that."

"I could never despise her."

"I know that, but she doesn't. You have to be the one to move this relationship forward."

As she rode home from the airport in the back of a limo, Anna took stock of her overnight getaway. If her only achievement had been reconnecting with Carolyn, it would have been worth the trip. And on top of that, she had met Vicki, and had seen for herself the kind of loving partnership they shared. Anna wanted that kind of happiness, now more than ever, and she was certain Lily was the key.

It wasn't all good news. Carolyn and Vicki each told coming out tales that left her heartbroken. Carolyn's was especially grim, leaving her estranged from her family.

A relationship with Lily would almost certainly cause problems for her father. He had guided her every step of the way as she meticulously planned her life, and he would be the first to decry this as not in her best interest. Martine's acceptance would be crucial to smoothing things at home. Without her support, this could drive a permanent wedge between them all.

As soon as Anna got home, she double-checked her tickets and travel documents for Germany. Then she unpacked her small bag from the Seattle trip and began the task of packing for nine days abroad. When she finished, she set her bags by the door and went to bed.

She was exhausted, emotionally more than physically. It was almost midnight, but her head was racing with thoughts of how she could get Lily to listen, and what she would say to convince her to give them a chance.

"I'm coming!" Lily couldn't imagine who on earth could be knocking at this hour, but rolling over in bed and ignoring it hadn't made it go away. When she looked through the peephole, every cell in her body awakened. Anna was on her doorstep.

She had already turned on the lights and yelled through the door, so it was too late to pretend she wasn't home. As soon as she released the latch, Anna burst through without waiting for an invitation. By her frantic look, something urgent had brought her out so late. "Anna? Is everything all right?"

"No, Lily. It's not all right."

Lily's heart was hammering. "What is it?"

"I can't stand what's happened between us. Everything's changed. I want us to be close again. I need it."

Lily's own need for Anna was almost overpowering. She wanted to give in, to accept on Anna's terms the simple offer of friendship. But she had to guard her heart. Meeting Anna's eyes with a steel resolve, she answered, "I can't, Anna. I want to, but I can't."

"What can't you do, Lily? Doesn't this hurt you like it hurts me?"

"Yes, of course it does. But being with you just makes it worse for me."

"Is it because of Todd?"

The tears Lily had been holding back since Tahoe suddenly filled her eyes. She sank to the arm of the couch and looked blankly into the dark living room, unable to meet Anna's eye. "Yes," she whispered. With that confession, she readied herself to let the chips fall where they may.

Anna strode silently to the couch, and grasped her hands. With a small tug, she coaxed Lily to her feet. "I don't want Todd. I never did. I only want you."

As if in slow motion, Anna's head tilted forward. Her lips parted and disappeared from view moments before making contact with Lily's waiting mouth.

Chapter 10

For Lily, their kiss was more than just a meeting of lips. It was an unmistakable confession, and she was completely overpowered by the sensation. Anna's mouth was soft and warm, the sweetest she had ever kissed, and her tongue took the word caress to a whole new level.

Too soon the kiss ended, both of them short of breath. Not willing to give up this intimate embrace, Lily buried her face into Anna's neck. Though anxiety simmered that Anna would suddenly have doubts, the words replayed in her head. *"I only want you."* If there was a chance on earth they could really be together, Lily would do whatever it took to make it happen.

Anna pulled her closer, cupping her head with her palm, swaying ever so slightly in a way that kept the sensations alive. They held each other like that for several minutes, not uttering a sound. Gradually, Lily felt the strain of the last six weeks recede. In its place was quiet, like a settling of her soul.

"I've been crazy without you," Anna whispered. "I've missed you so much."

They stood together silently for another few minutes, soaking up the calm. For Lily, the kiss had served only to whet her hunger. Leaning back, she studied Anna's visage for signs of awkwardness or uncertainty. Finding neither, she brought her face closer, her eyes darting between Anna's eyes and lips. Turning her head slightly at the last instant, they shared a breath as their lips met again.

The second kiss deepened with fervor as both were swept up again in excitement and wonder. Lily's hands remained still, holding firmly to Anna's shoulders. This wasn't about sensual passion. It was about knowing for certain Anna was there.

When they broke again, Anna kissed her nose gently and rested a cheek against her forehead. "I have to go. I need to leave for the airport at six."

"No. I'm never letting you leave."

"Dad and I are going to Munich tomorrow for nine days. I'd like to go thinking you and I were okay again."

"We're okay, Amazon."

"And when I get back, we're going to talk about everything."

"And kiss some more?"

"And kiss a lot more."

Lily was running on pure adrenaline, charging into the office by seven thirty.

"Where did these bagels come from?" Pauline asked.

"I picked them up," Lily answered, amused at Pauline's surprised expression. They had probably gotten used to her surly behavior of late, but those days were behind her now.

Another thing that was behind her—at least it would be when Anna got home—was the sixty-hour work schedule she had fallen into to get her mind off how much she hurt. In place of those thoughts were all-new sensations—the kisses, the embrace, and Anna's soft words of assurance. Unable to sleep after Anna left, she relived them all again and again. A part of her feared if she went to sleep, she would awaken and none of this would have happened.

It was Lily's nature to be insecure. She grudgingly accepted that as the legacy from her biological mother, the one who had abandoned her. Her anxiety took her to horrible places, as she had lain awake worrying that Anna had freaked out after driving home. A simple phone call this morning would have set her fears to rest. Why hadn't Anna just—

No. She would not screw this up with expectations about how Anna should act.

Nine days felt like an eternity to Lily. Her only contact with Anna had been three "thinking about you—hope you're doing okay" messages left on her voicemail, once while she was in court, another while she had been in the shower, and the third while she was taking out the garbage at home. Now resigned to let her garbage reach the ceiling, Lily planted herself on the couch all day Saturday waiting for the phone to ring.

She had no idea how she would survive four more days of waiting. Mentally, she was preparing herself to wait even longer, given that Anna would have so much to do when she got home. Her plane got in at 4:07 on Wednesday afternoon. She would probably be exhausted from her trip, and go straight home to rest. Then she would want to go to the dealership because she needed to check on things. And she would probably have to sleep more on account of the jet lag. And see her family. Lily figured she would be lucky to see Anna again before next weekend, but at least they could talk to each other from the same time zone.

Her misery was interrupted by the loud ringing of phones all over her small apartment. She had turned the ringers to the max to be sure she wouldn't inadvertently miss another call. Her hopes soared when the caller ID flashed "out of area."

"Hello . . . This is she . . . No, I'm not interested." The salesman was persistent, but Lily wouldn't give an inch. And she wanted him off her phone. "No, the only thing I dislike about my current phone service is you having my number." Irritated at the inconvenience, she hung up the receiver, immediately noticing the blinking message light. A quick dial of her voicemail confirmed her fears. She had missed Anna's call again.

Frustrated beyond measure, Anna steered through the restaurant to where her father was waiting. She had tried to guess when Lily would be at home or at her desk, but no matter when or where she called, she always got voicemail. The time difference made it difficult, and the seminars left her with little free time to keep trying. She had hoped it would be easier to connect on the weekend, but even today's call went unanswered.

Or maybe Lily was avoiding her calls again. Anna hadn't wanted to consider that possibility, but it had taken her a week or more after Tahoe to realize that getting bounced to voicemail was no accident. But what could she have done to create this distance again?

By the look on her father's face, he had noticed her unpleasant mood. And why wouldn't he? Five days ago, she had been cheerful and upbeat for the first time in weeks. Now she was sullen and distracted again.

"Sweetheart, is everything okay?"

"Of course. The seminars are good. Your company is fabulous. It isn't snowing. What more could a girl want?" She pasted on the best smile she could muster.

Unfortunately, he wasn't buying it. "It's just that you seemed so happy when we left, and now something's clearly bothering you."

"It's nothing to worry about, Dad." Anna didn't want to have this conversation. "It's just a small personal problem. I'll work it out."

Too late, she realized that was probably the worst thing she could have said. She wasn't ready to talk about Lily to anyone, least of all her father.

"Anna, I've been watching you worry about things all by yourself for thirty-two years. I want to help." She wouldn't meet his eyes. "Please let me in there."

She sighed. She had brought this on herself by being so transparent, and delivered her own coup de grace by calling it a personal problem. If she clammed up now, it would hurt her father's feelings. "You remember my friend Lily, from the earthquake?"

"Yes, of course."

"Well," she started hesitantly. "We had a misunderstanding, but I thought we had it cleared up before I left. Now I'm not so sure."

"Was it over what I said? If you want me to, I'll apologize to her."

"No, we got all that straightened out. I told her you were mistaken, and that I did all the hiring at the dealership anyway. And Kim told her you were off your medication that day and didn't know what you were saying." She enjoyed the look of surprise on his face.

"Off my medication?"

"You know how Kim is. Lily knew she was kidding."

He visibly relaxed. "So what was this misunderstanding?"

She covered his hand with hers to ease his worries. "That's the personal part, Dad. It isn't something I want to talk about."

He shifted in his seat and leaned forward, clearly agitated. "Anna, I understand Lily is important to you, but if she's causing you distress, maybe it's time to start putting that terrible earthquake ordeal behind you. You can't let misguided obligations rule your life. Some things you just have to let go."

Now it was Anna who was upset. Her evasive characterizations of the problem with Lily had led her father to assume the worst—that Lily was somehow pressing her into an unwanted friendship, and making unreasonable demands. Nothing could be further from the truth.

Standing abruptly, she gathered her jacket and purse. "I think I'm going to blow off the rest of this and head home." Monday was only a half-day of seminars, followed by a luncheon, then a cocktail party for the North American dealership owners tomorrow night, and networking meetings all day Tuesday. "I'm just going to go back to my room and call the airline. Do you want me to change your ticket too?"

Her father scowled. "Anna, just calm down."

"Dad, I need to go home and deal with this. If you want to stay until Wednesday, that's fine."

"We have meetings with important people. We need to stake our ground with the new owners in the California group. We can't let them form exclusive alliances with other dealers and squeeze us out."

He was right, but Anna couldn't think about business. Why hadn't Lily just answered her phone?

Lily spun in her chair and pulled the computer's keyboard tray closer. For the last few days, she had watched the weather in Europe, anxious about a snowstorm blowing in from the North Sea. It was due to hit Germany on Tuesday, so Anna's flight home the next day might be delayed, extending the torturous wait for her return.

Her stomach growled, announcing its displeasure at the late hour. It was almost eight o'clock, and the cleaning crew had started on the second floor offices. She was more than caught up with her work, but killing time in her office was better than being at home. How she would stand the next two days—or longer if the storm hit as scheduled—was anyone's guess.

She hadn't shared the news of Anna's late-night visit with Sandy and Suzanne, wanting first to be sure it wasn't just a fluke. She could almost convince herself it had never happened, and if Anna came back with seconds thoughts, that's exactly what she would try to do.

But it had happened. Her proof was the burning memory of Anna's lips on hers. No illusion could have created a sensation so sublime.

Despite that moment, missing all of Anna's calls had her imagination on overload. What if she was calling to say the kiss was a mistake? Her messages on voicemail had been nice, but she hadn't said anything that couldn't be explained away as just friendly and polite. Certainly, there was nothing of a more intimate nature.

Exasperated with the pessimistic path of her thoughts, Lily checked the weather report one more time before logging off for good. With her briefcase in hand, she was about to turn off her light when the phone rang, scaring her out of her wits. Who would be calling the office at this hour?

"Lilian Stewart," she said formally, reaching across her desk to slap the button that activated the speaker phone.

"Lily, it's Anna."

She dropped her briefcase and hurried back behind her desk, scrambling to pick up the receiver and disengage the speaker. In her haste, she very nearly disconnected the call.

"Lily, are you there?"

"Anna? God, if you'd waited thirty more seconds I would have been gone. And I would have missed you again." She sank back into her chair, trying to calm herself. "This has been so frustrating. I'm going to be so happy to see you."

"Then you may want to look out your window."

187

Lily sat up straight and craned her neck, but the angle of the blinds prevented her from seeing the street. She stood up and stretched, parting the slats with one hand. There beneath a streetlight, Anna leaned against the fender of a limo. With her phone in one hand, she waved her fingers in Lily's direction.

"You're here."

"I'm here."

Anna paid the driver in twenties and thanked him for his patience. He set her bags on the curb just as Lily arrived.

"Welcome home," Lily said, beaming.

They fell together in a tight hug, Anna relishing an end to the anxiety that had built over the past few days. "It seems like all I ever do is miss you."

"The only way to fix that is for you to promise never to leave again."

"Believe me. I'm not going anywhere." She hooked one arm in Lily's and picked up her shoulder bag. Lily grasped the handle of the large suitcase and dragged it behind her as they walked toward the parking lot. "I've been going crazy trying to reach you. And then I got scared you were ducking my calls again."

"We still have to talk about all of that, Anna. I'm so sorry for how I acted, especially that night we had dinner. I was a flaming asshole."

"No, you weren't." Anna didn't care about anything in their past. Lily's excited smile was all the assurance she needed to know the misunderstanding was behind them. "We don't have to talk about anything unless you really want to. But you're going to die when I tell you why all of this happened."

"What do you mean?"

"I mean when Todd followed me into the kitchen at Tahoe and kissed me, right out of the blue. I set him straight, and I was going to tell you all about it, but you left without even saying good-bye. I had no idea you saw that."

"God, I was an idiot." They reached the X3 and Lily opened the hatchback to stow the bags. "If only I hadn't—"

"Forget it. I understand why you left. If I'd seen you kissing someone, I probably would have done the same thing." Anna dumped her shoulder bag and held her arms wide for another hug. "But I don't care about any of that now. All I care about is this."

Anna loved the sensation of Lily in her arms, for the first time not feeling dwarfed by a man who presumed to be her protector. It was a different awareness, like that of being a true equal . . . and it felt very right.

"I don't suppose you're hungry," Lily said.

"I ate on the plane. But I'll go with you."

"I can hit a drive-thru. Are you tired?" Lily walked around and opened the passenger door. "Stupid question. You've been flying for fifteen hours."

"Yes, I'm tired. But I'm not expected back at the dealership until Friday, so I can sleep all day tomorrow." She dropped her purse on the floorboard and turned back to Lily, who was waiting to close the door. Though a streetlight cast shadows across her face, her smile was unmistakable. "We have so much to make up for."

"Let's just start with this." Lily stepped closer and gently cupped the back of Anna's head, pulling her face down.

Anna hesitated only a moment before closing her eyes and meeting Lily's lips. What did it matter they were kissing out in plain view of anyone who cared to look? The only person she worried about seeing her was still in Munich.

Anna was getting used to Lily's couch. Since her return from Germany over a week ago, they had seen each other every day, including two nights like this one when Anna hung out at Lily's apartment while she prepped her cases for court. They had slid easily into their old playfulness, the tension of the last six weeks forgotten.

Looking back, Anna realized she and her husband had never shared this kind of compatibility. In fact, any casualness she and Scott enjoyed as they got to know one another seemed to disappear for Anna once they moved their relationship to a romantic level. At that point, she became more self-conscious, more focused on saying and doing the right thing. With Lily, she felt comfortable just to be herself.

Tonight, she was stretched out reading the current issue of *Car & Driver* while Lily sat nearby on the floor reviewing a stack of legal briefs. Neither seemed to need the other's attention, but Anna relished the quiet closeness.

Her physical desires for Lily were growing, albeit slowly. *Scratch that*, she admitted sheepishly. Her desires were soaring. But the part of her that wanted it all paled next to that which goaded her sexual insecurities. It wouldn't be enough to give herself to Lily, as she had to Scott and Vince for their pleasure. This time, she wanted to take pleasure for herself, and give it equally in return.

As if reading her thoughts, Lily reached over her shoulder and absently stroked Anna's thigh.

"I'm not going to let you get your work done if you keep that up," Anna said, gesturing toward Lily's hand.

"What are you going to do?"

"I might just have to pull you up here with me."

Lily withdrew her hand and turned, arching her eyebrows suggestively. "Then maybe I should put my work away." She let the papers fall and climbed onto the couch, draping her entire body along Anna's frame.

Anna loved the feel of Lily's weight on top of her. When their lips met, her hands began to roam from Lily's thighs to her shoulders in an unbroken caress. As their kiss lengthened, it deepened, and soon Anna found herself responding to the exchange, moving her hips in a slow rhythm against Lily's thigh. Lily's hand found her breast, and she moaned, arching upward for more contact.

"God, you're incredible," Lily said as she suddenly stilled.

Anna had never felt such heated passion in her whole life—and this from only lying together on the couch. For the first time, she felt powerless over her physical desires. If Lily hadn't stopped—

"I could get lost in you, Anna." She pulled away and sat up. "That idea scares me half to death."

Anna caught her elbow. This was the part Carolyn had warned her about, that Lily wouldn't be able to trust her to stay. "What scares you?"

"Having you . . . and losing you."

"Please don't be afraid, Lily. I can't promise you what will happen to us, but everything about this feels right to me. And it's never been like that before."

"Not ever?"

Anna shook her head. "I can't explain it, but ever since I kissed you I've felt like my whole life was a lie . . . like I would never have found the right man because there isn't one." She sat all the way up and took Lily's hand. "I'm not ready for what almost happened just now, but I'm not afraid of it. And I don't want you to be either."

"How can you not be afraid, Anna? Everything you're facing is new."

"It's new because of the way I feel about you. But there's a difference between fear and anticipation. And yes, I'm anxious about some things . . . especially sexual things. That part isn't new for me at all. I've always been that way, but you excite me like no one ever has."

"Whew!" Lily fanned herself with her hand. "I can tell you a thing or two about excitement."

Anna chuckled. "Do you have any tips on how to leave when you don't want to but you should?"

"Don't ask me something like that, Amazon. I might have to lock the door."

Anna pulled her into a tender kiss. "One of these days, I'll help you do that."

"Lilian Stewart," she answered crisply into the receiver, not looking up at the display. She was due in court this afternoon to help Tony with jury selection in a housing discrimination case.

"Hi there, sweetheart. How's your day?"

Lily nearly swooned at the endearment. "Hi, yourself. It just got better when I answered the phone. What's up?" She stretched from her desk to push her office door closed.

"I wanted to ask you about something. Kim just called and invited me to dinner tonight. I want to tell her about us, if it's okay with you."

They had decided—actually Anna had asked—to keep their relationship quiet until they were more certain of their feelings. Lily took it as a good sign that Anna was ready to share things with her sister. On the other hand, it was also a risk, because Kim's disapproval would be difficult to overcome.

"Of course it's okay." More tentatively, she added, "Will you at least tell me how it goes?"

"Sure, but I wouldn't worry about it if I were you. Kim's already in our corner. I just want to tell her how we're doing."

"How are we doing?"

"I'm doing fantastic. And you?"

"Ditto." Lily was grateful for the reassurance. "How would you feel if I talked to Mom?"

"Go ahead. I know how close you two are. I guess it was silly of me to ask you to wait in the first place."

"It wasn't silly. This is all new for you, and it'll take some time to get used to it." She didn't want to be the bearer of bad news, but Anna needed to be prepared for some of the problems she might face as more people found out. "I know you've been worried about your dad, but he's not the only one who might not like the idea of you being with me. Some of the folks you've known for years might look at you differently if they knew about us."

"I'm not worried about that."

Lily took her dismissal with a grain of salt. Anna would worry when she faced these prejudices firsthand. "Still, you need to be ready for it."

"There's only one thing that really scares me, Lily. And that's me making another gargantuan mistake for everybody to see."

Lily's heart almost broke at the admission. "Anna, we don't have to rush into anything, okay? We'll take our time and do what feels right. I want you to be sure."

"So what's it like making love with another woman?" Kim was not one to beat around the bush. She had always seemed to enjoy the fact that Anna embarrassed so easily, especially in public places like the restaurant where they were meeting for dinner.

"I just poured my heart out to you about this sweet woman who has touched my soul. And do you want to hear more about that? No. All you want to hear about is the sex."

"Yeah, yeah. So? What's it like?"

Anna sighed and dropped her shoulders in surrender. Kim was incorrigible. "Do we have to talk about this?"

"Yes. I want details."

"I don't have details. We haven't gotten that far yet."

"Well, what are you waiting for?"

"It's not a race, you know. Not everybody gives in so easily to their animal instincts, like two people I know who can't even keep their hands off one another in public."

"We can talk about my sex life later. I know how much you enjoy that. But for now, let's talk some more about yours."

Her sister was the only living soul with whom she had shared the details of her intimate experiences with Vince and Scott. To her infinite embarrassment, Kim then went on and on about the things she and Hal did between the sheets. Anna wasn't able to look her brother-in-law in the eye for a month. "We are not talking about my sex life, Kim. I know you'll be devastated to hear this, but I don't happen to have one."

"Yes, you do. You just don't bring it out to play enough."

For Anna, sex had nothing to do with play. It was a huge, dramatic production that rarely involved fun. "We're not there yet. I don't even know what Lily wants." She mumbled the last part sheepishly.

"You're a woman too. That should give you a clue."

This conversation was going downhill fast for Anna. Once Kim tasted blood, she usually badgered her until she was too embarrassed to speak.

"Think about it, Anna. You told me what kinds of things you liked best, and as I recall, none of them involved a penis."

Anna covered her face with both hands to hide what she knew was a deep red blush.

"You like orgasms, don't you?"

Anna dropped her hands and rolled her eyes. "Do I even have to answer that?"

"Seriously, Anna. Aren't you dying to know what it's like with Lily?"

"Curiosity is a stupid reason to have sex."

"Maybe, but it's perfectly normal for two people who care about each other to want to express that physically. And you obviously feel that way about Lily, so what's the problem?"

She grimaced. "The problem is I have no idea what the hell I'm doing. So here I go again, just like all the other times I ever suffered through this. It's going to be about where everything goes, how something feels or whether or not everyone is being properly stimulated. It's not going to be about the person. When I—" She looked around the restaurant to make sure they weren't being overheard, and lowered her voice. "When I make love with Lily, I want it to be about us, not . . . it. Is that too much to ask for?"

Kim sat back and gave her a welcome look of understanding. "Believe it or not, if Lily is the right person, it's going to be about both. And all of a sudden, sex is going to be something wonderful that you'll want all the time, whether it's just to share your passionate love or to have plain old fun."

"I don't think I'm like that, Kim. I just don't get what's so great about it."

"I just told you. It's about being with the right person."

"Maybe you're right," she said quietly. She looked around again to be sure no one was listening. "Things have been heating up lately, and I'll admit it feels different . . . more exciting. And I told Lily that the other night."

"Let it happen, Anna. Lily's the right person."

"Dad's going to freak."

"Let him. You deserve your own life."

"Will you come visit me if he has me committed?"

Kim laughed. "You don't have to worry about him. He doesn't get a vote here. You said it yourself—it's all about you and Lily."

"Maybe so, but I don't want to lose my father."

Kim stretched a hand across the table and laid it on Anna's forearm. "We both know Dad. He may buck a little at first, but when he realizes he isn't going to get his way, he'll come through for you."

That's the way Anna saw it too, except for the bucking a little part. She expected a full-blown rocket launch.

❧

" . . . so we're taking it slow, but we're definitely going somewhere," Lily said.

"I told you she'd be worth fighting for," her mother replied. "And I can't say I'm a bit surprised. I knew from the way she looked at you that she had feelings."

"You never told me that part."

"Would it have made any difference?"

Lily thought about it. If she had known for certain Anna had feelings for her, seeing her kissing Todd would have been even worse, because it would have seemed like a concerted effort on Anna's part to deny it. "You know what? I don't have to wonder about that kind of stuff anymore."

"So when are you two coming back up?"

"I don't know. It's your turn to come down. I've started doing my hikes on Saturday because Sunday is Anna's day off. I haven't gotten her out on a trail yet, but I will."

"I walked up St. Joseph's hill last weekend with Bill Mueller."

"Bill Mueller? Your doctor friend?" Lily had met him a few times. His wife had died of cancer several years ago. "Do you two have something going on that I should know about?"

"I don't know. We're going to dinner Friday night. Ask me again in a couple of weeks."

"This is interesting." Her mother hadn't had a companion in years, not since the curriculum director who took a job at Arizona State. "I like Bill."

"So do I."

"That settles it. I'll talk to Anna and see when we can come up. I have to find out his intentions."

"And I have to find out hers."

Lily's X3 was the first to arrive from the valet at Empyre's. Anna gave her brother-in-law a kiss on the cheek before getting in. "Thanks for dinner. It was fun."

"Our pleasure," Hal said. "Hard to believe it's been a year since the earthquake."

"And a year since Anna and I first met," Lily added, following Anna's lead to hug both Kim and Hal.

"We're so lucky to be celebrating tonight," Kim said with uncharacteristic seriousness. "So many people lost someone they loved."

Anna hugged her and whispered in her ear. "And some of us found someone they loved." Then she climbed in on the passenger side. "We'll see you Sunday at the big house, right?"

"We'll be there," Kim said. "Something tells me we're in for an exciting night."

"Don't you dare say a word," she shouted out the window as Lily started to drive away. "He'll freak out!"

"You think she's going to tell your dad?" Lily asked.

"No, she's just trying to terrorize me."

"Your sister is a real piece of work. And what's so funny about her is that you always think she's joking, and then out of the blue she says something like that bit about people not celebrating because they lost loved ones. She pulls my gut out when she does that."

"That's Kim for you. She may kid around, but she never loses real perspective. She's an incredible woman."

"So is her sister."

Anna loved that Lily enjoyed being with Kim and Hal, and vice versa. Getting her father and Martine into that circle was her next challenge, but she wasn't ready to take that on. She saw no reason to put them through this before she and Lily knew where they were headed.

She almost laughed aloud at her last thought. There was no mistaking where she and Lily were headed. They would be lovers soon. Nothing stood in their way except deciding where and when it would happen.

Lily pulled into Anna's driveway and turned off the engine. "I

197

know you have to go, but I wanted to ask you about your sister."

Anna had a sales meeting at seven the next morning. "Sure. You want to come in?"

"No, you have to go to bed. I just wanted to know how your talk went the other night. She kept grinning at me like a Cheshire cat."

"I told her you made me happy." That must have been the right thing to say, Anna decided, because Lily now wore the most satisfied smile she had ever seen.

"So what did she say to that?"

"She was . . . inquisitive."

"You mean inquisitive like 'Are you happy with how things are going?' or inquisitive like 'What the hell do you think you're doing?'"

Anna's thoughts ran back to their dinner, to the moment she covered her face in embarrassment, and Kim's insistence she explore her new sexual side and report back immediately. Feeling a rising blush, she turned to look out the window. "No, inquisitive like 'What's the sex like?'"

"Oh."

This was stupid, Anna thought. Two adults who were presumably headed for a sexual relationship ought to be able to talk about it without one of them lighting up like a fire engine.

"Anna, look . . . I've been thinking about that since we talked the other night. I know you're kind of anxious about it. But I don't have any expectations. I just want to enjoy being together. If it happens, it will be wonderful. If it doesn't, I'm sure we'll be okay."

The conversation was no longer stupid. It had graduated to ridiculous. All of this talk about sex was making her even more anxious. And as if that wasn't enough, Lily had now concluded from her childish inability to speak that it might not ever happen. Anna needed to set her straight.

"Lily, come inside with me."

Lily followed her into the house, looking as if she was bracing for bad news.

Anna tried to allay her fears by pulling her into a hug. "Don't read anything into that stuff with Kim. She only says things like that to make me blush, and she's pretty good at it."

"So what you're saying is . . . you were embarrassed?"

Lily leaned back to look her in the eye, and Anna struggled not to look away. "I'm an idiot about these things. I've never been able to just talk like an adult without getting embarrassed. I wish I could. But just because I don't talk about it doesn't mean we won't . . . you know." Anna could feel herself turning red, though Lily probably couldn't see it in the soft light of the foyer. "Are you listening to how stupid I sound?"

Lily brought her hands to Anna's cheeks and kissed her chin. "I'm not going to tease you, I promise. I'm just glad to know you're thinking about me that way."

"Of course I am." Lily would probably laugh to know how often she thought about them making love. "If you don't already know that, then I'm not doing a very good job of showing you how I feel."

"No, you do fine. I'm just naturally insecure." Her voice grew quieter, and she buried her face in Anna's neck as if ashamed. "That's one of the lifelong gifts you get from a mother who gives you up."

Anna was gradually coming to understand the fragile state of Lily's heart. She loosened their hug and took Lily's hands, clutching them to her chest. Her heart was pounding with anxiety, but she couldn't let Lily doubt her feelings any longer. "I don't want you to be insecure about me. If you want to make love tonight, I'm ready. Just not here, not in this house. We can go to your apartment."

Lily closed her eyes and shook her head. "Anna, no. I want it to happen when it's right for both of us, not because I've made you feel like you have to prove something to me. I have to handle my own insecurities."

Anna relaxed, pulling her close again and resting her cheek against her head. She held her for several minutes, her emotions riding high. Talk of making love had definitely raised the stakes. "I love you, Lily."

Lily's arms tightened firmly around her. "I love you too, Amazon."

Chapter 11

Beneath the tablecloth, Anna walked her fingertips over to Lily's thigh and smiled when a hand covers hers. For the most part, the evening had gone well, except for her father blurting out how he missed seeing Scott at these family get-togethers. But the look on his face when she told him Scott had remarried made the awkward moment almost worth it.

It looked as if they were going to make it through the evening without further drama. With these casual family gatherings, her father would get used to having Lily around. In time, her presence would be taken for granted, and it would be easier for Anna to broach the subject of their relationship.

They were almost home-free when Kim quieted everyone by tapping on her water glass and clearing her throat. "If I could have everyone's attention . . . I think someone at this table is keeping a little secret."

Anna's stomach dropped as she locked eyes with her smiling sister across the table. Their father was going to have a cow.

"Secrets are fun, aren't they, Anna?" she asked, still grinning with mischief.

Lily let out a tiny yelp as Anna's nails dug into her thigh.

"But I think it's time everybody got in on the secret. It's time to welcome someone new into our family." She made eye contact with everyone at the table. "Hal and I are going to have a baby in July."

Anna's heart started beating again as she leapt out of her seat and darted around the table, all but forgetting about her father and Lily. "This is such wonderful news, Kim." She swept her sister up in a mighty hug and whispered in her ear. "I love you so much. And remind me to kill you later for that little stunt."

"Your sister is a terrorist," Lily said, holding the phone between her chin and shoulder as she turned off the bedside lamp. She had dropped Anna at her home and called again to say goodnight as soon as she got into bed.

"Tell me about it. She's been like that forever."

"But you're going to be an aunt. Isn't that exciting?"

"Oh, you have no idea. They've been trying for the last three years. Mom and Dad don't even know this, but Kim's already had two miscarriages. With the baby due in July, she's already four months along."

"Let's hope that means she's out of trouble."

"They must have gotten a good report, or I don't think she would have told everyone."

"I seriously thought she was going to tell your parents about us."

"I know. I almost had a stroke. I think I'm going to tell them soon and get it over with. I don't like having secrets."

"If you ask me, it isn't much of a secret. Unless your father always acts like he's being led to the gallows."

"Yeah, I think he has a pretty good idea of what's up, but he doesn't understand what we have."

Lily's heart warmed to hear Anna talk about what their relationship meant to her. "Why don't you tell me what we have?"

Anna sighed dreamily. "I have a girlfriend who ties me up in knots whenever I'm with her."

"I do that?"

"You do. And I think about you all the time."

Having Anna in her arms was the fantasy that carried her off to sleep each night and filled her dreams. But she couldn't imagine Anna entertaining thoughts like that. Though she didn't want Anna to have any sexual reservations, there was something charming and innocent about her shyness. "Tell me what you think about."

"I think about some of the things we've done together, like going out with Kim and Hal on the boat and cuddling under the blanket. I think about sleeping beside you on the camping trip . . . and holding your hand on the way back from San Jose."

"So what is it that ties you up in knots?"

Anna answered with a nervous chuckle.

"You don't have to tell me if you don't want to."

"I . . . I would like to tell you."

"Okay."

"Every time I look at you, I see so many things. I see this brave hero who risked her life to save me. I see a sweet, gentle soul who always makes me laugh. And lately, I've been seeing a beautiful woman who sets my body on fire."

Lily shuddered with emotion at Anna's confession. "I'm glad to know I'm having that effect."

"And I hope you're glad to know you're the only one who ever has."

"Is that really true?"

"It is."

"I wish you were here right now."

"In bed with you?"

"Yes." Lily felt a stirring inside. In the time since they declared their love for each other, they seemed closer emotionally, but Anna hadn't spoken again of making love. "Yes, I wish you were here in my bed."

Anna drew a deep breath. "And what would we be doing?"

Lily paused, measuring her words carefully, as it seemed Anna was finally ready to talk. "I'd be covering you with kisses," she said softly. "Every inch of you."

She waited nervously for Anna to respond. When she did, her voice was small. "You're tying me in knots again."

"I don't want you in knots, sweetheart. If you were here . . ." Lily closed her eyes and reached beneath the covers to touch herself. "I'd set you free."

"How would you do that?"

"By sharing the things that aren't meant for anyone else."

Anna's next breath hitched. "You wouldn't believe what you're doing to me."

"Oh, yes I would. Anna . . ." Lily hoped she was ready for more. "Touch yourself and tell me if you're wet."

It took her a moment, but when she answered, it was only a whisper. "Yes."

Lily's whole body shuddered in response. "God, I wish you were here."

"And would you let me touch you?"

"I'd make you touch me." Lily shifted beneath the sheets as her hand began to roam.

"What would you have me do?"

Lily's heart was pounding with excitement. "I'd have you kiss me with those beautiful lips."

"Kissing you is like coming home. It feels perfect."

"I want it to be home, Anna. I want your lips on mine. Then I want to feel them everywhere . . . along my cheek, down to my ear." Lily trailed her hand softly along the path she described. "I want to feel your hot breath in my ear. Your tongue and your teeth teasing my earlobe . . . then you'd be kissing my neck. I love to feel your mouth on my neck."

"Your neck is so soft and smooth. I love that."

"It makes me crazy when you kiss me there." The room was suddenly twenty degrees warmer and she sat up and peeled out of her pajamas. "I've just taken off everything, Anna. I'm naked and imagining you here."

Anna moaned. "I can see you in my mind's eye."

"I'm dying to feel your hands on me."

"I'm going to be all over you . . . touching you everywhere."

"On my breasts . . ." Lily pinched her nipple and gasped. "You'd touch me here, wouldn't you?"

"Yes."

"It would make my nipples so hard . . . I'd be begging you for more."

"You won't have to beg me, Lily." Anna was breathing faster now, and Lily knew her hands were roaming too. "I already want you so much."

"Would you put your mouth on my breasts?"

"I'd suck your whole breast into my mouth . . . and I'd bite your nipples until you screamed for me to stop."

Lily's body was aflame with the image of Anna moving over her. "I need you to touch me. I need it so bad."

"Do it."

"That's it." Lily's hand went from her breast to her center. "And while your mouth's over mine, I'd feel your hand slide down between my legs. I'm so wet for you right now."

"Oh, I know you are . . . I know so well what that's like."

From the low, raspy moans, Lily knew Anna was stroking herself, just as she was. "I've opened my legs wide for you. I want to feel you inside of me." She grunted as she plunged three fingers into her vagina.

"Yes . . . feel me inside you."

For more than a minute, they exchanged only gasps and moans as Lily imagined Anna inside her, stroking rhythmically as her excitement swelled. Mental flashes of Anna doing the same nearly made her explode.

"Now touch me on my clit," Lily gasped, her hips climbing as she circled her clitoris with her slippery fingers. "I want you so bad, Anna. I want to come for you so bad."

"Let me hear you."

By now, Lily was drawing deep rapid breaths to keep up with her body's need for air. Her spasms started as tiny electric shocks before erupting as waves of bliss. "Yes," she hissed. "Oh, you're making me come so hard, Anna."

As Lily rode the crest of her climax, Anna drew a deep gasp and grew completely quiet. It was only when she exhaled loudly and cried out that Lily realized she was coming too.

"Lily, I love you so much," she whimpered as she caught her breath.

"I love you too. I wish I could hold you now." She gradually lowered her hips to the bed as the waves receded. Her body was spent, but her thoughts remained attuned to Anna. Though they were miles apart, she had never felt closer to anyone in her life.

They lay quietly for a long moment until Anna spoke. "Lily?"

"Yes, I'm here, sweetheart."

"I want you to feel my arms around you, feel my whole body against yours. Think of me holding you tonight while you sleep."

Lily relaxed and lost herself in the comforting image. "I love you, Anna."

"I love you too, baby. Goodnight."

Anna was touring the lot with Holly, a new saleswoman she had hired last week. Holly had been one of the top sellers at the

BMW dealership in San Diego, and Anna was thrilled to see she knew her stuff when it came to the BMW line.

"Anna Kaklis, you have a call on line two. Anna Kaklis, line two." The normally animated Carmen always sounded so official and reserved when she used the intercom.

"Excuse me." Anna swung into an empty office to grab the blinking line. "This is Anna Kaklis. How may I help you?"

"Anna, it's Mother."

She was instantly concerned, because Martine rarely contacted her at work, sending invitations and messages through her father instead. "What's up? Is everything okay?"

"Yes, of course. I was calling to invite you back for dinner tonight. I'm preparing a London broil."

London broil was one of her father's favorites, but she had already called Lily this morning and made plans to spend the evening at her apartment. And after their phone conversation last night, there was a good chance she wouldn't be home until morning. "Is it a special occasion? Not that we need one . . . I was just wondering."

"Nothing special. I just thought we'd all get together again. We had such a good time yesterday. Kim and Hal are coming, of course, and we'll hear more about their plans for the baby. It would be nice if Lily could join us too."

Anna's stomach jumped at the mention of Lily. For Martine to include her without prompting probably meant she knew the score. "I think that would be very nice. Why don't I call her and call you back?"

A last-minute invitation on a Monday night was certainly unusual—especially since it included Lily. Martine was up to something. Anna only hoped it was something good.

Anna cornered her sister in the kitchen at the big house. "I'm not kidding," she said, making no effort to conceal her accusing tone. She and Kim had been sent to the kitchen by Martine to work on the salad, while Lily sat out by the pool with the rest of the clan, filling them in on the plans for the next Kidz Kamp outing. "It was almost like the whole thing was thrown together to get Lily over here again."

"It was, and before you tear my head off, I didn't say anything. They already know. Mom called me this morning and asked me if it was serious."

"What did you tell her?"

"I told her the truth. I said you guys were in love with each other, and that you were happier than I've ever seen you in my life."

Anna blew out a breath that sent her bangs flying upward. "Do you think she told Dad that part?"

"She probably didn't have to. All anyone has to do is look at the two of you together, or listen to you talk about each other. Everybody can tell you're in love."

Anna felt her face get red. "Should I say something? If they already know, it's kind of like an elephant in the parlor."

"I think this whole thing tonight is Mom trying to get Dad to accept it. I—" She leaned toward the sliding glass door to make sure everyone was still outside by the pool. "Hal and I heard them talking last night after you guys left. Dad thinks Lily's the one who put you up to leaving Scott."

"That's absurd," she said angrily. "I'm going to set him straight now."

Kim caught her arm. "Mom already did. She told him you weren't happy with Scott, but he didn't want to hear it. He kept saying Scott was perfect for you. And then Mom said she liked Lily better, because it was obvious you did too."

"This is worse than being a teenager and being told your feelings aren't real because you're not grown up yet."

"You can't listen to Dad, Anna. He's being a bully, just like when he kept trying to talk you out of getting a divorce, or when he ran Lily out of the house at your birthday party. You have to face him down on this."

"I'm not giving Lily up. That's all there is to it."

"Atta girl!" Kim chucked her shoulder. "Just remember, you promised to tell me all about the sex when you finally figured out what it was you were supposed to be doing."

"I never promised any such thing." Anna folded her arms in mock indignation, a pose she adopted often when dealing with her sister. "But I think I might be getting over my shy period very soon," she whispered, looking around to make sure no one else could hear. "I never felt this way with Scott. Not even close."

"I always knew Scott wasn't right for you."

"I know that now." But convincing others that Lily was right for her wasn't going to be easy. And she wasn't even sure what Lily wanted from all this. Maybe she didn't want to have to deal with people who didn't bother to hide their disappointment at her being Anna's choice. "It isn't going to be an easy road, Kim . . . especially with Dad."

"You know Hal and I are both here for you. And it looks like Mom is too."

"I appreciate that."

"And you may not believe this, but there's no hurry for you to get somewhere. I know how you always like to have everything planned out, but what if you just took this one day at a time?"

Anna chuckled softly. Her sister knew her so well. "You know, I've been working on that little planning obsession of mine for a while now. There's nothing quite like an earthquake to remind us we're not really in charge."

Kim suddenly went teary.

"Hey, what is it?" Anna took her sister's shoulders and studied her face with worry.

"Nothing. Pregnant women are allowed to do this for no reason."

Chapter 12

"Your father was nicer than usual," Lily said. "He really seemed to like the idea of Kidz Kamp."

"Especially when he found out he was paying for it," Anna answered with a chuckle.

"How was I supposed to know you hadn't told him?"

"It's no big deal. But he doesn't keep up with the books anymore. And I've stopped telling him everything we do in operations. He just worries about it, and he doesn't need to. We have everything under control."

Anna was driving them to her house in Bel Air, where Lily had left her car after coming straight from work.

"Seriously, he seemed very interested in hearing about the program," Lily said. "And he was excited when Hal offered to take a few of the kids out on the boat. He even said he might come along."

"I liked the part where you told him the kids would be less likely to steal BMWs if they had a positive image of the owners."

"That was just outrageous bullshit that I made up. You don't think he actually believed me, do you?" When she was invited to sit out by the pool with George and Martine, Lily caught on pretty quickly that she was on some sort of hot seat. She played along, determined to win over Anna's father, if not with her pleasing personality, then with her sardonic sense of humor. The latter had actually seemed to have a greater effect.

"Before we left, I told them I'd be back one night this week to talk."

"That means tomorrow night, doesn't it? Don't you leave on Wednesday for South Carolina?"

"Yeah, I guess it does."

"And you won't get back until Sunday," Lily said dismally. Her brain had already stored the fact that Anna would be gone on Saturday, her thirtieth birthday.

"My plane gets in around six. If you'll pick me up at the airport, I promise to make it up to you."

"I don't know. I'll be very old by then. I probably shouldn't be out driving by myself." Lily didn't like hearing herself pout, but she was disappointed that Anna would miss the cookout Sandy and Suzanne had planned for Saturday afternoon. It would have been a great opportunity for Anna to meet her friends. "I still don't understand why you're going."

"They're previewing next year's models."

"I thought that's what you went to Germany for."

"That was different. The design center in Munich showed us what the next generation of cars will look like, but those are about three or four years away. I've already seen these cars in South Carolina, but we get to take a last look at the changes before they roll them out."

Lily loved the intonation of pride in Anna's voice whenever she talked about her cars. It always made her smile to remember a mechanical engineering nerd resided in that beautiful casing. "You sure you don't want to wait until you get back to talk to them?"

Anna sighed. "I don't know. There's something appealing about dumping it on them and running out of town for four days."

"I can see that." And when she got back from her trip, there would be no more barriers. "What are you going to tell them?"

"That I love you . . . that I intend to be with you whether they like it or not . . ." She snorted. "That I haven't lost my mind."

"And then what?"

"And then we'll talk about Kim and Hal's baby. That should leave them in a good mood."

An entire corner of Anna's office at Premier Motors was devoted to putting the Chamber of Commerce records in order, as after two consecutive terms, she was happily passing the baton to the incoming treasurer. It had been a busy year for the Chamber, especially as businesses continued to recover from the earthquake. Anna knew she had made an impression on the members with whom she had direct dealings. Several were pressing her to run for vice president next year, which would mean an automatic ascension to president the following year.

"Anna, do you have a minute for your old man?" Her father poked his head into her office.

"Do you have an appointment?" she asked, only half joking. She looked at her watch, already feeling overwhelmed by the things she needed to finish this afternoon before heading out tomorrow morning. She had decided to put off talking to her parents about Lily until she got back, since Kim had called her about seeing "the perfect house" after work.

"I can come back later if you want." It was almost comical seeing him pout.

"No, silly. I'll always make time for you." Anna stood up to move a pile of paperwork from one of her extra chairs. "I'm just trying to get these files in order for the next treasurer."

"It was good experience for you to serve as treasurer. It's possible they'll want you soon for vice president."

"They already do, but I need a break. Maybe I'll think about it in a year or two."

He sat down and cleared his throat, obviously waiting for her undivided attention. "I've been giving some thought lately to how I interfere sometimes in matters that really aren't any of my business."

In her thirty-two years, Anna couldn't think of a time when her father had come to her with such an admission.

"Anyway, I think I may have jumped the gun a while back when you were going out with Steve French."

What?

"I talked with Steve the other day. He really is a nice young man, and I'm sorry if anything I said about him dissuaded you from seeing him again."

"Steve French?" A knot in her stomach told her this wasn't about the account manager at all, but about Lily.

"Yeah, he's really a very interesting fellow. You two probably have a lot in common. I mean, with both of you in sales and marketing and all. Sure, he drives a Jaguar, but we know how to fix that." He winked at her, but this time, his usual charm fell short. Way short.

"I'm not interested in Steve, Dad." Though they maintained their professional relationship, her memories of the trip to San Diego still gave her the creeps.

"You should give it a chance, darling. He offered us skybox tickets next week to the Dodgers' home opener. I told him you and I would come together."

Yes, this was definitely about Lily. Anna saw clearly through her father's charade, and was appalled at his unrelenting attempts to manipulate her. He had always done this, granting or withholding his approval as a way of bending her to his will. Enough was enough.

"You're right, Dad."

He smiled and started to stand, no doubt thoroughly satisfied at how easily he had accomplished his mission.

"You do sometimes interfere in matters that aren't any of your business." Anna stood and began to pace in her office. "We both know this isn't about Steve French. It's about my relationship with Lily, so why don't we just put it out there?"

Her father grimaced at hearing Lily's name. "You haven't been making good choices recently, Anna. I'm worried about you."

"What is a good choice? Whatever makes you happy?"

"You've always been so levelheaded. But ever since the earthquake, it's as if you've lost all perspective. You threw away a perfectly good marriage. You—"

There was nothing perfectly good about her marriage, but Anna wasn't going to open up her private life for her father's judgment. "I made a mistake marrying Scott, a mistake so big it would have kept both of us from ever being happy."

"That's not true. Scott was very happy with you. I spoke with him many times and he never wanted a divorce."

Anna felt a surge of anger. "You had no business meddling in my personal life. That was between Scott and me."

"I thought you needed help, Anna, and so did Scott. You were so confused when you came out of that earthquake . . . like you'd lost your sense of priority."

"You've got it all wrong," she said, her voice softening as she struggled to get her temper under control. "Yes, I was changed by the earthquake, but not because I was confused. It was just the opposite. For once, I found my priorities. I learned—" He started to interrupt, but she quickly sat beside him and put her hand on his arm to quiet his objections. "I learned I was strong

214

enough to do whatever I had to do, no matter how hard it was. And I realized I didn't have to stay trapped anywhere I didn't want to be—not in a dark pile of rubble . . . or in a marriage that was all wrong."

His face showed only anguish. "I'm just afraid you're being led somewhere that's only going to bring you sadness."

"I'm not being led anywhere at all, Dad. I'm going with Lily of my own free will. I love her."

"Anna, this is not who you are."

"Yes, it is." She still hadn't answered questions for herself about whether or not she was a lesbian, but loving Lily was who she was. "When I married Scott, it was because I believed it was all I would ever have, that I would never feel more love than that for anyone. But it wasn't enough to make me happy. I wanted the kind of love I see with you and Mom, or with Kim and Hal. I didn't have that with Scott. We were just going through the motions."

"He loved you." He stared numbly at his lap.

"Dad, look at me." She waited until he met her eye. "You're my father. And I need to have you in my corner on this, not Scott's."

His eyes misted with tears.

"Everything changed for me when I fell in love with Lily. Now I have what the rest of you have. I know what it is to really love someone, and I'm not giving her up for anyone."

"I do want you to be happy, sweetheart. But I . . ."

As far as Anna was concerned, that was the important part. In time, everything else would fall into place. "No buts, Dad. Lily's the one who makes me happy."

Lily waved good-bye to Lauren and her husband, the last ones to leave the party. It had been a wonderful day, perfect but for Anna's absence. At least Lily had been able to talk openly about their relationship, and to promise another chance soon for friends to meet her.

"You have quite a haul there, lady," Sandy said, gesturing to the pile of crank gifts that commemorated her passage over the hill. There was a jar of wrinkle cream, a tube of denture adhesive and a Lawrence Welk CD. "What did Anna get you?"

"I don't know. She said she was bringing a surprise from South Carolina."

"Peaches?"

Lily chuckled. "No, it'll probably be a BMW T-shirt, and a DVD on how to operate my car's features."

"Sounds romantic."

"Believe it or not, Anna could make an oil change romantic. She really hated missing this."

"Suzanne hated it too. She's dying to meet her."

"Anna said if she had any idea how to cook, she'd have everyone over for dinner. But then I reminded her that I wanted my friends to like her, so maybe we should all just meet somewhere and let the professionals cook."

"Why don't you just find out what night's good and bring her over. I'll handle the cooking."

"That would be great."

"So you want to get in the hot tub?"

"No, I think I'll go on home. She promised to call tonight, and they're three hours ahead of us in South Carolina, so it's"— she looked at her watch—"already ten o'clock there."

"Tell her I said hi."

"I will." Lily threw her arms around Sandy's neck. "Thank you for making my birthday a good one."

"Wish I could have given you what you really wanted."

"I think I'll last until tomorrow. But you guys made this day great."

On the short drive home from Sherman Oaks, she wondered how Anna might have handled an invitation to get in the hot tub with three naked women. Not that Lily would have let it happen. She wasn't going to share her first look at Anna with Sandy and Suzanne.

Pulling into her covered spot, she gathered the gag gifts and cards from the passenger seat. Despite her dark apartment, she didn't feel so alone this year. Even though Anna was three thousand miles away, Lily felt close to her, especially after the intimate step they had taken on the phone last weekend, and Anna's heart-to-heart with her father. The barriers were falling.

In her kitchen, she flipped the light switch with her forearm and dropped her gifts on the table. Disappointed to see the solid red light indicating she had no messages, she went again to her cell phone to make sure it was working. Anna had promised to call, but probably wasn't expecting her home so soon.

As if reading her thoughts, the kitchen phone suddenly rang.

"Hello," she answered cheerfully, recognizing Anna's cell phone in the display.

"Happy birthday to you," Anna sang.

"It is now. I was starting to worry you wouldn't call." She looked at the clock. "Are you finished with the car seminars?"

"I am, and I told them if they scheduled this rollout for the same week next year, I wouldn't be there because it's my girl-friend's birthday."

Lily couldn't have asked for a better birthday present than to know Anna wanted to be with her next year. "You just made my day, Amazon."

"Is that so?"

"Yeah, it's so. I love you."

"I love you too, baby. And I wanted to make your day. So I started thinking about what we could do on your birthday that was really special."

Lily loved it when Anna called her baby. "Oh, yeah?"

"Yeah, so when I tried to think of something really special, I started thinking about what we did last weekend on the phone.

Do you remember that, Lily?"

Lily shuddered, wishing she were upstairs in her bed. "How could I forget something like that?"

"There was only one thing I could think of that would be more special than listening to each other come over the phone."

"And what's that?" Her heart began to pound with anticipation.

"Why don't you come upstairs and find out?"

It was then that Lily first noticed a glow from the barely cracked door at the top of the stairs. Her bedroom light hadn't been on when she entered the apartment—she would have seen it from the walkway. She nervously made her way up the darkened stairway, trying to envisage what she would see when she got to her bedroom.

No imagination could have done justice to the sight that greeted her as she gently swung open the door. Anna sat in the corner armchair by the window, the picture of calm with one long leg crossed over the other, one hand raised so her fingers rested on her chin. Her features were shadowed by the dim light from the small lamp on the far side of the room. She was dressed in dark slacks and a long sleeved white shirt, her black hair draped loosely around her shoulders. Her elbows rested nonchalantly on the arms of the chair and her other hand held a cell phone in her lap.

Lily walked slowly into the room, stopping at the end of her bed, where the covers were already turned down. "I can't believe you're really here," she said with guarded excitement. If they both kept their nerve, they would be lovers soon.

Chapter 13

"A girl doesn't turn thirty every day." Despite her calm voice and seeming composure, Anna was quickly losing the bravado she had needed to set up this scenario in Lily's bedroom. Never before had she stood on this end of a seduction, but it was intoxicating.

Lily held her eye as she slowly crossed the room, stooping to place a calming hand on her knee. "Having you here is all I wanted for my birthday."

The touch of her hand was like fire burning through her clothes. This was the night she and Lily would lie together, the night they would seal their love. But Anna feared she had come as far as she could of her own volition.

Lily seemed to sense her nervousness, taking the cell phone from her hand and placing it on the bedside table. Then she grasped both of Anna's hands and pulled her up into a confident embrace. A gentle kiss followed, but it quickly grew deeper, and more passionate. There was no need this time to hold back.

Lily broke the kiss and held Anna's hand to her pounding chest. "This is only one of the things you do to me."

Anna returned the gesture, drawing Lily's hand inside the open collar of her shirt, knowing she would find a rapid heartbeat that matched her own. She looked down as Lily's fingers loosened the buttons of her shirt and pushed her collar back, revealing the lacy top of her bra. Then Lily pressed her lips into the valley between her breasts as deft hands gently tugged her shirttail free.

The anticipation of where Lily's hands might wander died as she suddenly stepped back. Without a trace of shyness, Lily stepped out of her shoes and removed her jeans and sweater, leaving her standing in dark green panties and a matching bra.

Anna nervously matched her movements, stepping out of her slacks and dropping them over the arm of the chair with her shirt. Then she reached behind her to unfasten her bra.

"Let me do that." Lily stepped forward and ran her fingertips over Anna's skin, leaving a trail of goose bumps as she reached behind her to find the clasp. When she released it, the bra slipped loosely from Anna's shoulders and fell to the floor. Lily lifted both hands to caress her breasts, and then brought her face once again to her chest, this time brushing her knuckle against a nipple that hardened instantly. "I knew you'd be perfect," she murmured, pressing her lips to the skin. Her tongue flicked the nipple gently before she drew it into her mouth.

Anna felt her knees go weak. Lily must have sensed it, as she pressed a hand into the small of her back for support. Anna quivered with excitement as Lily's breath cooled her wet skin. Desperate for more, she pushed her fingers through Lily's hair and held her firmly in place.

Lily gently kneaded the other breast before devouring it too. Then she wrapped both arms around Anna's neck and pulled her into another kiss.

Anna loved the feel of Lily's warm bare skin in her arms and against her naked torso. She had never been so aroused, and there wasn't a fiber within her that doubted she belonged here.

Lily broke their kiss and without a word led Anna to the edge of the bed.

Anna sat and watched Lily remove first her bra, then her panties. Her naked form was far more beautiful than she had imagined from their late night telephone interlude. Overwhelmed with the need to touch her, she ran both hands up Lily's waist, trailing her fingertips against the sides of her breasts. She realized now she had wanted this since the day on the boat.

Remembering perfectly the need Lily had described on the phone—the visions of which had dominated her thoughts since that night—Anna gently pulled her onto the bed and guided her against the pillows. With both hands, Lily drew her face down until they met once more in a hungry kiss. As Anna's tongue delved deep into Lily's mouth, her hand seized a breast, which she fondled with wonder, amazed to find it both soft and firm. When a nipple hardened in her fingertips, she was overwhelmed with the urge to cover it with her mouth.

Anna lowered her head and sucked the nipple between her lips, flicking it with her rigid tongue as Lily had done only moments ago. When Lily moaned her pleasure, it was all Anna could do to resist biting down hard.

She relinquished the nipple and went back for another kiss. As Lily clutched her back, she slid her fingers down the flat stomach and through the curly patch of hair. Lily responded instantly, opening her legs in invitation.

The wet heat of Lily's sex was more incredible than Anna's meager imagination had allowed. The soft folds were slippery and swollen, and Lily seemed to love her touch as she stroked the length of her sex. When she slipped her fingers inside, she marveled at her own body's excited response, and at the power she felt as she pushed her hand deeper and faster within. Lily writhed with need, and Anna shifted to the side to watch her body respond. When Lily's breathing grew rapid and shallow, she drew her fingers out to tickle the swollen clitoris, just as Lily had begged her over the phone. Suddenly, Lily's chest and neck were enveloped by a deep red flush.

"Oh, Anna," she murmured, her eyes closed tight.

With one arm underneath, Anna pulled her close. "Look at me, Lily. I love you." Their eyes met as Lily climaxed, forging the deepest connection Anna had ever felt.

In all the scenarios Lily had dreamed, none had entailed Anna touching her first. But when Anna took over, it was clear she needed to surrender or risk shattering Anna's new-found confidence.

As her tremors ceased, she tucked Anna's head into her neck and stroked her hair. "That was so beautiful. I can't tell you how many times I've imagined your hands on me." Her pulse quickened as Anna began kissing her neck, but she couldn't wait any longer to realize her dream of having Anna, body and soul. Her fingernails gently raked Anna's back, and Anna stilled her lips. Lily shifted both of them until Anna lay on her back.

Anna's nipples stood as dark brown peaks, beacons for Lily's searching lips. She gently pinched one with her fingertips and took the other inside her mouth.

Anna responded by holding her head in place, as she had when they were standing. "I've been waiting for this."

Lily imagined staying there forever, but her eagerness for more was pulling her in new directions. With her mouth still latched to a nipple, her hand reached down and slipped under the waistband of Anna's panties, gently scratching the tender area covered by her pubic hair.

Anna raised her hips and pushed her panties to her thighs.

Lily finished the task, sliding them down to her ankles and off. As her fingers found the patch of hair again, Anna thrust upward as if seeking more contact. Lily could barely resist plunging her hand inside. But she had something more intimate in mind.

She released the nipple and slid lower, circling Anna's navel with her tongue as her hands roamed her breasts. Anna continued to rock her hips and Lily shifted again, low enough to kiss the soft skin on either side of the dark triangle. The smell was overpowering, and Lily scooted lower still, parting Anna thighs to reveal the source of her excitement.

In her fantasies, she prolonged the anticipation with nips and kisses everywhere except the one place they were needed most. But the reality of Anna's glistening sex was irresistible. Lily pressed her mouth into the wetness, meticulously touching every corner with her lips and tongue as her arms came up to wrap around the rolling thighs.

Anna's soft moans and whimpers of desire were the most wondrous sounds she had ever heard. Anna lasted only a few seconds once Lily began flicking her clitoris. She cried out, pulling one of Lily's hands as she went over the edge.

Lily wasn't finished. She would never be finished. Her skilled tongue drew back, barely touching the tender spot as she waited for Anna to still. Then she pressed harder, drawing out a second climax and a third, the last one as she entered Anna with two fingers and stroked her deep inside.

Anna awoke before dawn and slipped into the bathroom. She and Lily had made love until after one, when neither could go on. That in itself was remarkable to her, since Scott had never continued their lovemaking once she had an orgasm. Lily had brought her to climax again and again, and she had done the same.

223

Splashing water on her face, Anna removed the traces of Lily's arousal from her chin. What an amazing experience that had been, to taste her and feel the softness with her lips. Her lack of reservation had surprised her, whether giving or receiving pleasure. Nothing was enough.

Remembering now the thundering physical sensations, the tender words and intense looks they had shared, and the way they clung to each other as they climaxed, Anna finally knew what all the fuss was about. Making love was about connection.

She still had questions, complicated questions for herself about her own expectations for where this all would lead. But right now, all she wanted was more sleep in Lily's arms.

Lily blinked back the sun that streamed in through the narrow window above the balcony door. She couldn't move for the long body draped over her, but it wasn't worth disturbing Anna. On the contrary, the chance to study her as she slept was too enticing to pass up.

Several hours ago, she had awakened when Anna left the bed and went into the bathroom. As the minutes passed, she had started to worry. What was Anna thinking now that they had shared so much? How did she feel about being with a woman? Lily wanted to get up and go see about her, but was terrified of finding her dressed to leave. If Anna was going home in the middle of the night, it was best if she left without the awkward words.

Traumatic imaginings had tumbled through her head of the awful possibilities. She first supposed Anna had awakened with guilt or disgust at what they had done last night. Or perhaps it was just disappointment because Lily hadn't lived up to her hopes or expectations.

With her imagination running wild, she was simply astounded when Anna returned to the bed and cuddled into her side. As she had lain there basking in the wonder of having Anna with her, she acknowledged the worst thing about her insecurities—they robbed her of energy she could be spending on more pleasurable pursuits.

Through the course of their lovemaking and falling asleep, one word had bombarded Lily's thoughts: forever. Every kiss, every touch, every sensation. She wanted them all forever. And she never wanted Anna to leave her arms.

Unfortunately, nature's call was adamant.

Lily squirmed out of bed and tiptoed into the bathroom, returning to find Anna stretched diagonally across her queen-sized bed, her arms sprawled to take up most of the space. No longer sleepy, Lily considered going down to make coffee and breakfast, but the temptation of lying naked with Anna was too great. Unfortunately, Anna hadn't left enough room on either side of the bed for her to get back in without climbing directly on top of her. On the verge of giving up, she caught the faintest hint of a smirk on Anna's face. "Hey, who are you? How did you get in here?"

Anna squinted at her with feigned confusion. "Isn't this apartment twelve? I was told to wait for the lady in apartment twelve."

"No, I'm afraid this is number ten."

"Does this mean I'm not going to get my money?"

Lily followed Anna out of the apartment and down the steps. "Where did you park last night?"

"In one of the visitor slots around back. I didn't want to spoil my surprise."

"I still can't believe you sneaked back like that. All day, I imagined you with your head under the hood of an SUV. And you were on a plane."

"Two planes, but who's counting?"

"Does anyone else know you're back?"

"Nope."

"And you're not telling me where we're going?"

"Nope."

"Or who you called while I was in the bathroom?"

"Nope."

Lily's first choice for a perfect Sunday would have been to lie around in bed and explore Anna's glorious body in the light of day. But Anna was hell-bent on sharing one more surprise, as if anything could top last night.

Traffic was light for a Sunday morning, and Lily soon realized they were headed to Anna's house. When they pulled into the driveway and stopped, she reached for the door handle.

"Just wait here. I'll only be a minute."

It was more like thirty seconds, as Anna retrieved something from her mailbox and returned to the car.

"What are you up to, Amazon?"

"You'll see."

They drove through the back streets and side roads until they reached Brentwood, one of LA's most upscale suburbs. On a quiet, tree-lined street, they stopped in front of a beautiful two-story Spanish-style home, white with a multi-level red tile roof.

"So what do you think?" Anna asked.

"It's gorgeous. Did Kim find this?"

Anna nodded. "I've got the keys. Let's go take a look."

Lily gasped when they entered the grand foyer. Stained and beveled glass above the door played colors all the way up the sweeping staircase. Anna led her through the empty house room by room. Downstairs, there was a large formal living room, a dining room, a family room with a cozy office off to the side, and an enormous kitchen with a breakfast nook set in a bay window. Both the family room and kitchen opened onto a beautifully landscaped patio and yard. The pool featured dark blue concrete and Spanish tile, with an attached hot tub. Anna pointed out the two-car garage in the side yard. Upstairs, there were four bedrooms, including a large master suite. The suite and one of the bedrooms had balconies overlooking the pool.

It was one of the most beautiful homes Lily had ever seen, not as sweeping and grand as George and Martine's, but more elegant and stylish than Anna's current home.

"So what do you think?" Anna led her back down to the foyer.

"Are you kidding? I think it's wonderful. Are you going to buy it?"

"That's my other surprise. I already have. Kim showed it to me the night before I left and I put a contract on it. By the time I landed in South Carolina on Wednesday night, the owners had signed off on my offer."

"So it's your house?"

"It is." Anna took her hands and looked her straight in the eye. "And it can be our home if you'll live here with me."

Lily was completely taken off guard and her stomach immediately flipped. Not the fluttering and sinking flip it did when she was nervous or anticipating bad news. This was a fluttering and soaring flip. She took a deep breath and tried to compose herself, fearing she might cry with the emotion that filled her. Losing the battle, she lunged forward and wrapped her arms fiercely around Anna's neck as tears of happiness started down her cheeks. "I'm going to say yes, Amazon, so you better be sure."

Anna twisted from side to side with Lily in a tight embrace. "I'm very sure, Pygmy."

Epilogue

Hal balanced a large box on his hip as he fumbled with the handle for the side door.

"I'll get it," Anna said, holding the door open as he entered. "You don't have to carry this stuff in. I've hired that muscle crew for the whole day."

"This was sitting in the driveway. It says law books."

Anna pointed to the small office off the family room. "It goes in there. Just drop it in the corner. Lily's going to have to sort through all that." She continued to hold the door when she saw her sister coming. "How are you feeling?"

"Like a bloated rhino," Kim said.

"You look great."

"You're full of shit."

Anna ignored her retort and greeted her with a hug. "Have you come to brag to everyone about how you found this lovely house?"

"Yes, and to thank you for paying full price. I made a huge commission."

"So glad I could help."

"I took a contract on your other house yesterday. They came in about eighteen thousand under your asking price, but if their finances check out, I think you should jump on it."

"Whatever you say."

Lily joined them in the family room. "Did George just run through here like his pants were on fire?"

Anna chuckled. "Now that you mention it, he said he was going out to get lunch for everyone. What did you do to him?"

"I found him wandering around upstairs and I offered to show him the master bedroom where you and I planned to sleep."

Kim laughed evilly. "No wonder his tires were screeching when he pulled out. Where's Mom?"

Lily tossed a thumb over her shoulder. "She's setting up the kitchen."

"Oh, right. Where would Anna be without her kitchen?"

Anna wrapped her arm around Lily's neck and pulled her close. "Lily likes to cook."

"And Anna likes to clean up," Lily answered with a smirk, seeing from the corner of her eye that Anna was frowning and shaking her head.

"You two are going to be quite a pair," Kim said, collapsing onto the couch. "Do you have any plans yet for all those extra bedrooms?"

"One of them will belong to my nephew when he runs away from home," Anna said.

Hal emerged from the office and fell onto the couch beside Kim. "He's been kicking like crazy these last few days."

"Just three more months, big guy," Kim said. "Then you can kiss your boat good-bye till he's old enough to live with Anna."

Lily took Anna's hand and pulled her toward the foyer. "Can you come upstairs for a minute? I want to show you something."

"Sure." As they passed the front door, they saw the movers folding the protective blankets and stacking them in the now-empty truck. "Looks like they're finished."

Lily led the way upstairs, through the master bedroom and out onto the balcony. "Notice anything interesting?"

Two chairs and a small table had been arranged so they overlooked the pool and spa. "What am I looking for?"

"Turn around."

"There's a crack in the wall!"

"Now look closely." Lily leaned against the rail while Anna located what she was talking about. Next to the small crack at the corner of the door, someone had scribbled the date of the Newport-Inglewood quake that struck Culver City.

"I'll be damned."

"Welcome home, Anna."

Anna traced the crack with her finger. "You think it would be all right to leave it here?"

"We should probably keep an eye on it and make sure it doesn't get bigger."

"Yeah, I'd hate to have the whole house collapse on top of us." She chucked Lily with her hip.

Lily grinned and chucked her back. "Whatever would we do?"

Publications from
BELLA BOOKS, INC.
The best in contemporary lesbian fiction

P.O. Box 10543, Tallahassee, FL 32302
Phone: 800-729-4992
www.bellabooks.com

ASPEN'S EMBERS by Diane Tremain Braund. Will Aspen choose the woman she loves . . . or the forest she hopes to preserve . . .   978-1-59493-102-4 $14.95

THE COTTAGE by Gerri Hill. *The Cottage* is the heartbreaking story of two women who meet by chance . . . or did they? A love so destined it couldn't be denied . . . stolen moments to be cherished forever.   978-1-59493-096-6 $13.95

FANTASY: Untrue Stories of Lesbian Passion edited by Barbara Johnson and Therese Szymanski. Lie back and let Bella's bad girls take you on an erotic journey through the greatest bedtime stories never told.   978-1-59493-101-7 $15.95

SISTERS' FLIGHT by Jeanne G'Fellers. *Sisters' Flight* is the highly anticipated sequel to *No Sister of Mine* and *Sister Lost, Sister Found.*

      978-1-59493-116-1 $13.95

BRAGGIN' RIGHTS by Kenna White. Taylor Fleming is a thirty-six-year-old Texas rancher who covets her independence. She finds her cowgirl independence tested by neighboring rancher Jen Holland.   978-1-59493-095-9 $13.95

BRILLIANT by Ann Roberts. Respected sociology professor, Diane Cole finds her views on love challenged by her own heart, as she fights the attraction she feels for a woman half her age.   978-1-59493-115-4 $13.95

THE EDUCATION OF ELLIE by Jackie Calhoun. When Ellie sees her childhood friend for the first time in thirty years she is tempted to resume their long lost friendship. But with the years come a lot of baggage and the two women struggle with who they are now while fighting the painful memories of their first parting. Will they be able to move past their history to start again?   978-1-59493-092-8 $13.95

DATE NIGHT CLUB by Saxon Bennett. *Date Night Club* is a dark romantic comedy about the pitfalls of dating in your thirties . . .   978-1-59493-094-2 $13.95

PLEASE FORGIVE ME by Megan Carter. Laurel Becker is on the verge of losing the two most important things in her life—her current lover, Elaine Alexander, and the Lavender Page bookstore. Will Elaine and Laurel manage to work through their misunderstandings and rebuild their life together?   978-1-59493-091-1 $13.95

WHISKEY AND OAK LEAVES by Jaime Clevenger. Meg meets June, a single woman running a horse ranch in the California Sierra foothills. The two become quick friends and it isn't long before Meg is looking for more than just a friendship. But June has no interest in developing a deeper relationship with Meg. She is, after all, not the least bit interested in women . . . or is she? Neither of these two women is prepared for what lies ahead . . .   978-1-59493-093-5 $13.95

SUMTER POINT by KG MacGregor. As Audie surrenders her heart to Beth, she begins to distance herself from the reckless habits of her youth. Just as they're ready to meet in the middle, their future is thrown into doubt by a duty Beth can't ignore. It all comes to a head on the river at Sumter Point.   978-1-59493-089-8 $13.95

THE TARGET by Gerri Hill. Sara Michaels is the daughter of a prominent senator who has been receiving death threats against his family. In an effort to protect Sara, the FBI recruits homicide detective Jaime Hutchinson to secretly provide the protection they are so certain Sara will need. Will Sara finally figure out who is behind the death threats? And will Jaime realize the truth—and be able to save Sara before it's too late?
978-1-59493-082-9 $13.95

REALITY BYTES by Jane Frances. In this sequel to *Reunion*, follow the lives of four friends in a romantic tale that spans the globe and proves that you can cross the whole of cyberspace only to find love a few suburbs away . . .   978-1-59493-079-9 $13.95

MURDER CAME SECOND by Jessica Thomas. Broadway's bad-boy genius, Paul Carlucci, has chosen *Hamlet* for his latest production and, to the delight of some and despair of others, he has selected Provincetown's amphitheatre for his opening gala. But Alex Peres realizes the wrong people are falling down, and the moaning is all too realistic. Someone must not be shooting blanks . . .   978-1-59493-081-2 $13.95

SKIN DEEP by Kenna White. Jordan Griffin has been given a new assignment: Track down and interview one-time nationally renowned broadcast journalist Reece McAllister. Much to her surprise, Jordan comes away with far more than just a story . . .
978-1-59493-78-2 $13.95

FINDERS KEEPERS by Karin Kallmaker. *Finders Keepers*, the quest for the perfect mate in the 21st century, joins Karin Kallmaker's *Just Like That* and her other incomparable novels about lesbian love, lust and laughter.   1-59493-072-4 $13.95

OUT OF THE FIRE by Beth Moore. Author Ann Covington feels at the top of the world when told her book is being made into a movie. Then in walks Casey Duncan the actress who is playing the lead in her movie. Will Casey turn Ann's world upside down?
1-59493-088-0 $13.95

STAKE THROUGH THE HEART: NEW EXPLOITS OF TWILIGHT LESBIANS by Karin Kallmaker, Julia Watts, Barbara Johnson and Therese Szymanski. The playful quartet that penned the acclaimed *Once Upon A Dyke* are dimming the lights for journeys into worlds of breathless seduction.   1-59493-071-6 $15.95

THE HOUSE ON SANDSTONE by KG MacGregor. Carly Griffin returns home to Leland and finds that her old high school friend Justine is awakening more than just old memories.   1-59493-076-7 $13.95

WILD NIGHTS: MOSTLY TRUE STORIES OF WOMEN LOVING WOMEN edited by Therese Szymanski. 264 pp. 23 new stories from today's hottest erotic writers are sure to give you your wildest night ever!   1-59493-069-4 $15.95